Sun-Tzu's Life
in the Holy City of Vilnius

Ričardas Gavelis

Sun-Tzu's Life
in the Holy City of Vilnius

Translated by
Elizabeth Novickas

PICA PICA PRESS

A portion of this work was previously published at Asymtote.com.

The translation of this book was graciously funded by a grant from the
Lithuanian Culture Institute.

ISBN: 978-0-9966304-3-6
Library of Congress Control Number 2018912894

www.picapica.press
Flossmoor, Illinois

Contents

Even as the cockle therefore is gathered up, and burnt with fire: so shall it be at the end of the world. The Son of man shall send his angels, and they shall gather out of his kingdom all scandals, and them that work iniquity. And shall cast them into the furnace of fire: there shall be weeping and gnashing of teeth.

Matthew 13, 40-43

1. The Yard

There shall be weeping and gnashing of teeth—that's for sure. There's already nothing here but pure weeping and a dangerous gnashing of the molars in sleep. When you look at the line of shabby flat roofs from below, Korals' eyeless buildings no longer look so shudderingly awful. It's true that they are falling and crashing onto the trashy yards or the unshaven passersby and could, at any moment, fall over on the entire world and flatten it like a rotten jellyfish. Return existence to the state of a primeval jellyfish, the pre-atomic dawn of the Cosmos, into the powdery dust between the stars, or perhaps even the primordial croaking of frogs. It's a prospect that thickens the blood and freezes the brain. Someone of a weaker spirit could get scared to death that he'll be crushed by the crumbling world at any moment. But I'm not at all afraid: I can hold those collapsing buildings in a vertical position by the strength of my will alone. I order them to stand in a dismal, eyeless queue, and they obediently stand there. Their oppressively shining windows lead nowhere and hide nothing. Korals hasn't had any charming secrets for a long time now; the only secret it doesn't reveal to anyone is me.

I surely am a secret, since even I can't manage to figure myself out. What's more, I can't figure out the hieroglyph of Karoliniškės' line of flat roofs. The essence of this malignant district can't be expressed in any hieroglyphs that could be written down and read. This world's essence isn't writable—it's faceless and wordless. Soundless, colorless, and scentless, like the deadliest of gases. Karoliniškės' poisonous sarin penetrates not into the lungs, but into a person's very soul, in order to burn out any life there. The sun doesn't rise there in the morning, and doesn't set there in the evening. Even the dogs there are achingly sad and quietly insane.

It was Apples Petriukas, the black wizard of Voodoo, the puny philosopher of Vilnius, who first nicknamed Karoliniškės Korals. It was only later that the wider public took up the name. Petriukas is the first to think up nicknames for everything; he's thought up at least half of the prevalent neologisms. He arrived in this wretched city from the Wonderland that Alice discovered. He still lives in that land—at least the majority of his time, which isn't measured by clocks. That's why Apples Petriukas so rarely errs—but this time he missed by a mile. There's no coral, no atolls, no reefs, no lagoons in this district—there was never a sea here at all, not even in the prehistoric Carboniferous period.

Perhaps it's fitting to call this moldy district Karoliai, after the Lithuanian word for a necklace of beads. Perhaps those rectangles of colorless windows really are bead necklaces, strung together on thousands of invisible threads, which is why individually they have no meaning. However, the people holed up behind that glass naïvely imagine their lives are meaningful and that their pale faces in the hallway mirrors secretly organize and influence the entire world's development. The poor, naïve people of Korals. Korals or Karoliai—if you would call this district of sighs by a slightly different name.

But at the time, your eyes fearfully closed during a sleepless Karoliniškės night, the only thing you could see with the eyes of your soul would be giant beads of amber. Amber and only amber, because in the land of blond-braided Lithuanian women you couldn't imagine any other beads even if you wanted to. In her old age, my demented mother doesn't recognize any other, only amber; ghastly amber beads sprawl stupidly on her scrawny neck. My stupidly silly mother herself once dangled on a silly swing in an advertising poster for the Song Festival, decked out in the national costume and grinning like the first attempt of a novice Angel of Death. The incomparable leer of an Angel of Death is my mother's trademark. Anyone trying to remember her remembers that perverted grin first, and only afterwards begins to breathlessly babble all sorts of sweet lies about her. Everyone fears my mother as if she were some sort of all-knowing spy. No one can utter a word of truth about her. Not even me.

Sometimes I think: maybe she really is the Angel of Death, and is constantly ingeniously threatening everyone from the other world, forcing them to spread honeyed lies about her. Whatever the case, my mother isn't here now; she lives in a luxurious retirement home and tries fruitlessly to seduce one of her nurses. Korals manages quite well without her; I manage without her, too. However, I can't get by without Karoliniškės, which in essence created me. Looking from below, the landscape of gloomy nine-story apartment blocks begins to sing in the inverse perspective of Russian icons. Things close up seem smaller and less significant, while the more distant ones are larger and far more meaningful. I perceive the world somewhat inside-out, probably because today is a festive day in my soul.

It's an important milestone today for Laima and me. It's not every day that a harmonious family marks twenty-five years of marriage, when they celebrate a real silver anniversary. On that kind of day you should eat solely with silver cutlery. And drink solely from crystal wine glasses. But what comes first is what's poured in those glasses and put on those plates. It's paramount to eat delectably and drink tastefully. It's one of the most essential laws of human existence. The gut regulates the quivers of a person's spirit and soul.

The second brain hides inside a person's gut. I always knew this, even though science only confirmed this recently. Rational

European science always was and always will be half-blind. It struggled for over a hundred years before it finally came across the magical second brain in man's gut. While I, without any modern-day laboratory equipment, determined a long time ago that a person's desires, mood, and even a portion of his thoughts are born within the second brain hiding there. A real human thinks first with his gut brain, and only afterwards engages the brain of the head too. It's one of the great fundamentals of humanity. It's a cypher key to understanding humanity's evolution. I discovered it thanks to untold investigations, innumerable sleepless nights, and mortal dangers. It wasn't at all easy; however, the end result was worth the fear and the pain. I discovered one of the most essential characteristics of human construction. Philosophically, it conforms with natural laws, but it's practically perfectly hidden from the eyes of curious bystanders.

It's senseless to go looking for gray masses or the typical convolutions of the brain. Even setting to it very earnestly, you won't find anything there except for the convolutions of the guts. But if you set to it still more earnestly... and still more, if you strained all the brains of your gut... if you were to set to it as earnestly as I did myself—perhaps you would at some point come across those at first inconspicuous nerve fibers and pulsating ganglions. They resemble lively little bugs—reddish, kind-hearted ladybugs, wandering through the diaphragm, through the entrails of the intestine, and even the half-blocked bile ducts cramping from excessively rich food. Perhaps you would realize that bundles of nerves of such size and unheard-of influence simply must unite into a seriously influential tissue.

This secret nerve tissue has a crucial influence on a person's moods, thoughts, and sexual prowess. It determines a person's actions much earlier than the brain. A person's brain sleeps most of the time, but the gut is always awake. A person acts first on what his gut cavity, his second brain, tells him, and only later does he consciously, and somewhat deceptively, think up a sensible basis for his actions—*post factum*. It's of utmost importance to firmly absorb this deep truth, otherwise you'll never grasp the majority of people's behavior. You'll never figure out anyone at all.

2. The Silver Anniversary

A man's flights and falls, the convolutions and riddles of his biography, the attainments he himself can't understand, are all decided by his gut. There's no point in grieving over or struggling with such a despicable cosmic human fate. However, it really is worthwhile to always dine as well as possible—if you can afford to. A fine meal is particularly appropriate before destroying a cockle weed, before making love to a woman, or before running for president. However, on your silver anniversary you must have the finest meal of all.

"Is your *carpaccio* sufficiently subtle?" I asked Laima, in no hurry and so drawling my words a bit. "Today you have the right to throw the most expensive dish in the trash, even if it's perfect. Just because it doesn't suit your momentary moods, or merely your illusions."

She knew this herself, but I could say whatever I felt like. We were sitting by ourselves at the table, so there was no need to dissemble or put on airs. That evening we had succeeded in escaping all the detectives. It was impossibly difficult; Petriukas and I made plans for a good two weeks, but in the end we won. That evening Laima and I appeared to have fallen into another world, as isn't a man's life normally nothing but dissembling and putting on airs? Perhaps we had behaved that way frequently ourselves earlier—but certainly not on that sanctified day. That evening we were as natural as plants. Only we weren't drinking the light of the sun, but rather the pale moonlight and the aromas of quiet music. We weren't manufacturing green chlorophyll, but rather human thoughts and passions.

"It's been quite some time since I've had any illusions," Laima finally answered, as if chewing her food with the utmost care was of supreme importance to her. "My illusions wilted and faded a long time ago. All I have is the reality around me, the pains inside me, and my legal husband in front of me."

"Am I annoying you?"

"Not for some time now," she calmly replied, and once again sank into contemplation of her plate's contents. "After all, I never see you."

She likes only subtle foods. I myself lean more towards the spicy: I ordered snails prepared Burgundy-style and cold-smoked salmon, inventively marinated in a soy sauce. An intoxicating steam rose from the hot escargots and the salmon had already been nibbled at, but put aside again. I simply didn't know what to take on first; I wanted everything at once, so I whipped everything into a single festive frivolity. White Moselle wine perfectly complemented this fairy-tale assemblage.

We surely would have changed wines later: *tagliatelle* with a black truffle sauce still awaited Laima, and I had ordered just steak. First class, *saignant* according to French cooking nomenclature. But I kept worrying: maybe I should quickly change it to *a point*? It's actually an important question: I just couldn't decide which shade of seasoning would suit the Chateau Margaux better. My memory lovingly cooed over *saignant*, but I don't trust my memory; it's deceived me too many times.

Sometimes I no longer remember either my name or my sex. I start quite seriously weighing whether I'm an innocent maiden, or a vicious frog, or, in spite of it all, this shabby country's president. Sometimes I no longer know where I've gotten to at the moment, what the place is called. But not that time; that evening I knew it all: this place is called The Astoria, and the woman sitting across from me is called Laima, and she is my silver wife. She really was silvered—but just a tiny bit. I saw silver dust and silver threads sewn into her black dress. Laima's hair is seductively light—it looks even nicer than it did in her youth. I know it's just good-quality hair dye, but after all, it's not my fault that dyed hair looks better than natural. That silicone breasts look sexier than real ones. That children started in a test tube are born healthier than ones made the natural way. I wasn't the one who brought the fashion for prostheses into this world. I hate that fashion, as I hate prostheses themselves. Only my beloved adopted amputees sincerely like prostheses. But my Laima is by no means a human prosthesis—she's my true, irreplaceable wife. I haven't been able to get enough of her for twenty-seven years now.

The candle on the table spread its sweetish fragrance; like it or not, it plunged me into dreams. The striving waiter stands off a way, following my every move, determined to read the slightest desire in my eyes. The hall was practically empty; that evening I was the supreme leader there—to me this is an agreeable and customary condition. Everyone knows me, perhaps only too well: I'm the only one who doesn't know or understand myself. That evening they couldn't recognize me; I had made myself up expertly. I could have had plastic surgery a long time ago, but I continue to prefer make-up. Philosophical reasons forced me to this decision.

I simply do not dare lose my face. A face is a person's distinguishing mark, his essential hieroglyph; nature stuck faces on us so that we wouldn't get confused among ourselves. And at the same time so we couldn't hide from demons, angels, or our just deserts. It seemed to me that changing one's face for eternity would be shameful—I'd be admitting I was a criminal by that alone. If, in spite of everything, I were to succeed, in the moment of triumph I could no longer show my true face. I would remain false and a stranger to myself for the ages. So I didn't change the features of my face; I just constantly alter it with make-up. Make-up is nothing more than a mask that you can wash off later. A mask doesn't change your face—it's merely the expression of an innate human desire for secrecy. And anyway, on that anniversary evening I wasn't supposed to be spouting metaphysics; I was supposed to be enjoying every last thing in turn.

I could enjoy the salmon, coerced Chinese-style; the rare, particularly expensive Moselle wine; but most of all I could enjoy Laima. All colors suited that woman: she looked like the ruler of this country of spiritual pigmies, but at the same time like a stunning frog goddess to whom offerings have to be made humbly. Every real man worthy of the name must kneel before her on his knees and kiss her most secret little corners. She has many such corners, and every one smells differently.

Everything of hers is suitable to be kissed all over. Laima is already forty-four, but she's as slim as an eighteen-year-old beauty queen. Her breasts are like two pigeons—but they don't smell of the pigeon droppings on Vilnius's streets, rather of the sweet fruit trees of paradise. Even from a distance her breasts entice me; Laima just now opened the crack between her breasts for viewing: that cherry-scented notch of her body drives me out of my mind. Knowing this full well, Laima also shows me her pearly teeth—I adore them too. I adore every little corner of her body, every one of her words, and even her unspoken thoughts. The men and women of this country of spiritual pigmies never managed to understand why I am so devoted to this woman. She looks like a frog, my evil-hearted colleagues would say to me in their cups, without even suspecting that they were merely firing up my passion. Of course she looks like a frog. Of course her nose is huge and stubby. But that way she can't be mistaken for anyone; she's unique—what do all of those shitheads know about my one and only wife? For many years she was my only joy; it was only much later that I discovered the great importance of reality in my fateful struggle.

"I'd really like to please you," I said to Laima. "I've wanted to please you all of my life, but I never did create a world worthy of you. I'm really sorry. I didn't even manage to become this wretched country's president."

"There's still plenty of time. Maybe you'll try it from your burrows?"

"But I don't want to anymore. There are quite a few things I don't want anymore."

"Like me?"

She's always so equally headstrong and seductive: she looked at me with such eyes that I instantly felt a sweetness in my loins. Her eyes are a pure blue, and as huge as my entire personal heaven. I would do anything for her. I have already done many strange and unfortunate things for her. But on that anniversary evening I got the urge, for some reason, to dissect her. To rip out her entrails with a curved hunting knife. To stuff a giant barbed pinecone inside her in place of myself. To simply carve her into the tiniest itsy-bitsy pieces, like some laboratory frog. Yes, exactly like some giant frog with youthful blond hair. To bestow upon her, on the occasion of our silver wedding anniversary, a melding with nature and the true essence of the world. After all, the ultimate purpose of the world is the growth of entropy and the final mortal equilibrium. That's why it's imperative to deconstruct all humans; but one must first disassemble them into their component parts. One must not think of this as ordinary murder—it's actually a search for perfection.

"Would you want to reach perfection?" I carefully ask Laima.

"In what sense—would I want to be divided into molecules? Or cut into little round slices and be evenly distributed in as large an area as possible?"

I was a bit surprised that she already knew this theory of mine, but only very slightly surprised. I've already mentioned that my memory was doing amazing things. I remember painfully too much; I'd really like to remember far less. However, even that surplus of memory doesn't exhaust all of my life, all of my thoughts, all of my sacred loves, or the innumerable women I loved, not physically, but in my thoughts. It is constantly turning out there are things in my life I'm completely unaware of.

"I love you," I said to Laima. "Nothing else is important."

The Astoria's hall shone with the pale light of reconciliation; the obliging waiter merely wanted to grant me as much pleasure as possible for the Radisson SAS Astoria's affordable prices; I was drowning in a gentle snailish bliss, alternating it with Moselle wine. I had almost forgotten who I am, and what I'm doing here in this world.

Before all else I am an aesthete; for the sake of god-like beauty I have frequently sacrificed wealth, glory, and even health. Sacrificing health is particularly risky, since health itself is an especially aesthetic thing. Sick people don't look good. But no one could convince me that my one and only beloved wife, the wife I lost at cards, isn't pretty.

3. The Revolt of the Snails

That dangerous evening had to end tragically; perhaps even with a bloody ball of twisted guts. Perhaps even with the flawless scalpel of a surgeon. I was overly confident in my disguise; I had ascended too high into pride and let my spirit loose. And worst of all—I completely ignored the danger of a snail uprising. Snails are dangerous for the sole reason that they're small, slimy, and have little moveable horns, but they're edible anyway. And as if that weren't enough—when they're well-prepared, they're tasty too. That is the ultimate horror of a snail uprising. That's how they try to get inside you, to melt into your essence and infect you with their snailishness. Sometimes they succeed at this. In fact, they frequently do.

They succeeded on the evening of our silver wedding anniversary. But this time the snails behaved in a particularly disgusting manner. They attacked us without even being eaten. They arranged a conspiracy that equaled the worst conspiracies of edible animals in the history of the world. That evening they colluded with the restaurant's entire administration, the waiters, and even some of the paintings on the walls.

It was the paintings that outraged me the most—I always used to get along well with them. I have always considered pictures living creatures, nothing less than a life form of my own race. It's particularly painful when your own race betrays you. A real black would consider a white's betrayal something that practically goes without saying. But betrayal by his black brother could crush him completely. I wasn't at all outraged that the snails betrayed and humiliated me, but the paintings' betrayal pierced my soul with black Voodoo needles.

It was those damned pictures that moved first. Those miserable schemers hung the walls with copies, or maybe imitations, of Francis Bacon. Old Francis keeps turning over in his grave whenever he thinks of them—it's actually quite painful for him: a million idiots have hung a million walls with ridiculous imitations of his figures. And in the other world he has to go on worrying about every one of them. There is no peace on the other side of the Lethe.

So, those wall-mounted perverts that turn old Francis in his grave slowly started to move. They didn't try to climb out of their frames; they didn't make faces, or even try to frighten us. They simply started moving, even though it was precisely their duty to sit there for the ages. Transgressing one's duty in this world is always dangerous and disgusting. It looked particularly repulsive that evening at the Astoria. The nearest painting's figure slowly tilted its sliced-to-pieces head, and leaned over, first to the left, then to the right. At that moment I still didn't suspect anything serious. I still didn't feel the revolting danger of the general scheme. I was just a bit surprised, and took a gulp of wine. Without hurrying, the head of the painting's figure assembled itself into a thing, and unexpectedly a second eye appeared that hadn't been there before. That man sitting on a tall chair took one numb leg off the other and sluggishly exercised it. But he never did escape from the double trap of the painting's frame and the dark blue cube he occupied within the picture. He didn't even try to escape. All of his metamorphoses were no more than a maneuver to distract my attention.

The movements of a painting hanging a bit further on were a deceptive maneuver as well. The elephantine figure in that painting didn't do anything stunning, either. That cellulite creature merely tried to stick stripes of the skin peeling from his thighs to himself. He moved so slowly and so moronically that you immediately saw there was no way he was going to succeed. The skin hung from his massive thighs in a truly unattractive way; a sight like that could make you start gagging instantly.

I should have paid attention to that painting as soon as I walked into the restaurant. No one hangs sickening images on the walls of a fine restaurant. I should have understood it all instantly from that obvious warning alone. But I was totally blind because all I was looking at was Laima. I saw through it too late, and when I saw through it I didn't immediately grasp what was going on. By the time I caught on at least somewhat, the snails started moving too. All six of them, proudly and treacherously, crawled out of their shells and stared at me with their metaphysical eyes. They were still steaming, as they had just been boiled in Burgundy wine. Their little horns, on whose tips the metaphysical eyes were hiding, writhed somewhat like underwater seaweed. I immediately felt like I was under water, and started gasping helplessly for air. Those snails were intentionally drowning me.

I'll share a solemn secret with you: snails are the Lord God's underwater sputum. On that evening, sacred to me in so many ways, that sputum mercilessly flooded my soul. Laima looked in horror at the reanimated snails and the figures in the pictures shaking out their cramps. She just couldn't understand it. I was the only one who more or less understood.

I could escape in a number of ways. To crash straight out the restaurant's veranda windows with all that glass would have been too dramatic, and too dangerous besides. They had prepared their plan almost to perfection, but they overlooked one essential thing: that I had been born and raised in precisely this quarter. It was precisely here that the immortal Sara taught me the art of metaphysical love. It was precisely the basements of this quarter that I knew better than any other thing on this earth. They could rebuild the buildings and rename the streets a thousand times, but I would know what these buildings were really called.

And how could I not know them? I gave them those names myself.

In this corner of the city no one could either catch me or corner me—in this regard they overshot by a mile. They completely disregarded Sun-Tzu's cardinal rule: they went to war with me in a territory I knew a hundred times better than they did. They didn't have a chance.

I was just sorry for the frog I love most in the world: Laima was looking about horrified, in complete confusion. She had been wronged; her celebration was irredeemably ruined, but I wasn't otherwise in fear for her: the snails' metaphysical eyes were staring at me, not at her. The fake obliging waiters naïvely believed they could physically corner me and catch me. Perhaps those skinheads were agents of some special government organization—that wasn't important. I made a joke out of them with every one of my movements. I trickled through them all like beach sand trickles through fingers trembling in excitement. I flowed through them like water through a sieve. They didn't yet grasp what spot I was in when I was already long gone. Their foolish bodies could only be in a single lone spot in space at a time. Their foolish brains were stuffed full of misleading knowledge about the immutable laws of physics, mechanics, and the unavoidable causality of events.

They never did understand a thing. I simply turned into wind and flew through them as if they were bare tree branches. I filtered myself through them, raising only a slight rustle— the way real thousand-year-old Chinese silk rustles. The poor things went after me when I was already at least twenty paces behind their backs. They turned around unbelievably slowly— like that cellulite fatty in the revived painting. They started after me even more slowly, knocking over the half-empty restaurant's chairs, frightening those few people who were unknowingly celebrating my silver anniversary.

Have you ever seen ten fat, clumsy cats trying to catch a single, nimble little mouse? I've seen this many times in my dreams. It was only on the evening of my silver anniversary that I realized what that dream meant. It unambiguously warned me in advance of that grotesque chase. No, those young men weren't at all fat or clumsy. They were well and regularly trained, nimble and physically strong. They clearly had never come across wind that instantly turns into sand, that turns into water, and then into wind again. No one had taught them that there are no separate movements—there is only the single, unbreakable movement of life, whose laws they would never manage to figure out. They couldn't catch me; all they could do was ruin the evening of my silver anniversary.

Later, in the peace of a rain runoff reservoir, I ruefully assumed I'd been recognized again. That is my torture and my damnation. The image of my face was once in all the newspapers and all over TV. My face had impressed itself on people's memory, or perhaps even on the retinas of their eyes. Before going to celebrate my anniversary I spent almost an hour on my hair and disguise, but my efforts were for naught. They recognized me anyway. It's been a long time since my tortured face looked as soft as a inflatable toy; it's no longer even pudgy. But they recognized me anyway. There's nowhere I can hide anymore—except, perhaps, inside my interim coffin.

4. The Interim Coffin

When I go out to eradicate the cockles of this world—I arise from my interim coffin. When I gather or burn up even a few wretched cockles—I lie down in my interim coffin again. There I think over and sort out all those who anger the gods, as well as the ordinary scoundrels, arrange them in my thoughts, count them up, and rearrange them again a different way. This deconstructional manipulation was taught to me by my first father while I was but still a child. For me, this ostensible selection and real, true eradication of human cockles takes the place of erotic dreams. I haven't experienced true erotic dreams for a long time now. That's good; it helps me concentrate like Diogenes, only in place of a barrel I have a coffin. It really is a good thing I don't experience erotic dreams anymore: a corpse with a permanent erection would look particularly unappealing.

Everyone is deceased and lives in his interim coffin; it's just that not everyone realizes this. Still others, in the depths of their souls, really, truly know this, but nothing can make them admit it, even to themselves. I'm completely open with myself, to the very bottom of my human essence, where the black worms and the thought-sucking leeches teem. Perhaps I'm not a man of divine courage, but I'm not a pathological coward either, like most people. I arise from my interim coffin to carry out my immortal task. It's only the work itself that's immortal, while people, according to divine definition, are interim. That's the definition of a human: a temporarily thinking reed. That's why it's handiest to consider yourself a dead man beforehand—then Death can't possibly catch you by surprise. It won't frighten you; it won't even surprise you. After all, you've always lived in a coffin; you were prepared in advance for Death's despicable attacks. It's truly pointless to hope you'll be the one the solemn bony creature with the scythe will overlook. There's no need to suppose you could become immortal. There's no need to fight with the gods; it's much better to simply collect and burn the cockles. Even if you were once—and perhaps still are—a despicable and noxiously rabid cockle. Or maybe it's the opposite—you're one of the thirty-six righteous men upholding the world's existence. The only one of them who has criminally deciphered his cosmic fate and as a punishment was quashed long ago.

Pushed along by these thoughts, I trudged home, dragging my feet and sluggishly cleaning off my make-up on the way. I've gotten so experienced at putting on and changing make-up that I could do it without a mirror, with my eyes closed, or in complete darkness. I change my despicable face almost automatically—without thinking and without even selecting a specific look for that day. I long ago accepted that I must always appear different—even though I'm frequently recognized no matter how I look. It's just that the time it takes to recognize me has grown considerably longer. After all, that's what you're after with make-up: that it would take as long as possible to recognize you, and in the end, when recognized, you would be taken for a completely different person.

My interim coffin differs from many other people's dwellings: there's no windows in it. But I got used to a coffin of that form when I was still in the Seimas. After all, the chamber where the Seimas sessions are held doesn't have windows, either; it used to feel even more oppressive, and certainly the company that would assemble there is nowhere near as cheerful as the one that gathers here. That cheerful company greeted me from afar with songs and various hoarse howls. And with Afrika's incomparable sweetish stench: those sensitive nostrils of mine picked up his scent from a hundred meters away. I entered through the first tunnel and immediately knew everyone was already home. They didn't know I was celebrating an anniversary today; they were celebrating their own joys and sorrows.

In the very center of the interim coffin stood a bulging five-liter wine bottle with a handle. My guys were drinking ritualistically: they sat shyly in the corners, only from time to time singing out some song's crazy little stanza. A single one would carefully get up and sneak over to the bulging bottle as if approaching a live prey that could dash off. Turning up the bottle, he would greedily suck down his gulp and proudly return to his spot. By no means would the next drinker approach the bottle immediately; they obeyed a rhythm I didn't understand, so each one would dally for some time before getting up. Even Braniukas and Serioga didn't break the long-pause rule. What astonished me most was that the wine was actually pretty good: it was the year before last's California Chablis. A bottle like that had to cost some hundred fifty litas; Apples Petriukas was the only one who could have brought it here.

I needed to down a good-sized gulp myself, but sadly, not understanding the drinkers' ritual, I froze. I didn't remain unnoticed. Albinas Afrika menacingly raised his right hand with the forefinger extended, and with his left quickly snatched up a small set of drums.

"*Attenzione!*" he brayed in his asinine voice. "The host has returned home. Let's all listen: I'm playing the basic theme for the newly-formed situation."

He drummed and swung like mad, his arms started wandering up and down and to the sides like hysterical hands. The echoes from the walls and heating pipes doubled and tripled the rhythm, and the drinkers pleasantly cheered up. Apples Petriukas bounced to the rhythm with his eyes closed. Afrika himself went completely nuts, waved and vibrated his hands so fast that they began to merge with the drums, and I finally felt the rhythm. I felt it with my spine, the tips of my fingers, and both hemispheres of my brain. Now I knew the pace at which I should drink the wine, what pauses to make and what cosmic order I should hold to. I carefully snuck up to the bottle, grabbed it, and greedily upended it. The wine was refreshing, with a hint of at least several fruits and perhaps even pumpkin. I wiped off my lips, and Afrika suddenly stopped pounding. However, the rhythm he had hammered in was still spreading in the complete silence; it had drilled into the space and my brain. Now I was giving birth to the rhythm myself with every cell in my body.

"That was 'The Marabou Salsa'," Albinas Afrika announced. "Because I'm a Senegalese Marabou myself, and Jennifer Lopez's little ass inspired our salsa hallucination."

I felt like a lost father come home. Serioga, accurately according to the rhythm still pulsating in my brain, tiptoed to the bottle and poured down his dose. Instantly I felt I had perfectly understood the entire structure of the intertwining rhythms of the world and a good portion of the secrets of the Cosmos. Albinas Afrika was already resting, his hands hanging limply, glittering with all his sparkles and beads. His Sudanese or Senegalese cap changed colors and his idiotic pseudo-African tunic spread a sweetish stench uniquely characteristic of Africa. It wasn't the smell of human sweat—only Africa's rotting soils, fertilized with rhinoceros dung, could stink like that. Albinas didn't just influence the world with rhythms, but with smells, too. Serioga and Braniukas haven't had the least influence on the world for quite some time now. Apples Petriukas gathered crystals of wisdom from the world as well as arranged special garbage dump pearls.

He would go to the dumps the way an archeologist goes to the excavation of an ancient city: to understand a people, or perhaps an entire civilization. He wanted to understand the

Lithuanian civilization—unlike me, he believed such a thing existed. Apples Petriukas supposed if he'd find the essence of this civilization, it could only be in the dumps or the garbage bins. He used to find his book titles there, too.

He wrote seven books; each new one was shorter than the last. There were all of three pages of text in the seventh one, and then Apples Petriukas no longer wrote text for books at all—he only came up with titles for them.

"A title is entirely enough for a book, if it's a suitable title," Petriukas would calmly explain, inhaling the smoke of some mild weed. "I'll be flawless only when I learn to write a book that will be no more than a title, and that title will have only one word, and in that word there will be only one letter. But that letter will have to be of such depth that a lifetime wouldn't be long enough to read it."

Apples Petriukas was probably a real philosopher, not a fake one. Although what do I know about him? All I know is why he hides underground and in the garbage dumps, and he knows why I'm hiding from people. We know too much about one another because we've known each other since the beginning of the world. Sometimes it seems to me that I knew Petriukas even before my first father; sometimes—that my first father was, at the same time, my first acquaintance with Petriukas. And sometimes I think that all in all, Apples Petriukas is my very first father.

"So are you drinking, or not?" Albinas Afrika asked peevishly. "It is your turn; I did, after all, play it clearly."

That evening I felt dreadfully tired: the sullen dog-faces from Francis Bacon's paintings ruined my wedding anniversary, and Albinas didn't play either a funeral march or a dance with swords for me—all he played was "The Marabou Salsa." I simply didn't know anymore what to do or how to feel inside my interim coffin. When I don't know how to feel, I keep trying to remember my first father.

5. My First Father

My first father was an interim coffin designer. But he didn't construct actual interim coffins; rather, he made spiritual ones—those that people confine themselves to of their own volition: the foolish labyrinths of human suffering. He tried to bond people's memories, used things, and old senseless dreams into a single object. Out of all this he tried to sculpt the image of a man, or his spiritual portrait.

But he was also the great destroyer of the world's structure. Although perhaps he was a reconstructionist: he wasn't at all interested in destroying anything—he just wanted to reassemble everything in his own way. He merely kept shifting our world around one way and another—the way children do with play blocks. He played perpetual Legos, with no beginning or end. My first father was a deconstructionist—only he didn't deconstruct someone's despicable written texts, but rather all the Lord's creation. He wrestled with the Lord in a purely constructive, not aesthetic, sense. My first father wasn't in the least concerned with his collection's beauty.

In a certain sense, he and Apples Petriukas are alike—the way brothers can be alike in the depths of their core when they don't resemble each other at all on the surface. That's exactly why I sometimes confuse the two of them. Perhaps I did get to know my father first, and only later Petriukas with his immortal Voodoo.

I remember very clearly how I stumbled into Father's secret deconstruction room for the first time. It seems to me that at that time we lived in a huge house where you could get lost. But perhaps it just seemed that way to me. However, that time I really did get lost in it, and accidentally found my first father. I meant to say—his special deconstruction room. You could get to it only by climbing up dusty, creaking stairs; they didn't even creak—they coughed, hissed, and laughed hollowly. They responsively socialized with you for as long as you trampled on their dusty spine.

Then you had to get yourself through the door. It allowed you in according to its whims, very cleverly and deceptively. Seemingly, it always let you in; it was never completely closed, but it ingeniously hid Father's real room. Every time you stepped over the threshold you could end up in a different dwelling. Some of those rooms had nothing in common with my first father, other rooms were unquestionably his—dining rooms, bedrooms, or offices. But only one single one was his special deconstruction room. That very first time I wandered into it totally by accident.

"The door let you in today, anyway," Father wondered somewhat innocently. "Come in, make yourself at home. Actually, you already are."

I myself wasn't convinced of that in the least; in those days I wasn't, in general, convinced of anything. I was a strangely spindly seven-year-old, fearfully trying to get to know the world, to name at least several of its more important characteristics more clearly. Unfortunately, it really wasn't worth hankering after clarity in our house. That kingdom of fly-splattered mirrors, shadows, and cobwebs wasn't at all suitable for seeking light and purity. My first father was completely incapable of explaining anything; he merely stood at full height in his deconstruction room and smiled miserably. I remember his morning jacket: made of silk, it had tiny rhombuses stitched on it, and inside each rhombus a tiny, barely visible ornamental coin. Just don't ask me what color that jacket was: all the things in Father's room appeared colorless, appeared to be constantly taking on some other color, appeared to be denying the existence of any color at all.

It was my mother who dressed Father in that jacket—at that time she hadn't yet taken up training and torturing me, so she tormented and controlled my first father. Gorgeous Rožė wanted to make an aristocrat out of him. That jacket suited him like a fifth leg suits a dog: my father grew up in a small town and remained in essence an unsophisticated village boy, right up until his end. That day he held an old silver teapot in his hand, like Hamlet his skull.

"I see all of the people who have drunk from it," he said to me sheepishly. "There were sixteen of them. They lived in a single house for all of three generations. They liked tea. All of them, except for just one. That one hated tea, but he was forced to drink it anyway, along with everyone else. He was a redhead and died of consumption."

Father gently set the teapot on the fourth shelf under his left hand, and then carefully lifted a disintegrating, rotting piece of wood lying one shelf lower and three positions further to the right. Later I practically memorized all those shelves and those positions. I used to dream of them, and even in my dreams I would deconstruct and refine the world. That first time I just gaped in astonishment. To me, a seven-year-old, there couldn't be anything more miraculous than all of those little shelves, drawers, and flasks jammed and crammed, overfilled and overflowing with the largest variety of mysterious things. Tiny naked silver-colored little humanoids quietly and nimbly scurried about over all those little shelves. They weren't really little humanoids; you see, they had rather long, flexible tails. My head swam; I actually started to get short of breath from the excess of all those oddities. I wanted all of them at once, I was afraid of those nimble, long-tailed humanoids, and I was desperately envious of my father for having such a plethora of miraculous things. I envied him, and felt a deep respect for him.

"Why do you have so much of everything?" I asked thoughtlessly.

"Is this a lot?" Father was sincerely surprised. "It's merely a millionth... a million-millionth a part of what I must collect."

He grew a bit sad, but nevertheless remained exceedingly dignified. On that occasion he unintentionally betrayed his great secret to me, which later he never wanted to admit to again.

"The world is dreadfully imperfect, my son," he said nearly syllable by syllable. "It should be made over anew, but that's too complicated. But it's possible to straighten it out a bit... To select some of its places and remodel them a bit, very carefully... You can disassemble some people, some sighs, some seas... Some insects, some feelings, some clouds... After all, scientists can disassemble atomic nuclei... God created those nuclei one way, and science remade them its own way... But after all, God also created frogs and cosmic nebulae. A lot of imperfect things."

He was probably talking to himself, or maybe just thinking out loud, but one way or another I heard all of it. Later he never again admitted to what he was doing. He would just call his deconstruction room a collection. At one point he actually naïvely tried to pretend to be an artist, and explained that it was a conceptional example of the art of arranging shelves. However, that first and only time he betrayed himself. At the time I didn't understand anything, but I took note of every one of his words.

The world really is dreadfully imperfect. Some people really are worth disassembling, as are some sighs. By no means all of them: the majority of sighs are urgently needed to support the structure of the world. When some sighs are erased or disassembled, it's not just that mountain peaks could disintegrate, not just clouds and insects, but the entire secret mechanics of atomic nuclei. It's much simpler to disassemble some people: most of the time this type of deconstruction doesn't harm anyone. Ideally, by now there could have been a number of dried humanoid mummies—as varied as possible—standing in my first father's so-called collection. From the very largest to the very smallest, from complete cockles to those who had only reached the very first stage of cockledom. That would have been more logical, and more useful to the world. But we all do what we can. My first father was only able to accumulate his deconstruction collection. Back in those days, forty years ago, everything around me seemed miraculous. The scents of unknown flowers and old clothes spread through the dimmed room. The number of shelves and nooks was endless; you couldn't even see where they ended, how far they stretched.

"There really are clouds and beetles here?"

"Really," Father confirmed.

"And sunsets at Palanga's pier?"

"And sunsets."

"And that dream where the wolves chase me?"

"And that dream of yours, too—inside a tiny jar."

I simply ran short of imagination when I tried to envision what else there could be there. Later, while secretly investigating Father's room, I kept running short of imagination when I tried to understand how my first father deconstructed the Lord's world. What he disassembled, where he arranged the components, and how he afterwards put everything together again anew. And most important—how he thought up, or at least dreamed up, the great plan of that new arrangement.

When they disassembled my first father himself, it was if as I started to grasp a thing or two, I don't know myself what. Perhaps that the deconstructor himself can be the deconstructed. Perhaps that the world really is too imperfect and unjust. Fundamentally unjust—demanding, insisting, that you essentially reconstruct it.

The world bit off my first father's head, and that, as regards myself, was terribly unjust. I was forced to get a second father in order to outweigh my wrong in at least some small degree. This time it wasn't an imaginary collection my second father had; it was a real one—a collection for the sake of a collection. This second one also hid in special rooms and also smelled of forgotten dreams. But you couldn't begin to compare it to the first. The same way you couldn't begin to compare my first father with my second. I became acquainted with Father's deconstruction room the fall I turned seven. I bade goodbye to its remains much more sadly, sobbing hoarsely without tears. I was fourteen at the time. My first father had died, and I desperately wanted to save at least a part of his legacy. That legacy wasn't just a heap of things or ideas: the deconstruction room was literally a part of my first father. As long as that room existed, a good part of my father survived as well. I hurried to my old house, actually stumbling on the way. Gasping for breath, I ran through Sara's yard at a trot, past the former strategic spots for ice cream vendors, struggled up the hill through the triple gates of the old monastery, and finally approached Father's spiritual abode.

I was overcome by a hideous foreboding, but what I saw exceeded my worst imaginings. The door let me in without so much as creaking—it had been finished off, too. I sprang into the room and froze in horror: it hadn't merely been murdered, but maliciously destroyed as well. Only murder maniacs behave that way; it's not enough to simply kill, they must mock their victims, too—before and after killing. With my entire body I sensed who that hideous murder maniac was.

She didn't kill just the room, she also finished off the last part of Father that was still alive. She demolished the entire world that had been stubbornly and painstakingly assembled on my first father's sagging shelves. My mother was never just a murderess; she was the Angel of Death itself, the carrier of death and its presenter in the home. It wasn't enough for her that the despicable world had bitten off my father's head; she needed to destroy all the remains of his spirit, too, all intuitions of his ideas, even the very possibility of remembering him. I mortally hated my mother, and she mortally hated me. In this sense we're equal and perfectly alike. I am truly my mother's child—that I don't doubt in the least.

6. Gorgeous Rožė

I don't know why Gorgeous Rožė so aggressively snatched up
my father for herself. Perhaps because he was so thoughtful
and mystically secretive, and she hadn't yet turned into either
the Angel of Death or a vampire. Or perhaps because even in
those gloomy times the newspapers and magazines wrote about
him: they worshipped the Lithuanians' incomparable star of
Soviet science. You see, in his free time from the deconstructive rearrangement of the world, my first father took up mathematics as well. At spare moments from research in his secret
room, he formed a high-spirited topological team at the university and even received several international awards. And my
mother always went mad over people with a famous name. Just
the smell of a man like that would give her a mild orgasm. It
was only because of people of that sort that she would descend
to earth; you see, she normally lived on completely unknown
airless planets.

On rare occasions she would descend from one of her
planets and unfailingly tousled my hair—I despised that habit
of hers. I never knew what to talk to her about—I was accustomed to talk to servants, and to me mother's manner and
vocabulary seemed foreign and tasteless. She used to descend
from her airless planet, tousle my hair, and pronounce some
astounding nonsense characteristic of deranged aliens.

"You've grown, kiddo," she would say nonchalantly.

"You're a real boy already. Maybe you've got girlfriends by now? Maybe you'll introduce us?"

She talked that way when I hadn't even gotten to know Sara better yet, just my courtyard and the playing field, where sturdy, sweaty girls with handballs scampered about. At that time I didn't have any sexual problems yet—only metaphysical ones. I was extremely intrigued by why Vilnius pigeons flew carried on wings, but clouds hover of their own accord. Why people sleep at night and walk around during the day. Why winter is cold and summer warm. I was already acquainted with my first father and his deconstruction room, but my mother was a complete mystery.

"Your fingers are long, like a pianist's," she would say, grabbing my hand. "You positively must become a musician. I'll make a world-famous player out of you. You'll bathe in money and glory. You can't even imagine what glory and money mean."

She talked in this senseless manner later, just at the time when I was already hugely interested in girls. Actually, not just girls, but more the very cosmic origin of womanhood. Everything around me, all the world's forms, reminded me of women. I couldn't imagine what I should or could do with those women, but I hungered for all of them with a suffocating, greedy desire. I hungered to touch, smell, and taste them; I wanted to simply melt within them and return no more to my repulsive body. Every last thing in the world was but women. Even the chairs in our dining room were women I desired. The trees in the courtyard had an astoundingly womanly form that drove me out of my mind. They resembled my naked mother. Sara was the woman of all women, even though she was only nine. And Mother babbled at me about a piano, in whose sounds there were was nothing more than women hiding in the highest vibrations.

Mother would pronounce her typical nonsense and clatter up the stairs. The magical stairs didn't chat with her; they didn't in general socialize. And she herself never said that what I expected from her, what I wanted from her. She was never a mother to me; she remained an alien from an airless planet, demonstratively enticing me erotically. She always forced me to do not what I wanted, but most importantly—not what this world needed of me. Gorgeous Rožė would clatter up the stairs, and I would stealthily creep up after her. I would secretly watch her changing her clothes. She took off her clothes slowly and gracefully; I learned what a real woman should look like from her perfect body. In my head, all the cosmic forms of women were made up only of my mother's body.

At that time my mother was stunningly beautiful. It isn't a veil of childhood memories and illusions; it's a sad, objective fact. My mother was Gorgeous Rožė, one of the first in all of Vilnius to turn beauty into a lifestyle. She shamelessly sold her beauty left and right, shone professionally in the high society of that time, and openly profited by it: with acquaintances, connections, or directly via expensive gifts. Without hiding it, she brought those gifts home and unwrapped them while Father watched. For that humiliation of Father I hate her. My first father was an abstraction-minded mathematician and a mad deconstructor of the world, but he was neither a fool nor a dupe. His intelligent face would fall, his lower lip would begin trembling rapidly, but he would never say anything, and afterwards he would go make love with Mother, too. Gorgeous Rožė would make him a gift of the incomparable sinuosities of her vagina just as liberally as she did all the others. I hated their creaking bed; that bed was a traitor that had made a secret plot with that dissipated mother of mine. That bed showed how weak and physically corruptible my father was. I wanted to see him as a demigod rearranging the world, and he showed himself to be nothing more than a powerless cuckolded husband, managing to silently come to terms with his spreading horns. He rearranged entire worlds, but didn't even try to rearrange his wife.

At that time, my hatred for my mother was no more than a puny, yellowish shoot, transparent and easily broken. But no one took up breaking it; it slowly grew and strengthened. I hated mother even more when secretly watching her change clothes. She burned me with the beauty of her naked body and my own hopeless shame. Pressing myself up against the crack in the partially open door, I would stare, my body completely numb, practically without breathing. She would carelessly take off her slip and then climb out of her panties. My body used to get so numb, it would turn completely spongy: if I had moved I could have sunk to the ground or broken into bits. I knew I was committing a horrible crime. I convulsively swallowed my spit and burned with shame, but I only watched even more attentively, not wanting to miss the slightest detail. My naked mother was stunningly beautiful: all the parts of her perfect body were just where they ought to be. I thought up my own names, mesmerizing, mysterious words, for all of her body's details. What I feared most was not even that I would be discovered and punished horribly; what I feared most was that afterwards my mother would shut the door carefully and tightly every time she undressed. If that had happened, I would have smelled her scent through the cracks in the door; I would have swooned merely from the quiet rustle of the discarded clothes.

Then one time my mother suddenly turned to me, naked and as beautiful as a goddess. I froze by the crack in the door with my completely numb body unable to even run away. I couldn't begin to imagine what she would do to me now. I had earned the very worst punishment. Mother came several steps closer without covering herself in the least, put her hands on her hips, and in a melodious voice asked:

"Am I really pretty? Would you want a woman like me when you grow up? Or maybe you're already grown up? Is there hair growing around your weenie already?"

She gazed at me with drowsy, somewhat tired eyes. But I

could not tear my eyes away from the rose in her crotch, which I saw for the first time from so close up. That rose of the crotch was like a mirror in which I saw myself—perhaps because it was just exactly from there that I had emerged into this world. It was only when I saw myself that way that I finally unfroze and was able to escape. I hated her and feared her. Gorgeous Rožė carelessly mocked my disgusting secret surveillance; it made absolutely no difference to her that I secretly stared at her naked. It didn't seem either indecent or shameful to her; perhaps she didn't actually consider me her son, just some curious adolescent. It was shameful to me, but horrible at the same time. At that time I was truly raving over the great idea of the cosmic woman, and to me all women resembled my mother. Just as beautiful and shameless as nature itself. With the incomparable mirror of the vagina, which reflects everyone who looks at it but can mesmerize as well, even transport you into the kingdom beyond the mirror.

But my mother's most shameless deed back then was the hideous advertising swing. She hung in that silly swing dressed in the national costume, with an amber necklace and with her hair woven into braids. It was perhaps the first official Lithuanian advertisement. My grinning mother advertised the Song Festival. It wasn't important to her what she advertised; she just wanted to end up on the cover of magazines and on posters, and in this way not just catch up with, but outdo my father's popularity. My sumptuous mother, the black panther of the Neringa restaurant, dressed up in the national costume for the first time in her life and grinned like a complete fool, or maybe like the Angel of Death. Many years later she was brutally punished for it: she really did turn into the Angel of Death and constantly hung amber necklaces on her neck, sometimes even two or three.

That summer Gorgeous Rožė was everywhere. I could barely go out of the house, because my Angel of Death mother stupidly stared at me from all the walls. She hung on a silly swing and caused me unrelenting shame. No one can understand how ashamed I was. She undressed herself even more disgustingly and openly than she would do in her room, knowing full well that I was secretly watching her. She shamelessly undressed herself in front of the entire city—she might as well have gone down all of Old Town's streets completely naked. It would really have been well worth it for Vilnius to see Gorgeous Rožė naked. That summer I no longer had a mother—only the creature of the advertising poster. I hated her. My hatred was no longer a puny shoot; it had grown into a slender but persistent tree—as tall as I was.

I followed her in the evenings. My first father sat in his deconstruction room and unhurriedly repositioned the world over and over again. I could read books, scamper about the streets with bad company, or die. In order to not die, I followed my dissipated alien mother. I don't even know what secrets I wanted to discover, but my inner voice whispered to me that sooner or later I would find yet more basis for my hatred. Following her wasn't at all difficult, because Gorgeous Rožė liked to walk. That beauty, who couldn't bear any work, could stride along for miles. Perhaps she thought she was exercising that way and avoiding weight gain. At that time there wasn't so much as a whiff of fitness or aerobic centers, and Vilnius's streets were boringly safe.

If she didn't hang out at the Neringa, she would go visit Irena; the two of them sipped liquor or wine for hours upon hours and chatted nonstop, interrupting one another. I couldn't hear what they talked about; I spied on them from the other side of a closed Old Town courtyard, pressed behind the pillar of a stairway. Their soundlessly talking heads stared out the window's rectangle as if it were a giant television screen. That sight was considerably more interesting than Soviet television programs. At least I could fantasize about what the two of them were talking about in there. In my fantasy they discussed Petrarch and Shakespeare. And then convinced one another how important it was to love their only sons with all their hearts, to understand their desires and secret fears. To know and approve that they secretly watched their naked mothers. To understand and to love, to know and to approve.

And one intoxicating evening, on the crooked Old Town window television, I saw something neither fitting nor beneficial for me to see. True, that sight didn't in essence change anything in my life—perhaps it just mollified my obsessive hatred for my mother. She and Irena were, as always, decently sloshed; the soundless television spectacle seemingly continued in its usual way, but suddenly I felt my body uncontrollably melting and turning spongy. It couldn't have been otherwise: unexpectedly, my mother began slowly and gracefully undressing. That sight had been seen many times, but at the same time it was unprecedentedly special. You see, that evening I should have had two bodies; the second had to melt and turn spongy too: Irena also started undressing slowly and seductively. I had never seen her naked, although I had imagined it a hundred times. She didn't look as beautiful as my mother, but her breasts were so large and heavy—I hadn't seen any like them in any pornographic picture. With two bodies, twice as spongy, not fully understanding what was going on, I watched that horrifying but gratifying erotic dance from beginning to end. That evening I experienced the first real erection of my life. I was ten years old; I attentively watched my mother dancing a love dance with her friend. I thought it was first and foremost a dance. I hardly remember much of that grotesquery; in that ballet there was plenty of nakedness and something irremediably painful. Those two women made love as if out of despair, as if they hadn't found themselves a suitable man, as if they could no longer find anything in this world: just ample liqueur and one another. The two of them, with immense care and for a long time, stared at one another's mirror of the crotch. The two of them very much wanted to see the most important secrets of womanly being in those miraculous mirrors. They would constantly lick one another's mirrors so they wouldn't cloud over, so they wouldn't, God forbid, miss seeing anything meaningful. That's probably all I truly remember from that evening. Naked bodies, an erotic dance, and the lustful licking of the miraculous mirror of the crotch.

After that lesbian ballet, Mother could no longer surprise me with anything. For some reason I no longer felt the earlier burgeoning hate for her; I simply obeyed her. Gorgeous Rožė was a dissipated alien from an unknown airless planet, so all there was left for me was to obey. I simply had no other alternative. And I meekly obeyed her: I allowed her to mold me into a young genius, the first and last da Vinci of Vilnius.

7. The Sufferings of the Young da Vinci

Gorgeous Rožė was weirdly disappointed in my first father. Father didn't in the least want to become what Mother pushed and prodded him to be. He didn't want to wear a silk jacket at home, one with tiny ornamental coins inside stitched rhombuses. Real, true French cognac, acquired through communist connections at the highest levels, made heartburn gnaw unbearably at his esophagus: Father's very body protested against Mother's snobbish intentions. All he wanted was to gather his deconstruction collection and carefully remake the world. That was the essence of his existence, and money for bread and butter and even caviar he earned at the university. He had no desire whatsoever to end up in the world of moneyed society and make a million useful connections. Better to make a million absolutely worthless connections with the things of his supposed collection, and the free connections left over—with me. I helped him arrange some of the things in his secret room. It seems to me that I sometimes helped him set himself to rights; I used to return him to the concrete world of Vilnius almost by force. My first father would at intervals forget who he was and where he lived. Arranging his cosmic solitaire, he would forget to eat or go to the bathroom. Undoubtedly he would feel something was amiss, he would feel some kind of discomfort, but perhaps he simply got confused between his carefully remodeled worlds; he no longer distinguished in which Cosmos and in what form he himself existed. At those times I would help him regain his awareness: he would always obey me, he never wanted to dismantle me. I suited my first father the way I really was.

Mother was the only one who tried to change me. She finally happened upon me on her airless planets when I turned eleven and all of my thoughts turned around the idea of the metaphysical origin of womanhood. I still remember my first, and at that time only, true manly erection, experienced in the stairway gallery of a closed Old Town courtyard, secretly watching my omnipotent and multi-gendered mother with her busty friend. But Gorgeous Rožė didn't offer me any answers about women's meaning in the Universe; she didn't even offer me any concrete women. I had to find and figure out Sara all on my own. Instead she started molding an all-around genius out of me, the first and only da Vinci of Vilnius. To send a child to art or music school was already fashionable at that time. However, only my alien mother from the airless planets could seek the absolute in her own way: she sent me to all the schools and forced me to take up everything at the same time. Unexpectedly, I turned into the most Renaissance teenager in Vilnius, a sickly da Vinci with eyes watering from ceaseless effort.

I had no idea why that was necessary. I felt an unfulfilled emptiness within myself; I felt as if I were pregnant with a teeny-tiny embryo—both physically and spiritually. That strange embryo took up only a thousandth part of myself, and everything else was cosmically empty. I wanted to give birth to an entirely different infant than the one Gorgeous Rožė pulled out of me with forceps. I had no idea to what purpose she drove me to art school and forced me to draw and to throw pots. Those things oppressed me. I started hating all pots in general—even the kitchen teapot. The worst of it was that I naturally knew how to draw, and even how to throw those wretched pots. Nameless, mocking gods inspired those talents in me. The art school teacher went into shock when, during the very first lesson, I drew a study of a Greek vase better than he could himself. But the mockery of the unknown gods was fundamental: all of my triumphs and talents didn't bring me the least joy, not even ordinary satisfaction. The more and the prettier the vases I drew, the deeper and the blacker that wretched emptiness within me spread. I was essentially vacant; my interior was irredeemably short of me myself. With every painted landscape of Vilnius, the black emptiness within me expanded even further, and inside me less and less was left of myself. It would have been better if I had never learned to draw a standard cone, a cylinder, or those shitty pseudo-Greek vases.

Unfortunately, I always knew and know everything, or almost everything, naturally—that was the curse of my life. When my mother, through a third-hand acquaintance, pushed me into a music school too, I started playing the piano decently in the second week. My fingers really are long and ridiculously well-suited to a pianist. All upright and grand pianos seemed like women to me, women I greedily palpated with my slender, agile fingers. While playing I would experience a long and painful erection; I would close my eyes and think about Sara; mostly about Sara. Sometimes about my naked mother, too, and Irena's heavy, naked breasts, and the lesbian ballet's frenzy. But this didn't fill my emptiness either; I felt energy struggling out of my inner being, but it was without any direction, as useless as the seed of a wet dream, unable to impregnate anything.

"Sara, I'll take you like a tornado," I would say to the piano, playing the Appassionata. "I'll fly into your most secret little hole like a typhoon."

For me, Beethoven always corresponded with Sara Mejerovič's plump red cheeks. Ludwig van truly knew some of women's cosmic outlandishness—it's no coincidence he was deaf. You'll understand women better in general when you're deaf, or simply can't hear their endless babbling.

"Irena, I'm so small that I'd drown between your boobs," I'd explain to the piano, sawing an Oginski polonaise or some Chopin opus for the thousandth time. "And when I drown there, I'll live within you, I'll be a part of you, the two of us will love Gorgeous Rožė together."

I don't know why, but every Polish composer, right up to Lutosławski and Penderecki, at once painfully reminded me of Irena's breasts. The latter two instantly called up a vision of the slender and firm behind of a light mulatto. All music was nothing more than a constant erotic torture to me, slowly growing into a pain of the finger joints.

After two years of this erotic torture, I won the republic's young pianist contest and brought home my first prize. Very soon all sorts of prizes no longer fit on the shelves in my room. They multiplied like cockroaches. I didn't understand very well myself where they came from and what they were supposed to mean. Some were given to me for playing the piano, others for mathematical olympiads, still others for art shows—they all tangled together and furiously tried to smother each other. I didn't understand what my mother wanted me to turn me into. All I understood was that I really didn't want to turn into a sickly and mad da Vinci with a boundless emptiness inside.

I didn't want to gouge out woodcuts or paint pictures. I didn't want to play those never-ending senseless little strings of notes. Mathematical problems seemed ridiculous to me, since after barely glancing at them I already knew their solutions, and sometimes even the answers. I knew almost everything naturally—it is the curse of my life, the mockery of the sadistic nameless gods. The more I accomplished on the surface, the less remained of me inside. I practically did not doubt that when I had accomplished absolutely everything, I would be left perfectly empty: all of me would be no more than a black emptiness.

But my mother wasn't concerned about any fulfillment; all she worried about was my prizes and trophies. She was always intoxicated by famous people, and here I myself was becoming more and more famous. I didn't concern her at all, but my empty glory sent her into ecstasy. Her conceited friends swooned out of envy when I would win yet another competition, yet another physics olympiad, yet another senseless basketball game. There was nothing more she needed of me. She even stopped undressing within my sight. I never understood why she gave birth to me. It was probably a thoughtless mistake; perhaps she didn't even realize what was happening inside her and was terribly surprised when I came out of her.

From time to time I would still follow her. Irena, together with all her boobs, ran off abroad somewhere, and Gorgeous Rožė didn't set herself up with any other friends. She simply wandered through the city, and sometimes she would get drunk all alone in some little hole in the wall. I no longer felt hate for her, but I couldn't support her, either. After all, who could support the blank panther of the Neringa, glomming onto others' rich and influential husbands in full sight of the entire city? When she used to vanish into the Neringa it would become impossible to watch her. The curtains were too thick, and staring there, glued to a fashionable cafe's window, would not have been allowed. I would idly return home; sometimes I'd read father's books, and sometimes go inside his secret room. He spent more and more time there. When I was seven or nine, he would stop by there only occasionally, as if going to a ceremony or devoting himself to a nearly religious ritual. But slowly he began stopping by there more and more often, and staying longer and longer. His invented deconstructive world pulled him out of the real world and no longer let him return. The deconstruction room sucked him out and muddled his pragmatic sense.

But I wasn't angry with that room; I didn't feel any hate or envy for it. It enchanted me and intimidated me somewhat. I felt attachment and something like respect for it. That room was more interesting than the outside world. In the outside world, there was nothing but school, piano competitions, and mathematic olympiads, as well as mother's worn-out evening routes. The things and smells in father's secret deconstruction room constantly arranged themselves into new combinations; in that room two plus two by no means equaled four, and a rock released from your hand wouldn't necessarily fall to the ground. A deep meaning hid within that room—unlike the outside world, which was categorically senseless. In father's deconstruction room I sometimes felt at least half-full, even if full of who knows what.

I tried very hard to find some kind of meaning in the outside world too. I tried much harder than that degenerate world deserved. However, it was completely fruitless: no one could explain to me what meaning there was, even in this kind of ritual: first you play the same concert ten times at home, by the way, knowing full well that others are forced to play it hundreds of hundreds of times before they manage to play anything at all. Then you dress up in a long-tailed jacket that resembles a tuxedo, a bow tie is fastened onto you, and you're pushed out onto the stage. Here, for the forty-seventh time, you play a deathly boring concert for the gathered crowd of wax people. They sit in sluggish rows; their eyes are empty, but they fervidly pretend they're holding their breath listening to your playing. Afterwards you stand up to bow, and they suddenly come to life again and applaud like mad. It's just that you don't hear the sound of the applause at all: you tried so hard to not listen to the concert you were playing that now you can't hear anything. Can there really be some kind of meaning in all that?

It's something else entirely to attempt to applaud with one hand. It's something else entirely to sit with father in his deconstruction room and carefully move things from one shelf to another, to perfectly remember the entire order of movements. It's extremely important to remember that order perfectly: the finger-sized green clay puppy definitely can't end up more than three rows from last year's dried bouquet of flowers. The bone from a child's forearm found in a village cemetery must always lie next to Tsar Nicholas's gold ten-ruble coin. Those rules were innumerable, and they were all equally important. If even one of them was unintentionally broken, an entire week's deconstructed world could unexpectedly disintegrate. It was as if the rock of Sisyphus could rumble down the slope, on its way breaking and destroying everything as well. When I was helping father, I had to be as subtle as the most painstaking of microsurgeons. I don't know why my first father needed that torture; one time I openly asked him that.

"It's punishment," father replied, sighing. "The world assigns punishment to every human—one's really awful, another's maybe completely ridiculous. Yet another human even gets a couple of punishments. I was given only one, but a very clear one: this damned collection, this library of Babylon without books, this work of art with no metaphor. It's actually a natural god-like punishment. Others call it a cross you are fated to drag along all your life."

"And absolutely everyone is punished?"

"Absolutely everyone."

"Even those who are rich and happy?"

"They're painfully punished with wealth."

"Even those who are just happy?"

"They're particularly punished. They're punished with a boundless foolishness, because, you see, they think they're happy. People can't be happy. The topology of human fate doesn't allow it. God created man unhappy; that unhappiness is what turns the wheels of the world."

This was one of my rare conversations with father; he opened the third eye for me. Suddenly I began to see, and in a flash I understood all of my life at that time. It was simply my punishment. The young musicians' competitions, the children's art shows, and my depraved memories of my naked mother—it was all my punishment. I was already twelve or thirteen; I was sufficiently grown to have my own punishment.

Later I also found out that the Lord's punishment can change. You aren't locked with chains to a single punishment. You can escape from one, only to fall into the clutches of a still worse one. You can redeem yourself out of one punishment with penance, but inevitably another will be waiting for you beyond the next corner. Man is truly a creature worthy of punishment, and the Lord never lets the opportunity to enjoy another's pain go by.

8. The Deconstruction of the Deconstructor

My first father proved to me that even a creature punished as severely as man is can live in harmony with the world. Humans are unique precisely because they are unpredictable and inexplicable. It isn't humanity's shortcoming, but rather its secret advantage. The second brain in a human's belly reacts to the world unpredictably. You can unerringly say that a lion, after eating its fill, will be content and snooze blissfully. You can firmly say in advance that a male gorilla, after seeing a competitor nearby, will go mad with anger. Only a human, savoring a choice delicacy for the first time in his life, can remain the unhappiest of the unhappy. Only a human can pervertedly enjoy secretly watching his one and only screwing someone else.

The last year of my first father's life was perhaps the happiest period of my life. I slowly started to feel that my insides were, little by little, filling with fundamental fluids. Father's deconstruction laboratory provided so many impressions that more and more of the real me started to appear. Inside, a human being slowly grew, filling all of me and searching incessantly for answers to every possible question. I tried to tame the tailed lizard people or rat people, but they didn't much want to have anything to do with me. They didn't fear me—I simply wasn't of interest to them. I didn't know what I could bribe or seduce them with. Father called them quarks, and explained that they connected the things in the collection between themselves. The faster they ran, the stronger the connection. My father's head was always engrossed in topology, quantum field theory, and similar nonsense. If only the poor man had stuck to just that! It turned out that in his time free from essential things, he also pulled off some unparalleled foolishness, but this became clear only much later. I didn't know anything about his secret pursuits, so I couldn't talk him out of it or restrain him. I didn't talk him out of anything in any case; I simply enjoyed my first father.

He led me not just through his deconstruction collection, but through the secret world of humans too. It happened entirely by chance—like everything in a human's life. Father never examined my drawings and never listened to my concerts. But when mother organized my first one-man art show, he unexpectedly came to it. He looked like a library rat lost in a gloomy forest. Although it was still quite warm, he had wrapped a thick muffler around his neck. He looked over my Old Town landscapes and hallucinations on a free theme with immense care; he actually sniffed at some of the pictures. I was a bit afraid he was going to peel off a piece of paint from one of them for his collection. On the other hand, when he left without stealing anything, I felt fairly mortified. Evidently he found nothing in the entire show that could change the world by so much as a hair's breath.

I didn't so much as imagine he would comment on it to me, or explain anything. But unexpectedly he spoke up that same evening, while obsessively, in a collector's way, trying to pair a dried butterfly with crumbling wings and a nine-inch nail.

"You didn't press the spring all the way down," he explained calmly, "and so it didn't expand with real force. Do you play piano just as impotently?"

"A lot of my works have been awarded prizes, and in piano competitions..."

"I haven't the least doubt about the awards and competitions. Really, I don't doubt them, nor your mathematical talents. But you see... How should I put this... Presenting to the world can be done with either perfect fullness, or perfect emptiness. But you aren't one or the other—neither hot, nor cold, just lukewarm. And the Lord spits those out of his mouth... Although that's at least better than being a cockle. You see, cockles are thrown into a smoldering oven, but being God's sputum is not at all dangerous. More like the opposite—they actually rain awards and diplomas on you."

"So how do I make myself hot, or even fiery?"

"It's possible to derive fire from distant gods..." Father thought for a little while. "But it's better to get it from from people. People's fire is truer and burns longer. Well then, let's go."

"Where?"

"Where, where... to Vilnius, of course."

If it hadn't been for that almost accidental conversation, Father would never have become my guide. Just a few months later his head was cut off and his collection splattered to bits. I could have never learned what heights he had managed to reach. I could have never found out how well-known other people's secret fires were to him. I never even suspected that Father understood Vilnius that well. I believed that between my childhood games and my teenage wanderings with Sara, I had explored all of Old Town's nooks and crannies. However, Father led me down an altogether tangled route: we went down some stairs into a basement in Gorkio Street and climbed out in Pasažo. In Arklių Street he spun such an underground ballet that, all told, I no longer knew where we had ended up. The little courtyard was three-cornered, narrowing to a point farther away from us, and the buildings around us were five- or six-storied. We were squeezed into a canyon that lacked pure air.

"We'll have to rise up into the air, son. There is no other out."

If he had said we were going to start flying like witches, I wouldn't have been in the least surprised. But all he had in mind was the fire escape ladder. It was wide enough for both of us. We climbed up, jostling a bit, until we finally hung opposite the second floor like two crazy grapes, or unduly intelligent monkeys.

"She always drinks tea alone; it's a unique sight. There's such strong despair smoldering inside her that the tea never cools. You must carefully scrutinize the wrinkles under her breasts and under her eyes. And listen carefully to what she says when she's talking to herself, too. Her name is Eleonora. She works as an accountant."

That was how, for the second time in my life, I saw the secret Old Town television. This time it didn't show a liqueur-soaked lesbian serial, but a horrifying study of loneliness, a continuation of avant-garde Italian neorealism. Eleonora sat stark naked at a giant crooked, blackened kitchen table. The table sat there in the middle of the kitchen, pressing down the floor so it wouldn't run away or wander off, a board at a time. It was practically impossible to exist in that kitchen, the air was so thick. But Eleonora existed; she sipped tea stark naked from a Russian cut crystal glass and patiently chatted with herself. At first I thought that she was going on to some cat or dog, but she was talking to herself; suddenly she leaned over, pulled out a bottle of "Moscow Special" from under the table, and sloshed it straight into the tea: a cocktail of unprecedented world harmony. When she leant over, the triple indentation of fat under her breasts briefly turned to double. Her left breast was much larger, almost the size of a soccer ball.

"Don't cut your boob off, Eleonora," she went on to herself sadly, "for the time being don't cut off that boob, let it live a while yet. After all, it so doesn't want to die. Now it remembers its youth, when it was firm and upright. It remembers all the men who caressed it. You do remember, little boob, don't you?"

She slurped the vodka tea down so thunderously, it seemed she'd shake us off our observation ladder. Loneliness and despair shone like a vague green light through her open window; they were visible, even perhaps touchable.

"Do you feel it?" Father asked matter-of-factly. "Do you see the green fumes? That's the spirit, it's emanating painfully, but smolders inside her yet. You ought to paint hanging right here, or better yet—in place of the lamp on her ceiling."

The skin under Eleonora's eyes constantly changed color: here it turned green, then blue, then as gray as damp ashes. Perhaps the growing metastasis of her cancer huddled under those eyes. Or perhaps the strong black tea chemically reacted with the hot vodka there.

"Just don't remember what you shouldn't, little boob," she said angrily. "Don't remember what you shouldn't."

It was a nearly perfect picture: a naked forty-year-old woman in a dreary kitchen with a glass of vodka tea and breast cancer growing right in front of your eyes. But that picture talked; that was its essential shortfall.

"Of course, this could be filmed," Father seemed to have guessed my thoughts, "but it would turn out a commonplace: just a documentary film. No, this should be painted; a true talent has to paint her chatting, and her smell, and even the taste of that vodka with tea. Now that would be a painting!"

It seemed to me that I really was hanging on the kitchen ceiling like a lamp lighting up the entire world. Besides the cut glass, a veritable still life of meat was arranged with obsessive orderliness on Eleonora's table. Next to a sliced ham cuddled at least two appetizing salami, some other roll of stuffed meat, raw pork fillet, a plate with some kind of stewed meat in a brown sauce, and, on the very edge of the table, a giant slab of smoked bacon. All of it looked lethally inedible, but Eleonora herself looked most inedible of all: the skin under her eyes changing color and the differently sized breasts. I never did manage to grasp her as a whole: she was just a collection of uncoordinated parts—like that meat collection on the huge table. At the time I couldn't have even guessed that a part of Eleonora herself would end up in my collection.

Lost in thought, I nearly tumbled off the fire ladder; Father thoughtfully held on to me. He smiled mysteriously while helping me climb down.

"I won't show you anything more today; you need to get used to it and think about it. But take note: all people are part of the world, and the world is made up only of people. Just the fumes of their spirits can lead you along the true path to the place of ultimate truth."

We wandered through the most secret courtyards of Vilnius many times yet, many times we again saw and smelled people's smoldering spirit. I don't believe Father was teaching me to paint or play music that way—he was teaching me something more meaningful, embracing the entire world. Father's somber magic when we secretly visited mystical Old Town families particularly sticks in my head. We would glide into a family like that without the slightest sound, and most importantly–without the slightest influence. We would simply quietly and meekly stand in the front hall or the corner of some room and watch how the family lived its life. They fought, cooked meals, and even made love in our sight, without ever seeing us. They were part of my first father's great collection, which he allowed me to secretly handle. He shoved me onto the path of destruction, and then left me entirely on my own.

Father got me better acquainted with Sara. One cold spring morning he accompanied me to a yard on the other side of Philharmonic Square, led me up some old stairs and quietly led me into a huge apartment where an enormous Jewish family lived. As always, we took shelter in a darker corner of a high-ceiling hallway and quietly observed the harmonious ritual of Jewish life. I was most surprised by that mute theater's movements: for the purity of the experience, Father would switch off the sounds of the world; we would hover in the strange space as if in a dream. Mejerovičius walked through the rooms with slow movements, constantly shaking his round, bald head. His slender little wife would fly about the kitchen pots even more agilely than my grandmother. A merry chain of children scampered through all ends of the house; I was always afraid that those inquisitive creatures would come across us, too. But Sara began to interest me the most. She was in my class, but up until then I hadn't paid her much attention—she was simply one more fat-cheeked Old Town Jewish girl. Observing her secretly, I learned several of her innocent secrets, so she unexpectedly became close to me. I saw her copying poems into a special album and putting dried flowers between its pages. I saw how hard she practiced solving arithmetic and even algebra problems—of her own will, not forced to or ordered to by anyone. I saw her talking to several paintings on the walls as if they were live creatures; unfortunately, I didn't hear her words. She was truly a strange girl, I was convinced of that more than once. Father managed to take me to five more families, but then a deadly lightning struck out of a clear blue sky. Our invisible visits suddenly and tragically came to an end.

To this day I still cannot believe what happened. I cannot find either a rational or a metaphysical explanation for it. It was so impossibly ridiculous that to this day it doesn't fit into my conception of the world. It was like a soundless frog's leap into the void. Everything collapsed in an instant: my father, with colossal courage and unsurpassed foolishness, leapt into the void, and ass-faced KGB agents started rummaging through our house. My entire world began to totter because strangers were idling about Father's deconstruction room, picking things up and not putting a single one back in its place. After no more than a half-hour, Father's room was so muddled that it practically lost its meaning. The work and research of decades was trashed in an instant. Those ass-faces were looking for physical evidence, or perhaps documents or codes.

First they interrogated Gorgeous Rožė, but she got herself

so prettified and bared herself so ingeniously, threw one leg over the other so, that the blinded agents only convulsively swallowed their saliva and couldn't manage to ask any decent questions. Later they took their fury out on me. I was already fourteen, which is why everything in my head was in a complete muddle. On one level, I knew these were security agents sitting across from me, that I needed to answer them especially cleverly, first to mislead them and then to definitively kick them in the teeth. On the other hand, the desire to explain the entire truth, the entire structure of the world to them was pushing and pressing its way out of me. And everything was smothered by an irrepressible urge to make fun of them. What would you do if a young man with an ass instead of a face sat down across from you and in that ass, as if it were perfectly normal, were beady little eyes and squirming narrow lips? Besides, that ass-face tried very hard to be blithely friendly.

"You never noticed that your father invited colleagues or other acquaintances over? You know, to drink tea or a bit of cognac..."

"Father didn't drink tea. On principle. He thought tea restricts the boundaries of human knowledge. And he also thought..."

"Wait, wait a minute, didn't he arrange some papers, or write notes in this...uh... laboratory?"

"It would have been silly to write some sort of notes here. Everything's clear as it is. Every object here is a sign of God. It was, until you mixed everything up."

"You say, God's? Then perhaps some priests visited?"

"No one came here. Father let only me in. The great collection must be carefully looked after, and most importantly of all—the positions of the exhibits should not be changed. That change could summon a global catastrophe. Perhaps it will summon it yet."

The ass-faced agent's face didn't show any emotion, nevertheless, by some impossible means, it reflected surprise. The poor thing couldn't manage to understand anything, but he was unusually curious. Understandably, he had never come across deconstruction rooms before. His little ass brain kept trying to fit a room of that sort into his ass world, without concrete results.

"And those things he collected and arranged here had some sort of meaning for him?"

"It was his very life."

"I don't understand... Was he mentally normal? Only an abnormal person could organize a nationalist organization with the stated intention to withdraw from the Soviet Union."

I remember I was grimly quiet at that moment. The assfaced agent had unknowingly touched upon the painful crux of the matter. Secretly I thought perhaps father actually had gone out of his mind; apparently, he really did organize an underground national movement. It was so supremely foolish that nothing could make me believe it. I could understand him spending evenings deconstructing this poor world, trying to make it at least a bit more acceptable to a thinking person. I could understand him turning topological spaces round and round in the subconscious and tying fivefold knots. I knew very well why he led me through Vilnius's courtyards and apartments, teaching me to recognize the real but ingeniously hidden contents of humans. But there was no way I could convince myself that he would stoop to organizing a national underground. I just couldn't believe he wanted to run away from the Soviet Union, taking all of Lithuania along. It's only worth running away from that wonderland completely alone, taking your topology or your piano along—I understood this perfectly, even at fourteen. My egghead first father made a fool of himself, perhaps went completely nuts, and in the end they cut off his head too. It didn't seem like life anymore; more like some film of the absurd.

There was even too much bloody absurdity in that film. From then on, everything happened at breakneck speed. They found my father in the bushes by the Neris, already starting to decompose a bit. His throat was slit from ear to ear; his head barely held on to his body. Security agents with calm ass-like faces stated they had just questioned him and let him go, and what happened later was the Soviet militia's problem. The Soviet militia didn't manage to investigate anything; apparently everything was all too obvious to that militia.

Everything was more or less cleared up for me much later, rummaging through KGB archives and repeatedly questioning old security agents. At the time, all I understood was that my first father's head had been cut off. It was an excessive punishment, one that no human deserves—even those living in Vilnius. I didn't deserve my own punishment either: for what fault did the gods allot me precisely that kind of father and precisely that kind of mother? That's a rhetorical question the gods haven't answered to this day, not even in my dreams. On the whole they don't answer any questions. You must give them and answer them all yourself.

They forced me to identify my headless father—that was the beginning of my true insight. The ass-faced security agents wanted to knock the ground out from under my feet so it would fly off into the void of the cosmos without me, but in reality they opened the third eye for me. They drove me to the morgue in Subačiaus Street and wanted to finish me off for the ages via the sight of my headless father. They wanted me to be broken so they could pluck me like warm wool and manipulate me like plasticine for the rest of my life. That was the punishment intended for me, an unnatural punishment: it wasn't allotted by the world itself, but rather by malicious people. They felt so omnipotent it didn't even occur to them that I could disobey. They wanted to blind me for the rest of my life, but I resisted, and saw through it with my third eye.

I couldn't look at my father with his head cut off; it was enough for me to smell him. The freezers in the morgue didn't work all that well, and Father already reeked a bit when they found him by the river. I made careful note of his true smell; I had memorized his smell in his deconstruction room, and how he smelled hanging on the fire ladder in the narrow, three-sided little Vilnius courtyard. The very last smell of my first father was disgusting and outrageous, but it was his true smell. I couldn't press my nostrils shut and not breathe, but I could shut my eyes. I saw my first father headless, thrown onto a dirty morgue gurney, for just one painful second. Then I calmly closed my eyes, but I saw everything with the third eye, the very truest vision of them all.

In reality my father was lying on something like a banquet table, heavily studded with tiny candles. He was unrecognizable, bizarrely spread out through the entire table like a a giant spongy pancake. The candle flames flickered and wavered, lighting father with a pale agreeable light. The contours of his body were rounded and pleasant. He hadn't vanished from the Cosmos or my thoughts at all; he merely withdrew from the temporary life of humans, leaving me almost everything he could leave. I probably loved him not just with a son's, but with a disciple's love too. Perhaps those quiet little candles were a reflection of my love, or perhaps he himself wanted to say goodbye to me in just that way. Studded all over with fragrant little candles, he slowly floated off into a boundless light or dark, because in those measures of space neither chiaroscuro nor colors had any meaning. Everything there was steeped in a uniform divine light; it was his true place. Quietly and sadly I saw him off there; all I kept for myself was father's severed head. I took it with me without anyone even suspecting. It had to accompany me for a good portion of my life yet, like the totem of a grim headless nation.

"Yes, it's my father," I said calmly to the ass-faces. "What papers do I have to sign?"

It seems to me that they were rather surprised. They were accustomed to all their malicious designs working, all their plans being fulfilled. I didn't tremble in horror the way they had expected; I didn't faint and didn't even get upset, so I seemed abnormal to them. They couldn't imagine even for a second that they themselves were the abnormal ones, and that a real human is able to defend and protect themselves from them.

"Well, what a nice little family," one of them sniffed. "The wife shows up in a hat and a neckline down to her belly button, and this offspring is as cold as ice... Here, here, sign this. Legibly. You don't have a real signature yet, anyway."

I was only fourteen; I actually hadn't yet signed any serious documents. It stayed that way for the rest of my life: I never signed any serious documents—even when I was Patris's right-hand man. I never needed any documents, anyway: a significant look, a suggestive word or a telephone call was always enough.

I left the morgue completely calm; the horror overcame me only as I walked down the street. Suddenly I realized that the deconstruction of the world deconstructor had to be carried through to the end. The obliteration wasn't entirely finished yet: after all, the deconstruction room was literally a part of my first father. I raced, stumbling no less, to my old house; on the way I nearly dropped my father's head. Gasping for breath, I ran through Sara's courtyard at a trot, past the former strategic spots of the ice cream sellers, struggled up the hill under the triple arches of the old monastery's gate, and finally approached Father's spiritual abode.

I was shocked by the glum silence of the stairs. They didn't as much as try to chat with me, or inform me of anything. The stairs were quite plainly no longer alive. My mother had killed them. I was engulfed by a hideous foreboding, but what I saw exceeded my darkest imaginings. The door let me in without a squeak—it had been extinguished, too. I burst into the room and froze: it had been maliciously demolished. Father's deconstruction shelves were broken and thrown all about the room. Almost all the collection's expositions had vanished: the bronze decorations and broken calculators, drawings of dogs in Chinese ink and father's appendix in a jar with a formaldehyde solution. Here and there the rat or lizard people with tails rolled about dead. I was most sorry for the jars and flasks in which father kept old dreams and the sensations of sunsets. The gang of civilization-destroying vandals broke even the test tubes with scents. Those scents didn't want to retreat from their usual spots; they didn't mix among themselves, each one lingered separately above the section designated for them on the shelves. I smelled them through my tears as I senselessly wandered from one wall to the other. With my entire body I sensed who the hideous murderer of the deconstruction room was. She had a name: Gorgeous Rožė. My first father's head was all she didn't manage to take away: I held it inextricably pressed to myself. It still smelled of my father; with my eyes closed, I could even think he was really still alive.

9. The End of the World

I desperately had to find out immediately whether they hadn't demolished all of my first father's world. His traces, Father's separate parts, were thrown about Old Town, actually throughout the entire city. I no longer remember by what means I found the narrow three-corned little courtyard in Arklių Street myself, without anyone's direction. I no longer remember how I clambered up the fire escape ladder to the second floor, or why I was convinced that Eleonora would definitely be waiting for me. She couldn't not be waiting for me; she couldn't not help me. She really was waiting for me, only me, occasionally slurping her vodka tea. The two of us had never spoken earlier; she would generally pretend she didn't notice father and me hanging on the fire ladder like two crazy grapes. But that time she spoke up immediately, and her voice was mortally wounding:

"Now you're alone, too," she said bitingly, "but your boobs are still alike, for the moment. Haven't you ever wanted to climb in with me, into my painting? I'm just a pathetic painting, didn't you know? A painting with smells, sweat, and tears. And meat, too."

I instantly obeyed; I nearly tumbled off that wretched fire escape, but through a miracle I scrambled up into her kitchen anyway. Eleonora was taller than I thought. She was taller than I, even though I had actually shot up quite a bit. She stood there stark naked with two differently sized breasts and carefully scrutinized me with her gaze. Hiding inside her was an immeasurably painful secret; it was just exactly that secret I needed.

"What's your name, my boy? Who's hurt you? Who would you want to kill now? Are you afraid of worms? Do you like vodka with tea? Do you love naked women? Or maybe just boys?"

Only then did I understand why I had clambered up in there: to make love to Eleonora. To spew out my sperm and accumulated fury. To foul the sacred picture, observed so many times, with whitish slimy paste and fury. All of that sacrilegious act while drinking vodka tea. Perhaps that was the accountant Eleonora's secret—that it was appropriate to act in just that way with her?

I peeled off my clothes and attacked Eleonora with all of the strength of a fourteen-year-old boy's wet dream. I was as firm as a stallion and could penetrate any woman through with my instrument of love. But suddenly I irretrievably froze and withered. Eleonora smiled with a La Gioconda smile and such a blue longing spread from her that no fourteen-year-old in the world could have so much as touched her.

"I'm dying, little one," she said sweetly. "Do you want to make love to a corpse? Maybe you're a necrophiliac? Come, come, I'll love you like no one else in the world, but then you'll be mine. I won't give you up again, to either the little Jewess Sara or the Lithuanian Laima. You'll be my one and only prince, I'll take you into the grave with me."

The rotten meat still lay on Eleonora's table, and she herself, with her differently sized breasts, was enormous and intensely predacious. She was a picture come to life, and at the same time a premonition of death. That was exactly why I so badly wanted to make love to her. They cut off my father's head, and I wanted to make love to dying meat. And at the same time with a painting come to life. To make love to Eleonora, even before my Jewess Sara. And that wouldn't have been a betrayal—I simply needed to understand the secret. Even then I obsessively searched for secrets. You would search for them, too, if they'd cut off your father's head. Differing-boob Eleonora became one of the people who influenced my life most. Exactly like Moses Malone from Chicago's southeast suburbs. Exactly like Gorgeous Rožė.

I never did do anything decent for her. I simply couldn't get it up, and worthless prodding and smearing myself with thin sperm meant no more than a great shame. The first macabre sexual experience in my life ended in complete defeat. That wretched defeat accompanied me all my life; I always lost to women—each one in a different way. And to the beautiful dead Sara. And to my one and only love Laima. Particularly to the one and only frog of my life, Laima.

10. The Frogs of Karoliniškės

The history of the founding of Karoliniškės is surprisingly dusty and grim. That neighborhood, like a sickly plant, formed out of dust and the heat of the sun. But yet another of its spiritual roots was the croaking of frogs. The grayish-brown drabness of Karoliniškės' buildings was born of dust, and the brownness arose from the croaking of frogs.

Only the chosen know this secret of Korals. Only the very first colonizers, the Karoliniškės pioneers of unheard-of courage, still remember the dark times of the froggery. At that time, all of this hilly spot was tortured by the sands torn up by excavators. Together with other newcomers to the neighborhood, I clambered up the steep sandy slopes, deathly afraid of the poisonous desert viper's bite. Every time I dragged myself home from work I would harrowingly risk my life. And then on top of that, the croaking of the frogs tormented me to death.

Back then it was always summer in Karoliniškės; a metaphysical heat always hung about there. And on quiet, dusty evenings the entire world would be drowned out by the stunningly loud croaking of frogs. Those frogs bellowed and roared like bulls, they howled like firefighters' sirens or thunderously droned like the giant pipes of the Cathedral's organ. They didn't just fill the human world; they filled the space of the galaxies too, and subdued the Milky Way itself with their croaking. It was one of the great cosmic secrets of Karoliniškės. I have been interested in cosmic secrets from the age of eleven, so I investigated Korals carefully and attentively.

Like the other pioneers of Karoliniškės, I knew better than to disturb those frogs. Secretly I believed they were the real masters, and we were no more than uninvited intruders. I myself was a particularly dangerous and unnecessary intruder. I had degraded from a wunderkind to a measly run-of-the-mill Soviet scholar. The frogs openly mocked me: they indivisibly ruled the muddled space and the ringing silence. But I didn't rule anything—not even my dreams. So I had to suffer their cacophonous cry. And I did suffer, suffered for an unbearably long time, but one evening I heard the commanding voices of angels. Sometimes the angels announce or command this or that to me.

In reality, there were no angels or secret voices; I just lost my patience. Patience is a sort of little sack wherein people's wrongs, humiliations, and anger quietly collects. Sooner or later that little sack overflows and rips open noisily. And sometimes when it's still nearly empty it gets torn up from inside by sharp thorns of uncontrollable fury. When the little sack of patience revoltingly bursts open, hideous misfortunes and even cosmic catastrophes pour out if it.

That evening, when my frog-tormented patience snapped, a cosmic catastrophe could have occurred, too. I had just returned from the office. I was sprawling stark naked on my froggishly green sofa, which converted to a bed after a lot of creaking and shoving. The desert heat was unbearable; I lay there helplessly and sweated, waiting for the sun to go down. It had already hid itself behind the one and only nine-story apartment building on the other side of the boulevard-to-be, but things still didn't cool down when it dived into the distant forest. All night long it would cool itself off in that forest, just so it could later attack Korals again like a maddened ruddy dog of the sky.

That evening I realized I wasn't going to bear that mocking

of the frogs any longer. The ruptured sack of patience splattered me with hate, uncontrollable irritation, and spiritual vomit. I leapt out into the stairway naked, at that moment completely forgetting what world I was living in. I had barely taken two steps when I came face to face with a girl. She wasn't in the least surprised; she looked me over curiously and rather carefully, her glance wandered to my crotch and returned to my face again.

"You're running to borrow some soap, or maybe you're looking for a towel?" she asked sarcastically. "Or maybe you're a conceptual streaker? Or simply a nut?"

"I'm running out to kill frogs," I said with parched lips, as if confirming her last supposition.

Her laughter turned out to be unexpectedly irritable and predatory. She herself was like a croaking frog with long blonde hair. It was only then that I looked her over carefully: she looked rather tall, rather slim, breasts too heavy for an appearance like hers. Against the background of the drying room window you could see right through her dark blue dress with white polka dots, but the rather low decollete, as if on purpose, hid in a seductive shadow. It wasn't that I saw as much as I oppressively felt the stunning notch between her breasts, smelled the intoxicating scent of her sweat, and actually trembled from the unceasing croaking of the frogs. Those barely visible breasts were no more than two giant, warm frogs as well, croaking their songs of love.

"Come by to see me some time," she said calmly. Apartment two hundred sixty-six. Just don't come naked, I won't let you in."

Laima always was, and still is, unflappable. She always managed to achieve what she wanted, and in striving, she'd calculate what use she'd have of it, too. She looked me over naked, impishly wanted me, and climbing up the stairs she was already thinking of how she'd profit by me in the future. I wasn't thinking of anything; I wanted to run outside naked as I was, but

I was afraid someone might stop me. Back then Karoliniškės was a grim and half-wild place, but civilization with all its conditions was already slowly coming to life there. Probably they wouldn't have let me get all the way to the froggery naked.

I pulled on some musty shorts and a t-shirt. Even though it was already getting dark, it was still despairingly humid. But the unceasing croaking of the frogs drove me to a still greater despair. It wasn't just swamping my skull, or the nine-story building that echoed from the slightest sound—it smothered the entire world; it had pushed out all the colors, the majority of the smells, and any remains whatsoever of conscience. Those frogs had extracted the entire essence of the world, leaving only a soulless husk, which probably ought to be thrown into a roaring furnace.

Back then I didn't yet rule the flames of heaven. At the time I was living through a gray period, which followed immediately after the pale blue one. I didn't rule even the crooked dusty path that led to the evening's heat-emanating ravine. The frogs' abode should be hiding somewhere on its bottom. Their grim hellish lair, their crushing kingdom, the teeming heap of a million insane frogs, should be lurking down there. I knew that in battling with them, I could suffer for it badly. To lose everything I had accomplished in life, to lose my emotions, my senses, even my mind. But I no longer paid attention to anything because my patience had finally snapped. A man whose patience has snapped becomes unpredictable and dangerous, even to himself.

I crashed through thickets of bushes and nettles, ignoring the pain of scrapes and the burning stings. I absolutely had to get to the dark lagoon and do battle with the myriad of murderous croaking frogs. I inexorably approached my destiny. It was a moment of great determination, and at the same time of life's most essential insight.

That insight was a vision worthy of complete insanity. I finally descended to the very bottom of the ravine and froze as if transfixed. The teeming heap of cosmic frogs lurked just exactly there. I choked and gasped from the blinding sight. The last rays of the sun still lit up the right-hand edge of the lagoon. That little pond was not much more than a thousand square feet in size. But not even that was the most distressing and insulting. A single, lone frog ruled that palm-sized pond. It wasn't at all the size of a bull—more like the size of a fist. It stared at me with eyes reddened by the sunset and shamelessly mocked me. And croaked unmercifully. It simply, madly, wanted to make love.

Its croaking really did thunder like a pipe organ and hoot like a fire engine. It was the loudest frog in the world; no African elephant's trumpeting could equal the vibration of its swollen throat. But it sat in the middle of the puddle all alone—tiny and completely unmoved. It wasn't just insulting and mocking; it was eerily somber, too. That metaphysical frog despairingly announced the approaching end of the world.

Probably the end would have overtaken the world that very evening, but it was saved from destruction by the divine Laima. She was never just Laima, but true *laimė*—Lithuanian for luck—my luck, the luck of the world, maybe even the essential base upholding the existence of the cosmos. I fell hopelessly in love with her that first evening, without even knowing her name, without even getting a good look at her, just by smelling her true scent.

She squatted uncouthly next to the pond, inquisitively watching me and the frog. She half-squatted, half-kneeled on one knee, with her legs spread shamelessly and an arm leaning on her left knee. Her crotch flashed in the glow of the sunset, forcing the question of whether Laima had covered it with anything at all. Her warm-blooded, but for that reason still more froggy chest bobbed mysteriously in the dusk falling on the ravine, calling for my comforting. Laima had run over to help me, so I wouldn't be tortured to death by sadistic frogs. After all, she, too, hadn't suspected that in the entire Karoliniškės world there was but one single frog. It was an unforeseeable secret of that time's world. It was only much later, when I had ended up in the world of high-level politics, that I profoundly understood that in the entire kingdom there could only be but one single thunderously croaking frog.

"Let's do in that spawn of hell," she suggested to me in a whisper that nevertheless drowned out the monstrous croaking of the frog.

When that woman spoke up, everyone instantly heard her—particularly if she spoke in a whisper. She managed to nail every man's attention without the least effort. Sometimes she really did look like a monster, but the notch between the breasts, the thick hair, and the froggy scent was always stunning.

"It's impossible," I answered in despair. "Finish one off—three will spring up in its place. That's not a frog, it's a metaphysical Hydra. That's a Gorgon jellyfish. That's the quintessence of Karoliniškės' insanity."

Laima laughed again, and that laughter scattered my last hopes. During those dark times, the gray period of my destiny, I had secretly sworn to myself that I wouldn't surrender to any woman's charms. That I would live like a wise man, a hermit, and get to know the world through the all-knowing gaze of the true solitary. I was completely convinced of this, right up until that froggy evening. Frog-breasted Laima, poised to leap, and the real sonorous-voiced frog, by now plopped into the water, essentially changed my destiny. I turned down a completely new path of life, marked by the number two hundred sixty-six. It was perfumed by Laima's miraculous crotch stalking me in the dusk. Deafened by the lone frog of Karoliniškės, which we later murdered anyway.

But not yet that evening. That evening the two of us made love like two insane frogs. Like two cosmic protuberances. I hadn't made love that way even with Sara herself. Not to mention that I hadn't made love to her at all, in the usual standard sense.

11. Varieties of Interim Coffins

Now Laima's and my interim coffins have separated a bit.
Their size, space, and most of all—their scents are different.
The refined aromas of her house supersede Gorgeous Rožė's
most secret dreams, and my interim coffin smells a bit differently. But after all, that's not vitally important. It's simply that
people kick and toss about in their interim coffins, senselessly
trying to escape them. They try to jump out of one coffin and
climb into another, as if this could change something in their
karma. People change apartments or houses, naïvely hoping
this will change their life. But in reality all they're changing is
the decoration of their interim coffin.

Some like wooden interim coffins in the bend of the river,
surrounded by pines and the chirping of birds, pierced by the
barking of distant dogs and covered with clouds resembling
stallions or silent flutes.

Others value solid, three-story brick coffins, gloomily bur-
rowed into the ground, angrily extended up all three stories,
intoxicated from the exhaust fumes of the newest model of
Mercedes instead of good hashish smoke, with as much elec-
tronica as the green aliens' flying saucer.

But the most human of all are the high-rise communal
coffins, in which many people bury themselves alive at the
same time. The feeling of communal demise is frankly incomparable. The coffin boxes there are as identical as the cards in

God's pack. You could change everyone's place, shuffle, divide, and change places again—the gods wouldn't bat an eye. The gods count interim coffins like that by the dozens, not individually. A dozen dozens is the magic pain unit of communal coffins. The most painful are the totally communal coffins—those like Korals. Birds never chirp and dogs never bark there, and if it appears to someone that they really do bark, it's just a peaceful doggy hallucination. There's never any clouds there and it never rains warm rain. Even the frogs died out there a long time ago, but the people held on. People hold on through everything. They endure all the varieties of interim coffins. Even the stinking high-rise communal coffins.

Once upon a time I used to ride through the red high-rise communal coffins of the blacks in southeast Chicago. I'd rumble by in the direction of the South Side neighborhoods from a suburban station, and every time I badly wanted to stop there and visit them. I sensed a significant secret hiding in those communal coffins that I couldn't learn anywhere else. All my life I frequently dreamed of an old, thin black man, sadly singing me blues whose words I just couldn't understand. I had practically no doubt that black man lived in the red communal coffins of Chicago; I could well-nigh smell him there. When I asked a fellow traveler about wanting to visit that neighborhood, the man had a ministroke. Supposedly even ambulances don't go there without a police escort, and whites would get completely ground to flour there. By the way, for some reason I've never feared being ground to flour. Someone could even cook pancakes out of me—that doesn't seem at all horrible to me.

My personal God really does exist: perhaps he's called Coincidence, or perhaps simply Bad Luck. The suburban Chicago train, for the first time in three years, suddenly irretrievably stopped—of course, right next to the red communal coffins. I was the only one to get out, and like a somnambulist, I walked off towards the dangerous high-rises of the blacks. Someone fearfully called after me, but I paid no attention; I had to find the black man of my dreams. I sensed he would impart an important secret to me. The most important secrets always hide in the very worst interim coffins. If someone only knew what secrets hide in our interim coffin, where our entire spirited company is now methodically and merrily dying!

Bent beer cans and used syringes were rolling about everywhere. At the time I couldn't even have imagined that in ten years Korals would look the same. I continued as if on the surface of the Moon or Mars, trying not to breathe; you see, I suspected there wasn't any air. There was as much air as you could want, it simply reeked of Afrika's incomparable smell; if you weren't used to it you could suffocate. Terrifying juveniles herded basketballs around me. They simply didn't see me: in those surroundings I looked like such an unbelievable miracle that it was impossible to believe I existed.

But the black man of my dreams with Morgan Freeman's face saw me immediately. He wasn't herding a ball, he was simply floating above the ground: not very high up—perhaps by a few fingers' breadth. Probably he had risen because he was smoking a long, stinking cigar. I started to feel really horrified because he reminded me of my first father: he was just as tall and lean, and smiled in the same sheepish way.

"At least you found the door, sonny," he uttered sheepishly, "Oh, you shouldn't have come here. Better sit in your own interim coffin and not wander about strangers'. Are you a collector already? You already collecting and burning the cockles of the world? How many fathers you have? What sign were you born under?"

Quite the old black guy with Morgan Freeman's face: he hung a bit above the ground, smoked a stinking cigar, and did nothing but ask questions, instead of revealing the essential secrets of existence. But suddenly he raised the forefinger of his right hand:

"If a white man finds old Moses Malone, it means the white man already knows at least some of his great destiny. It means the white man has already gone on the path of war and stockpiles the fluids of revenge. Your soul is already pregnant. It's already conceived and will give birth to an unheard-of love—the kind of love that will pulverize everything around it. Your steeds of Socrates have already drawn you in the direction of the true purpose. What they do to you, pale face? Rape your mother? Castrate your father before your eyes? What they do to you, and what do you want from them now? I see you'll take a truly terrible revenge. Your round little face don't fool me, it ain't easy to fool old Moses Malone. You won't fool yourself, either."

At least several long years had to go by before I finally understood the prophesies of the black man from my dreams. At the time he prophesied, I was a perfect omnipotent fool and Patris's main advisor. But the first shoots of virtue and justice were already sprouting inside me. They sprouted out in the most disgusting neighborhood of Chicago's municipal communal coffins, where my life was literally in danger. The shoots of virtue and justice always sprout out only in view of mortal danger. And if you don't want your head cut off, you must learn how to fight flawlessly. You must become a real Sun-Tzu. Not the character popularized in numerous editions of books, but the crafty and merciless multitalented military leader. Old Moses Malone with the craggy face of Morgan Freeman taught me this first. Besides, he literally saved my life: he led me out of that damned black neighborhood, where they would have simply finished me off, cut me into pieces, and eaten me without salt or pepper. Or cut my head off, like they did to my first father.

12. The Founding of the House of Rulers

I didn't begin digging myself an interim grave when they cut off my father's head and Sara dissolved alive from my gaze. I didn't run off to dig myself a grave even after what my second father tried to do to me. But actually I should have immediately dug out a grave in the damp, rich earth, a place where whitish worms writhe, just like my second father and his society of collectors. Instead I just closed my eyes and continued to live. However, I instantly went to dig out the great interim coffin as soon as I left politics and Patris. My second brain ordered me, commanded me to hurry. It gave birth to a truly grand interim coffin: it's the real House of Rulers, because inside lived, and continue to live, the true rulers of this country.

We are modest, but modesty doesn't obscure our good sense: obvious facts ought to be acknowledged, even if that acknowledgment sounds like a challenge. We are grand, and it behooves grand people to have a truly grand interim coffin. A real underground House of Rulers, a Palace of the Grand Dukes, in which, if desired, a good part of the world could fit, like in some Noah's Ark sunken long ago. I'd even say that no small part of the world has been accommodated here already: from time to time Lame Elena shelters with our indivisible society. But most important of all are the delicate cocoons, my beloved homunculi, the metaphysical inhabitants of my secret room.

At first I wanted to dig under the Cathedral: it's a strategic spot in the city, the handiest place to arrange attacks against the cockles of the world. However, the ghosts of Grand Dukes constantly loaf about there and disturb the necessary gravity of the cockle destroyers. I had decided to take up residence right under Gediminas Hill, but I simply lacked the opportunities. Some kind of initial cellars, some already existent initial hideouts were nevertheless needed at the beginning. I needed the initial underground framework—only then could Nargėla take on his work. Thank heaven, underground nooks like that are plentiful in the holy city of Vilnius. Thank heaven, his six years behind bars for the waste of fantastic sums didn't destroy Nargėla. That man really knew how to build—one way or another, he rebuilt Trakų Castle, and while rebuilding it managed to steal half of it, too. There's a man of truly great talent. However, even his spirit's strength wasn't boundless; even he needed construction support at the outset. After all, he had to plan and then build an entire underground world that would have room for not just all our boundless spiritual powers, but all of my collection, too, my little bubbling broths of the universe.

Of course, you're not going to create an interim coffin like that all at once—we dug, laid bricks, and fortified our underground palace for at least four years. It's not entirely finished even yet; it alters and changes daily, it improves itself like some living being. Our interim coffin strives to be the most eternal of all the interim coffins. Sun-Tzu taught us: equipping a great warrior's headquarters requires the sacrifice of all forces. Better to lay in ten redundant bricks than to leave even one little crack. Better to build threefold fortifications than to leave the enemy an open bridge over the river. Of course, our hideout wouldn't withstand the explosion of an atomic bomb, but we don't need that, anyway. Sun-Tzu clearly said: don't waste your strength trying to defend yourself from that which is wholly indefensible. Simply evade that overwhelming attack.

If attacked, I practically wouldn't have where to hide—except perhaps for one single place. There's this old friend from the Sajūdis days, Artūras Gavelis; we've always been linked by a rather strange metaphysical connection. He gave up all politics a long time ago; he's a philosophically-inclined bachelor and truly wouldn't betray me. In case of an attack, he's the only one I could at least temporarily hide out with. He is my hope.

So far, we've avoided all overwhelming attacks. That's why we can call ourselves the real rulers. Many in Vilnius know the location of our residence, but the paradox is that no one even suspects that's actually our residence there. Sun-Tzu said: if you know how to remain invisible even though you're walking without your face covered in the very thick of the crowd—you have already won. So far we've won. There aren't very many of us, but we're as real as death itself and as indivisible as painfully stinging bees. And like bees, we each bring our own honey. Albinas Afrika brings the drum sounds I find so necessary and his incomparable black man smell. Apples Petriukas brings thoughts and sometimes—shockingly good wine. Up to a certain point, the great builder Nargėla kept bringing mysterious improvements for the construction of our interim coffin. Lame Elena, as always, brings money. And likewise a thing or two specifically for me, as the great warrior chief: the body she is consciously destroying, together with all of its crannies. She has no end of money, but practically no sense of greed—only a true passion for work and one insurmountable attraction, on which account she fell in love with me. I was the only one—so the gods would have it—who didn't refuse to grant her a peculiar solace. She really needed it, and I could grant it to her. Morals or the rules of human society have nothing to do with it—it's our business and our concern. I guard her secret, and she guards mine. That's the highest mutual trust, and therefore the highest mark of humanity, too.

But most often the two of us make love like animals. I don't at all have something bestial or disgusting in mind—it's simply that the two of us like to imitate living nature by all means possible. If we can't think up a direct way, then we imitate it in words at least.

"Do you know that the sawfly larva's penis is seven times longer than its entire body?" she suddenly asks, nearly at the moment of climax, "In any case, those larvae are hermaphrodites, but during copulation they get so tangled it's impossible to untangle themselves anymore. All that's left is for the larva to bite off its little cock at the very base. From then on, it's left as just a female. You see how easy it is for bisexuals to turn into women. Could you manage to bite something off yourself?"

She babbles this more and more quietly, by the end she's nearly hissing: telling legends of animal sex is one of her methods of making love. She's a devilishly perverted expert: I actually start listening and unconsciously hold back ejaculation. She tells her sexual legends, or maybe explains actual facts of nature, that have erotic utility at the same time. She's insatiable and stunningly refined all at once. She wants many men all at the same time, and is not at all shy about admitting it to me.

"Just imagine, some female centipedes have little pockets created just for that purpose," she says to me after all is over, blissfully smoking a rolled cigarette, "Inside those pockets they carry at least a couple of little males that can make love at any moment. One biologist came across a female with fourteen of those little pockets—can you imagine it? Fourteen little guys always ready to serve you. Fantastic..."

"While male guinea-pigs, after making love with a female, leave a several-centimeter plug in her little hole," I retort. "So it wasn't some knights on a crusade who thought up chastity belts."

In its own way, this erotic chitchat brightens the somewhat dreary basement surroundings. Lame Elena's lunacy over animal sex isn't the worst of her insanities, but nevertheless it's practically incessant. She doesn't merely tell her tales, but tries to act them out, too. I'm not fond of some of those imitations—like her eternal desire to be banged by two or three in a row. She has written up some seventeen animal species whose males behave that way—from hedge sparrows to shit flies.

It's just that I really don't want to be either a hedge sparrow or a shit fly; I'm more likely to agree to be a red spider. I want the female to eat my sperm, even at the risk of being eaten myself. Lame Elena swallows my sperm with relish, maybe there will come a time when she really will eat me too. Sometimes it seems to me that I'd entirely agree to it; sometimes it seems I almost understand that passionate mania of hers.

Out on the surface of the earth I hardly even look at the girls; I feel too old, too tired, and busy with much more important matters. However, inside my interim coffin I frequently can hardly wait for Lame Elena; I even tremble with impatience to turn into a red spider, or at least some sexy larva. The smell of the underground and the sense of the nearness of death heats my hormones red-hot. At times I'm simply live testosterone.

Sometimes I obey Lame Elena's zoological mania, but most of all I like to stay human. I insanely like vaginas, because they are flowers. If only I could, I'd grow an entire garden of flowers of that sort. The underground interim coffin badly needs a garden. After all, you can't admire your collection's cocoons all the time. They're too lifeless and too abstract. They don't smell at all. All that smells inside my interim coffin is Albinas Afrika and my constantly approaching painful death. In that desert of smells, I most often think about vaginas and mirrors.

13. Eyes and Mirrors

Mirrors are vaginas, while eyes are penises—and the reverse. Eyes pierce mirrors and impregnate them. If there were no eyes, the contents of mirrors wouldn't exist, because no one would see them. Without eyes observing the reflections, mirrors would be completely meaningless. They would reflect and reflect and reflect—but all those reflections of the world wouldn't be seen by anyone, so they'd be completely unnecessary; in essence, they wouldn't even exist.

That's why mirrors stay empty if no one looks at them for a long time. I experienced this back in my childhood in the corridor of a damp Old Town house. I was so small and cowered so, that the mirror just didn't notice me. It didn't respond to me: I quietly snuck by, while it forgot, or was too lazy, to reflect me. Or maybe that mirror thought I had no eyes—a double penis that could properly impregnate it. It didn't sense any sexual attraction to me. I went down the corridor right by that damned mirror, but it didn't show anything: not me, not the corridor—nothing at all. All there was in that mirror was a void, a barren cosmic wilderness, nameless and soulless. Human eyes, the gaze of a human soul, were needed to revive it.

In their depths, all mirrors are soulless and nameless, just that the one from the corridor in my childhood home had more complexes and was more careless. It was tormented by sexual mirror complexes, which is why it betrayed the scared secret of all mirrors to me. Or maybe it simply thought I was still too small and wouldn't figure out any secrets. I didn't understand them back then, but I thoroughly committed the irredeemably empty rectangle of the corridor mirror to memory. I grasped the essence of that void much later, when I was already in my second father's house.

It was much later that I also found out about the second, and perhaps essential, secret of mirrors. Once upon a time the world of mirrors and the human world weren't as separate as they are now. They existed right next to one another, but neither their inhabitants, nor their colors, nor their shapes corresponded at all. They differed on a basic level—it was two very different worlds. The kingdoms of mirrors and of humans got along harmoniously: it was possible to go into the mirror and return again. You could be sure that no one would harm you on the other side of the mirror. However, one night troops from the other side of the mirror unexpectedly invaded the world. The army was extremely powerful, but after a bloody battle, the magic power of the Yellow Emperor celebrated victory. He chased out the plunderers, imprisoned them within the mirrors, and, like in a bad dream, ordered them to repeat people's every move. He took all the powers from the beings in the mirror and even their very image, humbled them to the level of complete slavery.

But sometimes the beings on the other side of the mirror manage to disobey the spell. Sometimes they try to act independently, or at least to not repeat people's movements. That's exactly how the mirror of my childhood home acted. It tried to revolt quietly, even if not at all violently.

But the time will come when the mirrors will free themselves of all the spells. People will spot a narrow little band in the depths of the mirrors, and the color of the band won't be like any known color in the world. Afterwards, all the other imprisoned shapes will wake up, one after the other. They'll slowly start differing more and more from our shapes; they'll stop imitating this world's people by coercion. What will happen then—no one knows. Perhaps the Yellow Emperor's spells will keep the kingdom on the other side of the mirror separate from the world of people. Or perhaps the soldiery of the other side will invade the Earth again—but this time it will be for all time.

The worst of it is that vaginas are mirrors, too. You stare and stare at them as if under a spell. You can see your own depth inside them, as you can your past and a portion of your future. Usually one looks at the vagina with the eye of the penis, but you can look at them with ordinary eyes, too—for hours upon hours, even with a magnifying glass. You can smell them for hour after hour, patiently trying to remember if you've already smelled a flower of that aroma.

Those are always my interim coffin thoughts. Sometimes I feel even more alone in it than I do on the surface of the earth. Up there, on the surface, you're at least doing something, moving senselessly from one place to another. That's an excellent way to kill time, a distraction from thoughts of the eternal. While below ground, those wretched thoughts and even more wretched memories are all that's left for me. First of all I remember those who determined that I am now a sacred warrior. I remember my first father and the differently-boobed accountant Eleonora. Painfully often I remember Patris, my curse and my ruin, and even more often I remember my joy and despair—Sara Mejerovič.

14. Sara Mejerovič

Vaginas are mirrors in which you can see your own depths, and flowers, too, smelling bitterly of lust and death. I figured this out this only thanks to Sara. She was the mathematics star of our school and the terror of all the boys in the class. To their shame, she cracked test problems and exams like nuts. I was the only one she couldn't beat; you see, I was unbeatable in general. One way or another, the two of us couldn't have avoided falling in love. More accurately, we could have turned either into mortal enemies or inseparable friends.

Sara and I were saved from the eternal religious war by the current of life. We were in the same class from the third grade on. First of all, we were firmly connected by my secret visits to their house, and later by the taste of marzipan at the Mejerovič's little shop. It was only much later that a silly mathematical competition flared up between us, but by then it could no longer ruin anything: we were already madly in love, to us all intellectual oppositions seemed funny, senseless, and merely others' inventions.

Sara Mejerovič was a prototype of the truly cosmic woman: I well remember that by the fourth grade her boobies were already fully matured. Occasionally during the day I'd secretly watch my mother undressing, but at night all I did was dream of Sara's never-seen boobies. Just at that time I was going through my rose period and Gorgeous Rožė's spiritual terror. I gathered prizes and trophies one after the other, poured watercolors, sat in father's secret room for hour after hour, but at night I dreamed of Sara. I believe that triad of childhood images determined a great deal of my future life. Oh Sara, Sara, you were goddess of the days and nights throughout my childhood and adolescence!

The gods were merciful; I didn't stay enclosed in the snare of night visions. Sara and I became friends, naturally and truly unavoidably. It was just at that time that the epoch of squeezing and pinching spread through our class. It was mandatory during recess to trap two or three girls in the class and lustfully shove them into a corner or between the benches. Then we were expected to furiously grope them while they screamed like they were being butchered. Neither we nor they understood why we had to do this; we didn't even feel any particular pleasure, but at the next recess we'd again trap some of them in a corner and maul them until they screamed. And they, for their part, would seemingly unintentionally stay in class after the bell for recess, on purpose so they'd be captured and hedonistically forced to shriek. During class the girls would be thoroughly flushed from memories of the screaming, while the boys would be proud and self-satisfied. I, too, willingly took part in this ritual, until one time I was left face to face with Sara. She always imperceptibly slipped out of class and didn't allow herself to be caught by anyone, and besides, she wasn't at all among the beauties considered suitable for the Great Groping. But that time she actually missed something in her backpack, while I, not having found better booty, chose her. Better I had, as customarily, grabbed long-legged Asta or whiny Violeta. However, my personal God shoved Sara Mejerovič into my arms. He had maliciously planned it all in advance. But no, my personal God doesn't feel malice or sarcasm; he simply plays intellectually, and weighs and combines events, colors, or people—just like my first father.

He weighed Sara Mejerovič on his secret scale of fate,

and put her into my arms. For the first time I felt with my entire body that her boobs were now completely mature. Her swollen nipples shook me through both our school uniforms with the electricity of the great secret. Sara's eyes were dark brown and orientally huge. Her small full-lipped mouth was always irritably pressed together, and her plump cheeks shone a healthy red. She didn't scream at all, she just sighed and quietly asked me:

"Now, tell me, who acts that way with girls? I don't like it at all, and your pinching will leave bruises. But if you want to touch me gently—I've got nothing against it. But that's done somewhere hidden by ourselves... Where no one sees... And no one hears..."

As she spoke, she kept pressing up closer to me, and suddenly I realized that the marzipans in Mejerovič's shop were not at all the biggest gift Sara could give me. Her matured boobs would be a much bigger gift, not to mention her almond eyes or that which I, at the time, didn't even suspect was hiding inside her.

"Come by to our courtyard today at five—we can go for a walk," Sara calmly invited me, still pressed up to me.

I was utterly speechless—I just nodded my head. That's how our secret meetings began, that's how our great love and the strange games began—now it seems to me that everything happened on one and the same day, the single day the gods allotted to me and Sara.

I dressed myself up like a peacock for our first meeting. I put on my velvet shorts for special events and tied mother's ribbon, which she sometimes wore with a black jacket, on my neck. I spent a long time considering knee-high white socks, but in the end I was put off by the fringe sewed on them. I wasn't ready to cut off the fringe, and an inner voice whispered to me that love games with little Jewish girls and golf stockings with fringe are fundamentally incompatible things. At last I went to the meeting with the ribbon and velvet shorts,

my bare feet stuck into shabby sandals. It was the truly smash-
ing style of an Old Town dandy. I don't know what would
have happened to the white socks while I was clambering
through the cellars, but I immediately irredeemably whitened
the velvet shorts.

Even though Gorgeous Rožė could have killed me for that,
nothing was important to me anymore, save Sara. Already on
that very first day of our love I not only saw but touched her
matured Jewish breasts. Sara very much wanted it; she was
even impatient, and hurried me somewhat.

"Do you know what these are? Do you really know?" she
kept asking me.

"The apples of Paradise and soft-skinned peaches," I
answered, and totally enslaved her.

She hadn't read comparisons like that in the cheap romance
novels that, as it turned out, she devoured literally gasping for
breath. Besides, she had two older sisters whom she would
occasionally spy on when they made out with boys. Poor Sara's
head was simply exploding with actual, perused, or imaginary
love scenes; she just couldn't find herself a suitable partner.
As I've already mentioned, the poor thing wasn't pretty. She
looked particularly funny to me at that first meeting: a chubby
girl with somewhat crooked legs, a short flowered dress, and
a transparent polyester ribbon woven into her hair, who was
constantly sniffling her nose in excitement.

But all the laughter vanished when I accidentally leaned up
against her body. She was giving off waves of such strength that
a careless little kid like me could have been shaken to death.
I survived it; I just jumped away from her as if I had been
scalded. Meanwhile Sara controlled her excitement by talking
incessantly, saying whatever came into her head.

"Are you afraid of me?" she asked in a whisper. "Are you
afraid of all girls? Are you afraid because they don't have a pee-
pee, or because they've got boobies? Have you ever seen real
boobies from close up? Would you want to feel my boobies?

Is your pee-pee really tiny, or a bit bigger? Would all of it fit in my hand?"

That day she seemed like a real sex maniac, that Sara Mejerovič. And if we were to say that all of the days we spent together were merely a single day as long as a lifetime—for that entire day she was one or another form of sexualist. She presented me with her body piece by piece, so that I could thoroughly enjoy each one. She allowed me inside herself in a devilishly slow way, perhaps that's why the time she stopped stretched into one single day.

I worshipped the gap between her girlish boobies—it was I who taught her to wear a bra so that her breasts would be a bit raised and that gap would acquire a shape to drive you out of your mind. I was already nearly crazy from the gap between my mother's breasts; I secretly called it the Tunnel of Wisdom or the Tunnel of Dreams, and sometimes the Honey Chute. I was totally convinced that burying my face in that tunnel, smelling it and especially licking it, I really would feel the taste of honey and my brain would be flooded with unheard-of intelligent thoughts. I couldn't test this with Gorgeous Rožė, but I tested it with that little horror Sara. It turned out that the Honey Chute smelled of cranberry and lingonberry leaves and its taste was salty, but piercingly subtle. Sara allowed me to lick the gap between her breasts everywhere: in the cloakroom at school and under low-growing frosty trees; during movie shows and in the stairway at her house that reeked of urine.

"Your tongue is rough and warm, like some animal's," she kept saying. "Maybe there's some coarse-haired animal living in your mouth? Maybe you swallowed one of the lizard people from your father's room?"

She always talked a great deal; she talked non-stop even on her deathbed—although at the time no one knew it was a deathbed. But until that time came, we still needed to travel many slippery winter streets, explore endless Old Town basements, and get into fights with at least a couple of cripples on carts. Those men without legs compelled me to especially love Sara's, particularly the dimples under the knees. I first discovered those dimples on Sara, and only later did I begin to devotedly explore them while secretly watching my mother undressing. I named those dimples the Dimples of Summer, as they were only approachable in the summer, when Sara went about with naked shins. The season of our single shared day changed like mad, but I most looked forward to a summer as warm as possible.

Not just because I could then nibble on the Dimples of Summer as much as I wanted, but also because in the summer I could suck on her big toes as much as I liked. Mother's big toes always stupefied me. I could enjoy them without hiding it; I would simply freeze and stare when she painted her toe nails. The other toes didn't interest me at all—just the big ones. Sara's big toes were chubby and unusually tasty to suck. They fit my mouth perfectly. I named them the Gates of Energy–you see, a relentless force from Sara's body really did flow through them. Perhaps I sucked out her life forces through the big toes. Or maybe I sucked them out through her madly stiffening boobies; Sara would bare them at the first opportunity, or no opportunity at all. She liked to be the goddess of suckling mothers, a tiny Hera of Old Town's crannies.

However, all of this seemed mere games in comparison to our most important and most consummate occupation. It was precisely during that endless single day with Sara that I learned to admire the intoxicating flower of her crotch. By twelve or thirteen I had already tried out all the little corners of her body; she presented them to me modestly and gently. The two of us spoke via secret signs, even during class. I would show her my fingers wound together a certain way, meaning I was now licking her nipples. Sara would close her eyes and get lightheaded; in forgetting herself, she would nearly fall off the bench. Or she would twist her little finger a bit, letting me know she was tickling my constantly swelling peter—then it would be my turn to swoon.

She knew how to do this like a knitter of the finest stitches. If only she wanted, she would tickle me in the most improbable places and at the most unlikely times. She would come by our house to supposedly watch television, and actually tickle me to death in the same room where Gorgeous Rožė and my first father were sitting. At least twice she wore me out tickling me in the back seat of old Mejerovič's Moskvič while we drove to the Žaliųjų Lakes. But most of all she loved to do it in the light of day, after undressing me entirely, just so she could see every little tremble of my peter, every new hair sprouting next to it. She would do this only when she wanted; she was my ruler—my goddess and my queen.

"There now, we're waking up," she would chatter without letting my crotch out of her sight, "there now, we, my little one, are awake. After all we, the boys, must answer to a girl's temptations. We must stand up straight and show how stiff we are. After all, the girls like that very much, especially if that girl's name is Sara. And maybe even the boys themselves like it."

She could go on like this in a sing-song for a good ten minutes, although generally such a long wait wasn't necessary. In the morning of our endless day, or maybe even midday, my thing wouldn't just tremble; it would shoot an aching bliss through my entire body and collapse. But on one particularly meaningful occasion it finally fully effectively spat straight at Sara's face leaning over it. She had just then finished it off by tickling it with her loose curly hair. I was afraid she would be angry, but she was only unusually cheerful. She wiped that whitish gruel from her red cheek and curiously tasted it.

I believe it was afterwards that she finally showed me her miraculous mirrored crotch for the first time. Her vagina was a magic mirror in which I could see my own depths. I would stare at that miraculous flower for hours upon hours—or at least it seems that way to me now. I would smell that flower of a thousand scents without ever getting enough of it. It was incomparably more perfect than all the flowers in the world. Flowers always smell the same, while Sara's crotch smelled different every time. Sooner or later flowers wilt, but Sara's vagina only flourished more every day. There were so many hues and colors, wrinkles and crinkles in it that all the words of human languages wouldn't have been enough to name everything. It wasn't just mirrored, but eternal as well—at least that's how it seemed to me. At the time, my first father was still alive, I would occasionally secretly watch while my mother dressed, and bored to tears, I'd put on my little imitation tuxedo for concerts—everything continued to seem eternal and changeless to me.

I would stare at Sara's vagina from close up, maybe from ten centimeters away. I wanted to not just see my soul's reflection inside it; I wanted to dive into it entirely, to disappear into it for the ages. But I didn't have the right to even touch it. Exactly so, just so: Sara did not allow me to even touch her vagina. I gawked at it, eyes goggling—this she allowed. Once I even examined it through a magnifying glass—Sara especially liked this, she spread her legs so that I even felt all the beating of her veins. But I never touched her miraculous flower of the crotch, as if it could have disintegrated or wilted from my touch. The two of us never did make love in the usual sense. I hardly believe it myself, but that's how it was. The first time in my life I made love physically was with the different-breasted accountant Eleonora. I made love very unsuccessfully, but that was my baptism into the struggle. And afterwards I again spent hour after hour staring at Sara's untouchable vagina. After some thirty years, that sight and those scents finally pushed me onto the road to war. I suspect that my conversion into Sun-Tzu was most influenced by Sara's mirrored flower and the war invalids on carts.

15. The Invalids on Carts

They rode through Old Town as drunk as skunks. It was perhaps around 1955. Not many of those war invalids lived that long, but a few still stubbornly gadded about Old Town's dirty little streets. It was particularly difficult for them to get uphill.

Their legs were amputated right at the joints of the hip. In a manner my childish brain couldn't understand, they tied their stubby little bodies to homemade carts and furiously pushed on forward. On their hands they used to put gloves with wooden knuckles made for the purpose. Or else convulsively press wooden stumps in their hands for pushing themselves along. Decorating themselves with war medals and ribbons, they used to panhandle at the Aušros Gate, and afterwards they'd drink at Mejerovič's shop. He was the only one who'd let them run up a tab. I had no doubt that they knew the secret, approachable only by them, of legless existence, which they wouldn't voluntarily reveal to anyone.

Sometimes I badly wanted to torture one of them a bit, like a wingless fly, into giving away that secret of theirs. When I met them in the street, I kept inquisitively trying to draw even with them, since they were almost my height. My height—but with grown-up faces. There were circus dwarves with the faces of old people that were my height, too, but their proportions were disfigured, while the invalids on carts were simply legless. Their prostheses were boards on wheels, or more accurately, on ball-bearings ripped off from who knows where, which would grind horribly on the stones of the pavement. Sometimes a drunk one would thunder down from Aušros Gate louder than a Roman war wagon.

One of those war wagons blocked my path when I was on my way to the first date I'd ever had in my life. Sara Mejerovič waited, or at least was supposed to wait for me in her yard, and I had to boldly march over to her all by myself. I had to cross the street, then the square opposite the Philharmonic, and then go up the hill on the Mejerovič's little street. On the corner of that street my path was cut off by a Roman war wagon.

"Listen, kiddo," severed-legs said to me in a rough, nasal voice, "you're going the wrong way entirely. Don't start with the little Jewish girls. They're all poisoners. It's a known fact."

After this insight, legless guffawed in a hoarse, barking laugh. Obviously he sensed that forty-five years later he'd emerge from the hatch of the drunkards' fountain in Korals. Already then he unerringly sensed it.

"I love Sara," I barely got out. "My love is like the sea."

I wasn't that horribly frightened, I knew the shorty Ivanas on a cart by sight, and I really had seen the sea: my first father took me to Palanga, and on the shore he explained the concept of infinity to me at length. All I understood was that love and the sea had to be alike in some regard.

"Well, I love my legs," that wheeled Ivanas explained to me, "and my love is like a forest. Let's go look for my legs, huh?"

The offer was so astonishingly unexpected that for an instant I forgot Sara. Of course, she was an extremely sweet chubby Jewish girl with puffy cheeks, and maybe she would bring some candy from her father's shop to the meeting. But looking for the wheeled invalid's legs seemed much more attractive to me. They undoubtedly lived comfortably in some fairy-tale world, or maybe they were hiding somewhere close by, in the underground lairs of Vilnius.

"I love my legs," the wheeled one repeated sadly. "That's

why I killed them. For a great love you always start killing in the end. Pay attention, boy. Better not to love anything—it's safer to live that way. I loved my legs too much. I ran with them, jumped high and far; I used to win prizes at sports festivals. I danced with girls and climbed mountains with them. I didn't want to share them with anyone—that's how much I loved them. And then I took them to war and murdered them. We won't find them anywhere, kiddo; they're not alive anymore. Take care, my man: if you really love something, you'll surely kill it."

Legless suddenly shoved off with his wooden knuckles and slowly clattered down the sidewalk, towards Mejerovič's shop, while I sluggishly plodded on to seduce Mejerovič's daughter. That was my first childish friendship; I still had no idea about either boobs or the flower of Sara's crotch; at the most I thought about a possible marriage. If we married we could take over Mejerovič's store with all its teas, "Bear of the North" candies, and sugared nuts. But first Sara and I had to get past seven rounds of ordeals.

Those legless men really did have a strong influence on my life: they gave me an incurable mania for legs. I love and honor my and others' legs; to me, legs are simply divine things. It's depressing and sad to look at my own feet: blocked-up blue-violet capillary veins are furrowing them more intensely all the time. My legs are slowly dying, getting heavier, and thereby trying to drag all of me into non-existence. Sometimes I've overwhelmed by a hysterical desire to get rid of them: in my dreams I run around legless and as light as a feather; I never used to run around that easily, even in childhood.

All my life I was likewise hopelessly charmed by slender, sturdy or chubby girlish legs. Perhaps the most horrifying lack of fulfillment in my life is the eternal and unfortunate unattainability of those legs. When I was a child or a teenager, real women's legs were as unreachable as the sky, as the peaks of far-off snowy mountains. I was simply too young; all the owners of those charming legs didn't pay the slightest attention to me. The best I could have done was to forcibly cut those legs off and bring them home to enjoy in secret. When I finally reached the age of love and endless sex, I was completely conquered by my one and only Laima. Miraculous girlish legs were completely within reach, their owners threw seductive and coquettish glances at me, but in my everyday reality none of them existed; Laima alone existed for me. Now, while I inexorably age every day, slender and sturdy girlish legs have become unreachable again; their owners again no longer pay attention to me, because to them I look too old.

There's no justice in this world, and who knows if I can expect it even in the other. No matter how many times I celebrate wedding anniversaries, even Laima's legs are no longer attainable. All I have at hand is the lame Elena, my victim and patient, the damned sexuality biologist who's always turning me into a grub here, a goldfinch there, a red spider anywhere. I can't even love her legs, because Elena's legs are nothing more than a horrible and dangerous experiment of the gods.

16. Lame Elena

Elena was my irreplaceable assistant and confidant during the time of the Great Rule, the red period of my life. Every minute of my prominence in government actually was marked by a red danger signal, just perhaps I didn't perceive it at first. Patris and I fiercely battled with the Commie Reds in public, but in secret we'd write agreements of Oriental craftiness and deceptiveness with them. We allowed the frightened Reds to live a while longer in their luxurious apartments, a bit more time to wave in public, and even to pretend they hadn't been up to anything bad. In return, they shared their seized factories, gas pipelines, and harbor loading docks with us. To this day I do not know where Patris hid his money, diamonds, and stocks. I myself chose a perfectly ridiculous solution: everything I managed to loot for myself is registered in Elena's name. I stole the wealth of this country's people with no regret or gnawing of the conscience: I never was a Christian, so the Decalogue doesn't apply to me.

In any event, Elena was no more than an assistant who was head over heels in love with me; she didn't have to fill out and publicly announce any declarations of income, no intelligence agencies were ever interested in her—they didn't even try to recruit her. She was a living alibi, not just for herself, but for me, too. For those who don't know the story, I'll mention that the Commies suddenly became active again and even returned to government, so they wanted to scrape out a thing or two from me that they had gifted in fear. But Elena protected me like the magic shadow of a slain warrior. She had long since disappeared from view in the government offices, mercilessly drove business at some dozen locations in Lithuania, and scooped up gold by the handful. She was always lucky at cards—even back when Minister Mureika and I played poker for her. Elena was already insanely successful back then: only I always won her.

Back then she hadn't yet put a ring in either her clitoris or the nipples of her breasts—only two elegant gold rings protruded from her belly button. Elena's belly button was attractively perverse; perhaps I was seduced by her precisely because of her belly button and those little dangling belly button rings. At the beginning of the red period I was still obsessively faithful to my Laima. Politics and government broke and corrupted me. Those two things taught me and convinced me not to obey God's rules of morality. Oriental treachery and Sun-Tzu's teaching slowly became my essence.

The Decalogue commands you to not steal, but really, it's impossibly stupid to obey a precept like that if you're in government. Diamonds and lumps of gold roll under your feet, you don't even need to bend over: helpful toadies always appear to pick the riches up from the ground and hand them over to you directly. Don't tell me some reasonable person would start thinking about who should really own those treasures. All ownership in the world is infinitely complicated and confused, while wealth you're already holding in your hand is unbelievably straightforward and meaningful. You don't even need to take it out of somewhere or take it away from someone: it simply falls into your hands from the heavens. Or rises up from the ground.

The Decalogue orders you not to commit adultery, but it's unbelievably stupid to obey a rule like that if you're in government. Both young and mature beauties swarm around you; you don't need to either seduce them or court them—they seduce you themselves, and satisfy any fancies you may have. You can be coarsely sadistic or quite hopelessly passive—anything suits them. They don't desire for your physical body; they merely want the smell of power, power's mysterious aura. Perhaps only Elena really desired me for myself. She seduced me in a ridiculously ordinary way, in my own office, in the middle of the work day. She simply sensed that I was already matured and ripe for my first betrayal of the wedded state. She locked the office door from inside and, swaying her hips, strode over to my ergonomic work chair. Lifting her full skirt, she revealed her lack of panties or stockings—just her astonishingly juicy vagina. Her clitoris was huge—perhaps half the size of my finger. That practically hermaphrodite vision did me in: I grabbed her and rumpled her like some bundle of rags. She melted entirely and screamed and shrieked. Afterwards, when I went out into the corridor to recover my breath, I immediately realized that half the halls of state heard those shrieks, but I shrugged it off. That's the true feeling of power: when you can shrug anything off. The greatest pleasure isn't to command or control; the great pleasure is to scorn and stomp.

Elena was one of the few people I didn't scorn or stomp on, perhaps that's why she helps me to this very day. But also, of course, because I'm the only one who satisfies her most secret desires. Lame Elena is an incurable apotemnophiliac: she relentlessly hungers to injure her body—she even wants her left leg cut off below the knee. But she isn't an acrotomophiliac: she isn't at all attracted by legless or handless amputees. If she were twice as old, in her youth she would have watched Old Town's legless men on carts with mortal envy. She wouldn't have desired them in a sexual way, but she would have wanted to become one herself. I never told her about the legless men on carts, although in general I've told her a lot, probably too much. Financial secrets aren't all Elena manages to keep; she can keep personal ones as well.

When I first saw the first little ring on her half-a-finger-sized clitoris, I still foolishly believed it no more than chasing an unhealthy fad. When Elena started to cut her belly and thighs with a razor and be delighted with her scars, I understood that my great lover was hiding a strange attraction. It was only much later that I carefully studied at least several scholarly articles about apotemnophilia and acrotomophilia. But back then she simply seemed just as nuts as the rest of this stinking country. With an obsessive relish she injured herself and was proud of her self-injury, too. On top of that, she aesthetically appreciated the shapes of her self-inflicted scars. This suited the overall metaphysical image of Lithuania remarkably well.

Back then I sometimes used to bonk her right on my work desk. On the same one where before and after I bonked all of Lithuania. Lame Elena and lame Lithuania seem similar in many ways to me yet. This drunken country begged and pleaded with me to injure it as badly as possible. It nearly became routine to me. But when Elena gently asked me to cut off her left leg below the knee, I was astonished anyway. In the red period of my life the world still managed to astonish me.

Elena always succeeded: she asked the only person who could have helped her. The national microsurgeon, blinded by her money, actually could have cut off her leg. Some melancholy psychiatrist could have shoved her into a madhouse without blinking an eye. But she turned to me, so she was both blessed and saved. I talked her out of the amputation then, and one way or another I've talked her out of it to this day. But back then, at the end of my red period, I was already tediously engrossed with the gut's second brain; I knew how to competently hold a lancet in my hands. I offered Elena a perfect compromise: to not cut off the legs, but just ruin the ligaments a bit and lame her. It was very difficult for her to limit herself to lameness, but she really did love me, so she obeyed me. She holds my commands sacred to this day. I can order her to do whatever necessary, and she'll do it all. At least in my underground I'm an omnipotent ruler, a true demiurge.

I've thought many times about my experiments and about Elena, lamed by my hand. My conclusion is actually quite simple: I have ruined or even destroyed many people's lives. When I was in power, I'd spiritually destroy several dozen people a day. And I didn't worry about it a bit. Although actually, on rare occasions I did worry: I was sorry I didn't rule some place like Russia and didn't spiritually destroy several dozen thousand each day. The one laming of a single maniac is truly a trifle compared to the spiritual blinding, or even destruction, of thousands of people.

I destroyed thousands upon thousands, butchered dozens upon dozens, and drove as many out of their minds. With my abominable evil, I truly rise above the majority of people; I truly approach the gods. This does not provide me with great pleasure; it's more like my fate, or even my duty. It's my punishment—the great punishment of the world, which my first father spoke of so sagely.

17. Sara's Great Punishment

Those godly punishments of the world have fallen to me much too often. In attempting to understand myself, I always recall them, but I can't manage to entirely explain them, anyway. I inherited not just my first father's deadly inclination to collect things, but his demonic powers, too. And that's not to mention his severed head, freezing me with a piercing gaze in all my dreams. Perhaps every demiurge is a demon at the same time. Perhaps every warrior battling with the world's cockles, even with perfectly practiced blows, occasionally hurts innocent people. Or maybe I simply questioned Sara too much and too often. My rose period had already been brutally interrupted by then; on the whole I no longer understood the colors of the world. I even began to fail to recognize Sara's angelic voice, particularly when she would ask:

"Did they really cut off his head? In these times, the second half of the twentieth century—even if it is in the shitty outskirts of Europe?"

How could I have answered her? She didn't need an answer anyway, she knew everything herself; she could spend hour upon hour explaining the essence of the world to me. It was only through Sara that I found out how miraculously flexible and changeable the human body is. In the course of maybe a year she turned from a fat-faced, chubby little Jewish girl into a slender-legged, big-eyed beauty. I, at least, had never seen anything so beautiful before in my life. I badly wanted her to become the first exhibit in my life's collection. At that point I still didn't even suspect what a bloodthirsty desire of mine this is. True, it wasn't the most important one. My greatest desire was purely physical. I was already fifteen; I wanted to make love to Sara for real. But just then she gradually began avoiding me. The two of us spent most of the time on our one and only endless day together, but in the evening of that day she really did begin to distance herself from me. She revealed her already quite womanly breasts to me less and less frequently, and then she stopped showing them to me altogether. I could expose them to the light of day only by cunning, or even by begging. To beg her to tickle me to the blissful point of releasing sperm seemed on the whole humiliating and shameful to me. And Sara herself would treacherously forget; she would present me with what once used to be such an ordinary blessing on the rarest of occasions, hurriedly and somewhat furtively, without any pleasure.

She wouldn't even let me suck her toes anymore!

She was becoming completely grown up too quickly, and in place of our favored depraved body games took up mysterious words. Sara was most likely destined to become a philosopher, she truly could have written books as good as Hannah Arendt's.

"All naturally satanic people look for their own Jews," she explained to me, comfortably settled on the couch or in an arm-chair. "Those so-called Jews don't have to be Jews at all; they can be Negroes or invalids, or Chukchi, or simply women. All that's important is that they can be marked with a sign cho-sen for that purpose. Not necessarily the star of David—maybe a magic pentagram, maybe a swastika, or maybe a despicable face-covering that women are forbidden to remove. It's impor-tant to oppress and to despise. And even more important is the despicable or even deadly marking. It's the irrepressible incli-nation of people's satanic nature. They cut off your father's head, regarding it as his most important organ. Primitive people used to castrate a man in these cases. I'll most certainly write a book about castration, injury, and slow killing. Those are the basic means of the little Satans' activity. You're lucky the little Satans in Lithuania aren't very powerful."

She could talk this way endlessly. Sara no longer cared in the least about mathematics; in eighth grade she even began to get mediocre grades. At times I began to not understand her, but I could no longer free myself of her. She completely enchanted me still; I never even got angry if I came across her with some considerably older Jew. Not even if they were holding hands, not even if one put an arm around her waist. Sara knew how to redeem all of her sins. She continued to allow me to admire the flower of her crotch, allowed me to smell it, and look at it as if into a miraculous mirror. In that mirror I saw both my own and her own future. The little people beyond the mirror in her vagina lived their lives and sent me secret signs I could not understand. She would spread her legs in her giant armchair and begin her unending monologue. I would watch attentively and sniff, and only later listen. In this way I nearly let the most horrifying news of the epoch by: Sara and her family had decided to leave for Israel. They already had almost enough money saved or borrowed from relatives for bribes.

In Vilnius, permission to escape from that hellish country was fairly easy to get for cash. Local Jews who wished to emigrate patiently parceled out bribes to everyone. First of all they paid a large bribe to the state—supposedly for a school certificate, a university diploma or scholarly degrees. Then they would throw bribes at several clerks too, a couple of security agents—and the road to the Promised Land would miraculously open up. Old Mejerovič decided to drag Sara down that road, too. That was his fatal mistake.

I couldn't let Sara go anywhere. My world was already spookily empty: Father's collection ravaged and destroyed, the Little da Vinci period long gone—I couldn't even kill time with boring piano practice or by daubing soulless still-lifes anymore.

I couldn't so much as look at Gorgeous Rožė anymore—neither naked nor indecently dressed up. All that was left for me was Sara with her stunningly scented flower of the crotch and her profound speeches. We were completely insane. Our classmates attended biology or physics clubs, played basketball, and kissed on the landings. Some tried to collect good grades; others snuck smokes in the school bathroom and in the evenings downed cheap wine right out of the bottle. But there was really no one like me and Sara: as soon as classes were over, we'd run over to her house; she would spread her legs in the giant leather armchair like a dissected frog and start monotonously prognosticating, while I madly examined her mirrored vagina, without the right to even touch it.

"I can't stand this disgusting country," Sara said over and over. "I can't stand this city's crooked, dirty lanes. I can't stand those unwashed peasants who don't know who Chagall is. I can't stand those dead Jew killers who have secretly penetrated into the brains of innocent young Lithuanians. Sometimes I hate you, too—most of all because I love you."

At times it seems to me that she repeated this a thousand times, and at other times that it was barely a couple of times, or just one single time. But maybe a few at least—I keep remembering how things slowly disappeared from the Mejerovič apartment: paintings from the walls, crystal from the buffet, and later even the leather divan. They methodically sold things because they had been assigned a single railroad container to transport all of their belongings. Sara, hanging her froggishly-spread legs over the black leather chair's arms, displayed her mirrored vagina to me on a constantly emptier stage. I was horribly afraid that Mejerovič would sell that enchanted armchair. And sometimes it seemed to me that he could sell Sara herself: then I would have attempted to buy her. And in the meantime I tried to absorb her into myself with my eyes, starting with the rank-smelling flower of the vagina.

"And I hate that desert-to-be even more. I really don't want to go to a desert," Sara would groan monotonously. "I'm afraid of Arabs. And worse of all—I just can't imagine that many Jews in one place. I only grasp my Jewishness meaningfully when it's full of non-Jews around me."

"But you're going to Vienna first, to the very heart of Europe. And then lots of Jews head for New York. Maybe you won't even have to see that miserable desert. We're already looked over enough deserts of intelligence and spirituality here."

Then we'd be quiet for a long time, only intensely staring at each other. It seems to me that Sara and I unconsciously wanted to invent a new nation that only we two would belong to. It seems to me she didn't want to be a Jew at all. My great disappointment with the Lithuanian nation didn't happen until a long time later. And at that time, I simply obsessively didn't want to let go of Sara. She seemed not just more important than food, but air too. First of all I wanted to make love to her, because I had convinced myself that if I didn't, I'd never manage to make love like a man to any woman, only to helplessly poke a bent pee-pee at all of them, in the belly or thighs, as I had once poked the different-sized-boobs of Eleonora the accountant. However, Sara's theatrical surrender at the last moment before leaving—maybe even the last night or day, like in some second-rate movie—wouldn't have suited me at all. I wanted all of her, for all time.

"Just before the end I'll be a Jewish *vaidutė*, a vestal virgin for you," Sara joyously explained. "When this room is entirely empty, we'll light a sacred fire here. Maybe we'll burn both our paintings and our kimonos in it. Their smoke will go straight to heaven, and there we'll be joined together forever more."

It was just exactly then that the first evil thoughts began to stir in me. She shouldn't have mentioned fire, because I immediately got the urge to burn something. To burn something alive and howling in pain: to burn up the philosophical Old Town dog, like some giraffe in a Dali painting. Or cut off someone's head: cut it off just like they'd cut off my father's head, and then stick burning candles into the remaining headless body.

But most of all I wanted to gently release all the blood from Sara, to desiccate her in a special way so she wouldn't lose a single characteristic of hers, so all of her spirit would be preserved. To transform her into a peerless cocoon of the soul, with which I could begin my great collection, and which would, perhaps, be the first and only exhibit in that collection. I truly wasn't dreaming of Madame Tussaud's wax figures—perhaps about magic Chinese mummies that could preserve a human's spirit and his true nature for thousands of years. If it wasn't my destiny to have the living Sara, I had to at least create her a magical cocoon like that, smelling, for entire centuries yet, of the miraculous flower of her crotch.

I loved her so that I would have eaten her heart. I said this to Sara herself many times, and all she would answer me with was a wan smile. There was more and more Sara in the Mejerovičs' musty old room, but fewer and fewer things. At last all that was left were two leather armchairs, a leather sofa, and a gigantic mahogany cabinet with creaking doors.

True, I nearly forgot the paintings. They hung on opposite walls and gazed attentively at one another. If I had started a sacred fire for my Jewish *vaidilutė*, I would surely have burned them first. In the painting on the left, three different sized skulls rolled about on dirty snow and some kind of newspaper scraps. Startlingly alive skulls: there were teeth, or at least the remains of teeth, sticking out of every one, so it looked like they were smiling wryly. Sometimes I'd unconsciously turn my gaze from Sara to those toothy skulls; a hundred times I counted each one's teeth. One had fourteen, another eleven, and the third, the very smallest, had seven. It could have been the skulls of the Mejerovič family: father, mother, and the only child Sara. Only extremely unhappy people could hang a painting like that on the wall.

There were neither dead people nor their remains in the second one, but that painting looked singularly sad, too. In it, little wooden Vilnian Shanghai houses flew in a purely Jewish manner. They soared sadly, even resignedly—not at all energetically, not at all dreamily like Chagall's. You saw immediately that they had only just barely gotten off the ground and were flying with difficulty, swaying dangerously. At any moment they could lose their hold in the air and slam into the ground with lethal results. It was a portrait of houses committing suicide.

And it turned out my *vaidilutė* herself was a slow suicide. Now I recognize people like that after my first conversation with them; sometimes I literally distinguish them instantly, no matter the size of the crowd. Back then I couldn't even have suspected people like that existed.

"I won't live in that desert," Sara repeated to me, "I'll wilt there anyway, like a flower that's never bloomed."

I blame myself most for her death, but she did put in a great deal of effort herself. She wanted me to suck out her life force with my gaze. And she also wanted us to turn into Chinese and speak in a special Chinese language understandable only to the two of us. She was the one who pulled those weird robes or kimonos out of the creaking cabinet, instantly threw off all her clothes and put on the feminine one. It was the first time I saw Sara undressing, and then completely naked—like I used to see my mother. Sara was already considerably thinner by then, but I didn't realize it: after all, I didn't have anything to compare with. And I didn't compare anything; I just quietly undressed myself and put on that silly Chinese robe or kimono too. That's how we became not a Lithuanian and a Jew, but just two Chinese who didn't speak a word of Chinese. Who didn't recognize a single one of the hieroglyphs both our robes were strewn with. They were silk; besides the hieroglyphs, there were also red flowers and yellow dragons drawn on them. That was how we would become Chinese, but we would still speak

Lithuanian anyway. More accurately, we would think in Lithuanian, since for the most part we didn't speak at all.

Most of the time we listened to Chinese music and danced Chinese dances. Sara herself came up with the music and then sang it: I'll never forget that doleful cooing and screeching. I'll never forget her trembling, either, when we would press up against each other, dancing half Argentinian tango, half American foxtrot—that was what we called Chinese dances. She trembled with the sickly quiver of the dying. She faded away, retreated from this world at an amazing speed, while I, without even realizing it, helped her by every means possible. When she undressed, I sucked her out and destroyed her with my gaze. I should have understood everything, but I intentionally remained blind.

On our single endless day, she changed into her Chinese robe with hieroglyphics a thousand times. Millions of Chinese hieroglyphs snaked in front of my eyes. Sara looked thinner each time, and each time the smell of her miraculous flower of the crotch became more bitter. Her cheeks sank and her eyes flashed with a fevered fire. Her head ended up resembling the skulls in the horrible Mejerovič painting—just with all her teeth. Or maybe it came to resemble my father's head, which would sometimes show up in Sara's room, right on the table, and stare at her crotch with me. My first father's head never deserted me.

Sara went out like that *vaidilutė's* flame we never did manage to light, because that was impossible. Sara was my second punishment of the world, given in advance for what I was only just getting ready to do sometime. I dreamed of it a thousand times: with no horror, even without any real regret, like in a movie film by a master of restraint, whose main character I apparently was. But just a character—certainly not a real player in actual events.

She died quietly in a corner of the leather armchair still left in the room. Sara ended up so dried and withered that she actually fit in the very corner. God preserve us, she wasn't staring froggishly spread-legged—she hadn't shown me her mirrored crotch for a long time. She put on that silly pseudo-kimono, curled herself up into a fetal pose and calmly departed. I didn't even realize she was dead. She didn't remind me of my father with his cut-off head in the least. I didn't pierce her with burning candles; Sara was so thin that I couldn't have stuck them in anywhere—unless maybe I glued them on.

The doctors explained that it was an unbelievably rare sudden death syndrome. They said Sara hadn't been ill; they had examined her by the most thorough means and determined that she was clearly perfectly healthy. From a medical aspect, she looked absolutely excellent; this tragedy was, all in all, incomprehensible and scientifically inexplicable. Both of the elder Mejerovičs choked back tears and asked everyone how it could have happened.

"Why did this have to happen to us?" they asked me.

"But why would it have to happen to someone else?" I answered their question with a question.

It's a good thing they didn't ask me what had actually happened. I probably would have told them everything, given everything away. Back then I hadn't even heard of Sun-Tzu's teaching about the necessary disguise of crucial thoughts. I was excessively crushed by what I had seen and what I had done myself. I had sucked out Sara's soul and destroyed her with my fatal gaze. I didn't want her to leave, so I didn't let her go anywhere. It was better to finish her off so she'd stay inside me forever. So to remember her better, I cut off a tuft of Sara's miraculous pubic hair. Its smell hasn't worn off to this very day. In my nostrils it always mixes with the smell of father's decapitated head. Even here in my underground, I can always sniff my Sara and my first father. The only thing I can't do anymore is look into Sara's all-revealing mirror of a vagina.

18. My Second Father

I met my second father for the first time at Sara's funeral. He knew the Mejerovičs; on the whole he knew all the Jews of Vilnius, and particularly well—those running away from the dying country of those days. Aleksas bought up paintings, antique furniture, and antiquarian books from them. He had squirmed deeply into the government's security labyrinths, like a pale slimy worm. He would get permits for Jews to escape in return for the exclusive right to buy up collector's treasures cheaply; they wouldn't have been allowed to take them out of the country, anyway. Aleksas was strangely similar to a fat white worm that had mistakenly squirmed into a person's body. He was disgustingly revolting, but at the same time gentlemanly, exceedingly gentlemanly. At Sara's funeral I couldn't have even suspected yet that he would shortly become my second father.

He charmed Gorgeous Rožė at once, and then unfortunately tried to charm me, too. At Sara's funeral he stuck to me and my mother, and kept stroking me in sympathy. The hand stroking me was plump and smelled of damp earth—that's what worms' hands are usually like.

"She was your girl, my son? All of us at times experience the pain of loss. It's particularly terrible when a young person dies," Aleksas spoke like this, or something similar, with one hand stroking me and at the same time plainly hypnotizing my mother.

Gorgeous Rožė was attracted to the point of pain by Aleksas's wealth, his gold rings with precious stones, and his restrained confidence in himself. I was instantly charmed by the fact that he was a collector, like my first father. Aleksas's collection was even twice as large as father's: it didn't just take up an entire giant Old Town apartment, but spread into other city spots, and even into a moldy basement. Aleksas kept piles of bronze candlesticks, bas-reliefs of obscure nobility, and even silver vases in an old courtyard woodshed in place of kindling for the hearth. The space around Aleksas was crammed full of antique treasures, worm-like collectors like himself, and graceful, helpful young men—who served everyone just about anything with polite smiles.

I was blindly jealous of those young men because they were much handsomer than I: tall, rangy, wide-shouldered men with the lazy movements of pumas or panthers. And they were even more blindly jealous of me: in King Aleksas's mansion they were nothing more than servants and pages, while I instantly became the prince. That's how the orange period of my life began. I don't even know why orange—perhaps because gold and oranges always seemed like they were the same color to me.

Now that I'm over the hill, in the gloom of my underground I boldly remember all the details of my slimy love for my second father. I was afraid to even think of them for at least several decades. The years I spent in government reconciled me to Aleksas. His slimy wormish knowledge about all possible, past, and future government corridors and hideouts came in very handy for me. When I was in government, I could instantly recognize all the pushy Aleksas types, guess at my enemies' intentions, and torture those below me with relish. Aleksas bestowed me with considerably more knowledge than Machiavelli, even if Sun-Tzu undeniably exceeded them both.

"The first thought upon meeting some little guy is inevitably this: what use can this slug be to me? But only a one-dimensional person would immediately reject someone who didn't offer him any direct use. You see, after that first thought, this one must come too: in what way can this little guy be of interest to me? Then yet another thought could come: how can I harm or humiliate this guy? It's uniquely delightful to trample all sorts of insignificant little people; however, you cannot trample them just for the sake of trampling. They should be trampled with relish, with inspiration, with artistry, I could say. The aesthetic feeling inside a real man is almost as strong as sexual attraction—whatever Kant might have to say on the subject. Do you understand me, my son? Are you sensing the magic in my words?"

Aleksas had no children of his own, and he insistently called me son, particularly in front of other people. I was horrified by losing Sara, but no horror took away my dry mathematical intellect. I calmly weighed what use a kid like me could be to King Aleksas, what it was that so attracted him to me, in what way could I be of interest to that all-around slug. I calmly weighed how my second father was planning to harm and humiliate me.

At the age of fifteen I already had no illusions about this world and my place in it. I was a smallish young man with deep eyes and a meaningless, chubby little face. Not for a second did I believe anyone should love me *a priori*, or do me only good. I looked askance at those around me; I wanted to bite through some of their throats, and for good measure strangle the rest. They cut off my father's head and quietly did away with Sara. They didn't deserve any of my sympathy, respect or even restrained politeness. I had no one close: my second father was a sumptuous slug, and my mother—a sumptuous traitorous slut. She was Queen Gertrude three times over, the undoing of not just my first father but his collection too, and even the manuscripts of his theory of deconstruction. And I was Hamlet without his Horatio, surrounded by nothing but a crew of Rosencrantzes and Guildensterns. Conspiring with all the doctors of Vilnius, they had killed off my Ophelia, infected her with a mysterious cosmic dwindling virus.

I was probably infected with that virus myself, because dangerous changes began to show up in my brain. I frequently tried, without success, to discern myself in the mirror, but I couldn't find myself there. None of the inhabitants of the kingdom beyond the mirror took up reflecting me and slavishly imitating my movements and expressions. The world knows many sad and disastrous stories about people who have lost their shadow—I lost my image in the mirror. It wasn't my alter ego gazing at me out of every mirror; only a sexless and senseless creature for whom now only a made-up name would do.

During those years I felt like Emperor Caligula's stepson. I was amazed and oppressed by Aleksas's feasts served on silver or Meissen porcelain dishes. I was grimly irritated by the handsome accommodating young men who didn't leave the house night or day. They used to to wash up in the shower in twos or even threes, strangely sobbing and moaning behind the shower curtain. I was for some reason attracted to them; I wanted to dash in behind their secretive shower curtains and then wantonly sob and moan together with them. I slowly grew accustomed to living in that collection of paintings, giant vases, furniture, and bodies, and I even grew attached to Aleksas in a peculiar way. He himself was something like an exhibit in the collection: a giant, corpulent caterpillar, studded with precious stones, brooches in erotic forms, bead necklaces, and little gold rings. All of it was pinned directly to his pale parchment skin. When the hundreds of brooches fixed to his body pierced his skin, no blood ran—just a pale pungent fluid seeped out. An Aleksas like that came into this world straight out of one of my dreams: only his face remained clean, without anything pinned to it, the way it really was. His face and his sexual organs.

In Aleksas's house, exhibitionism wasn't just a norm of life—it was the meaning of existence too. Those people desperately tried to raise whatever they had to the top: money and

clothes, dishes and rings, as well as their own wormish or pan-
therish bodies. Aleksas himself displayed his stumpy sexual
appendage wherever possible. His penis wasn't at all small, just
thick and stumpy—unlike mine. I was just then going through
the age of sexual measurement, comparison, and juxtapo-
sition; I was shocked more and more each day by the handsome pages of the mansion. They flashed by here and there
with their robes undone. There was literally an uncountable
number of them; they probably fulfilled the function of the
lizard people in Aleksas's collection. My mother feasted her
eyes on their bodies openly and shamelessly. She was already
somewhat past forty, but in a more obscure dimness she would
wriggle out of her clothes too, and secretly join in the frenzied
public exhibitionism.

"My child, you don't need to be afraid of your body," she'd
cunningly explain to me. "any body is beautiful, as long as you
aren't afraid or ashamed of it. After all, you yourself used to
secretly stare at me when I got undressed—don't pretend you
don't remember. And now you turn your eyes away from me.
Do you find me disgusting now?"

Gorgeous Rožė wasn't at all disgusting; she had miraculously preserved her perfect shape, only her skin had withered
slightly. I quite intentionally didn't look at her so I wouldn't
arouse an incestuous passion in myself. My mother was the
only woman in that medley of naked bodies. Aleksas didn't
keep any women servants—the young men with puma movements even cleaned the rooms for him. I desired all the women
in the world, and the world annoyingly saddled me with just my
naked mother and dozens of naked athletes with puma movements and impressive puds. This reality drove me out of my
mind; I could escape only in my dreams. I dreamed of Sara's
miraculous mirrored vagina and I'd wake up soaking wet, my
face steaming with sweat and the sheets drenched in sperm.

My incestuous passion instantly disappeared after I stumbled upon Aleksas fucking Gorgeous Rožė in the ass in a giant

Renaissance bed. Rožė lay spread face down and moaned softly: it hurt her, but probably not particularly badly. Aleksas roared much louder; the precious stones on his body shimmered, the throbbing brooches quivered, and the necklaces tinkled like little pearl bells. He insolently looked right at me and smiled wryly. I didn't retreat, and, like in the most disgusting video-tape, attentively watched the spasms of their orgasm.

"When someone watches, it's peculiarly intimidating, but pleasant, too," Aleksas shortly explained to me, carelessly wrapped in a robe. "Did you enjoy watching? Are you a real voyeur, or did you just come across us by accident?"

I couldn't even answer right away, I just quickly gulped down the offered wine. Aleksas looked particularly caterpillarish, but his slimy gallantry seemed attractive to me. He caressed my thigh repeatedly as if by accident, and as if by accident I remembered what his handsome pages got up to in the shower. Suddenly, with impossible clarity, I thought: and how could this caterpillar with a body incrusted with brooches and precious stones be of use to me? Suddenly, with impossible clarity, I experienced a painful erection, which Aleksas instantly felt with his hand. That was a fraudulent signal of my body, directed not at all at him—but after that day and that wretched erection, I no longer had the slightest possibility of squirming out of it.

At least now I no longer deceive myself—that I suspected nothing, that I was naïve and didn't realize what my second father wanted from me. I don't even deceive myself that I appreciated Aleksas's intentions then like I do now: pragmatically and indifferently, like an old movie, someone else's concocted story. Back then my second father's caresses and flirtation horrified me; one day I wanted to run away from home because of it, the next I wanted to kill myself. When Aleksas pressed up against me with his entire body, I would break out in a sweat and want to die right there, or better yet—to kill him. I didn't have the slightest illusion about his intentions, but I ran nowhere and killed no one. The great horror of that story was purely inside me: I submissively agreed with everything going on.

Most often I picture my great ordeal with Aleksas as a magnificent dark-toned painting. It's much easier and more beautiful to me that way. Aleksas, with a crown on his head, clambers over me ingeniously; his gigantic threatening body shines darkly. But his body's brooches and necklaces shine particularly brightly—earlier I had thought they were pinned or hung on, but now they have literally grown into his body, they are a part of the black caterpillar, an expression of his beauty and his depths. I'm extremely frightened and hopelessly curious; I kneel on all fours under his giant body and try not to make a run for it, because most of all I want to escape. The other variant on that painting is even more grim, but also more beautiful: my head has just been cut off, blood seeps from my bent neck, I'm no longer kneeling, but lying spread under Aleksas's powerful body, the way Gorgeous Rožė had been lying. Just that I'm not moaning, I don't make any sound at all—after all, this is a soundless painting, and not some wretched old movie, someone else's life story. I give up completely now; I gave up a long ago, but my mother always has to tear everything apart—even this painting, both its variations. She destroyed my first father's laboratory, demolished my life up until then, and then she broke off the murderous connection I was forming with Aleksas, too.

It was just that moment that Gorgeous Rožė floated into the room in a brilliant orange mist and pronounced in a hoarse, perhaps even truly agitated voice:

"Get off my son, you pervert. My boy, has he used you many times already? He'll pay a million for each time."

"Not yet. Not even once yet, mama. That time worth a million hasn't happened yet."

That was the holy truth, even though my mother didn't believe it. Now in my underground coffin I look at all of that philosophically, but back then I was simply going out of my mind. I was only fifteen years old, and I had already gone through a few too many circles of hell. My father's head was cut off by security agents, and I didn't even make love with the love of my life, I just watched her mirrored vagina for a long time. My one attempt to make love with the accountant Eleonora ended in a shameful fiasco, and then my second father tried to fuck me in the ass too. That was my emotional and spiritual biography as of that instant.

Aleksas had prepared my initiation very carefully, bringing no less than three creams to slick and soften the anus. I was probably internally ready for anything; I had looked over the handsome young men's caresses in the shower as much as I wanted, I had even come up with a morbid theory which explained that I'd never be able to make love to a woman. That my sexual powers were mystically destroyed by my endless staring into Sara's mirrored crotch. She sucked out my masculine powers, and I sucked out all the life out of her. Caught by my mother, I felt I'd never be able to make love to men either; at that time I mostly thought about whether I should cut off that wretched sexual appendage of mine.

Aleksas didn't even think of getting excited or otherwise tormenting himself. A gem or two immediately quieted Gorgeous Rožė, while as for me, he just calmly decided not to tempt me anymore.

"It's too bad," he went on sadly, throwing himself into his favorite soft chair, "I had a truly charming idea. Some men fuck a woman and her daughter side by side. But what a pearl of invention it would be to fuck both a mother and her son at the same time! I would get weak as soon as I thought of it. Although, to tell the truth, you aren't all that attractive. I was seduced by the undiscovered possibilities in you and the incomparable perversion of the situation. But on the whole it's more interesting to talk to you rather than to rumple you. Those walking mannequins are much more sexy. You attracted me as a rarity. To fuck you was a matter of honor to me—like fucking some innocent priest."

To fuck priests he would go to Kaunas—as if Vilnius was short of them. A more disgusting or headstrong creature than Aleksas I never did meet. Patris was perhaps even more headstrong and actually more obstinate, but he very much lacked Aleksas's incomparable sliminess. And even more Patris lacked the brooches attached all over Aleksas's body. Those brooches were like the hieroglyphs of an unknown language.

Back then was the first time I moved into Vilnius's underground for a bit. I didn't want to see the surface of the earth or the people crawling on it anymore. It was much more peaceful in the basements of Old Town; there only the rats got in my way. Rats are much more lovable creatures than people, which is why all worthwhile people are either physically similar to rats, or try to crawl underground in their free time. These days I meet the most interesting people in my life underground, in my interim coffin. Back then in the basements of Old Town I simply pondered the structure of the world and my place in it.

This was the question that worried me most: did Sara really dwindle away from my staring at her body's mirrored essence? Maybe I really am a spiritual vampire or some Abaddon, destroying everything with my gaze? I was also terribly worried about my second father. I was horrified by Aleksas, but I didn't by any means reject him. I attempted to guess the riddle of why I was punished with a stepfather like that. Why did that pleasant slimy caterpillar in a man's body so desire to use me homosexually or bisexually? Why did he specifically go to Kaunas to fuck priests? But I was tortured even more by another mystery: why did that whitish caterpillar-man appear to me to be pinned with precious stones—brooches and bead necklaces? That's the kind of questions that should stir and excite humanity.

Unfortunately, I was the only one to seriously delve into those questions. In my underground adolescence world, I decided the brooches on Aleksas's body were meaningful hieroglyphs I simply didn't know how to read. I also remembered the hieroglyphs on those strange Chinese robes Sara and I had. All the world's secrets that were allotted to me, all of its most important pronouncements, were coded in hieroglyphs. Hieroglyphs, and nameless signs of God.

19. Hieroglyphs

Hieroglyphs insidiously overran my brain in my tragic underground adolescence. Before the Mejerovič robes—superficially totally ridiculous, but they'd brought sure death—I had only seen them on Chinese postage stamps, and my impression of those hieroglyphs wasn't at all enchanting. They were wan, banal, and meaningless, like all of the Chinese People's Republic of those days.

My first father had twenty-eight identical pale pink Chinese postage stamps commemorating the Mao Communists' decade of power. Those stamps, as is appropriate, were absolutely identical, but my first father saw a profusion of differences in them. He searched for differences in them as if they were rebus pictures. And those differences would actually turn up. At the time I thought he scraped them himself with a tiny needle or some other secret, perhaps even invisible tool. It was only much later that I found out some people know how to alter objects with their gaze. Later I learned this myself—to my horrifying ruin. I had so eerily changed Sara's body with my metaphysical gaze that her body refused to work anymore. You can change postage stamps rather safely with your gaze, but after all, she wasn't a Chinese postage stamp, just a slender-legged, boundlessly intelligent Jewish girl. And it was the hieroglyphs of the robes in her constantly emptying room that first insidiously beset me. Later I mastered a truly unhealthy number of them.

The hieroglyph I like the best is "a frog's shadow on the moon." Despite the powerful croaking of the frogs, there was, on the whole, no moonlight in early Karoliniškės. I moved over there just as the district was coming into being, and lived in a cooperative apartment purchased with Aleksas's money. My second father had already lost all interest in me, so he didn't make any effort to look for a good apartment for me. He only fixed me up in Korals at my mother's urging. The spiritless hieroglyphs of the identical buildings seemed completely unimaginative to me, but multidimensional and polysemous anyway—otherwise they wouldn't have been hieroglyphs. Multidimensionality and intangibility—those are the etymological characteristics of hieroglyphs. The meaning of the world is of multiple essences and intangible, because it is nothing more than the intricate, sinuous hieroglyph of God.

It's a rare person who's even allowed to see that sign of God. And probably no one at all is allowed to read it. But a person must decipher that sign all his life—otherwise it will be difficult, perhaps even impossible, to justify your existence. Existence without justification is miserable to bear, and ought to be painfully punished, too.

Punishment is expressed and defined by entirely different hieroglyphs than "the frog's shadow on the moon." Perhaps the hieroglyphs on the Mejerovič's Chinese robes or kimonos expressed the punishment Sara and I shared. If I had been as wise thirty years ago as I am today, I most certainly would have kept those pseudo-kimonos for myself. I would have always had hieroglyphs signifying the worst human punishment at hand. They must have been completely different than the hieroglyphs on the twenty-eight pale pink postage stamps my first father monotonously collected. He constantly collected identical things he would later make totally different by just his gaze alone. He was always saying that I, too, am at least several dozen different people, which he saw perfectly well with his miraculous world-changing gaze. It was only to all those around me, those half-blind little people, that I looked innocent, and continue to look like a single, unchanging person. Even in my childhood my first father had already perceived all of my several dozen essences. Later I myself learned to see them in a mirror.

I'm probably not even a human, just a hieroglyph I've never in all my life managed to read and translate into a normal European language. But I try hard, really, I try very hard.

20. The Angel of Death and Politics

My mother hasn't been Gorgeous Rožė for a long time now, only a lonely crazy Angel of Death. She imagines I'm still floating along, way, way up high in government, so she does nothing but scold me for all the bad things in the world when I call her on the phone. I haven't been able to visit her for a long time, but on occasion I call her—if I succeed in swiping a mobile phone and the owner doesn't cancel the number immediately. I cannot visit her anymore, but sometimes I spend entire hours carefully watching the colorful circus of her life in a retirement home. A captain's spyglass isn't the most convenient way of socializing with one's mother—but after all, an optical sight would be even less convenient.

Most of the time at least several foolish agents are waiting to see if I'll come visit my mother. I run into them immediately whenever I take to missing that wretched Angel of Death and drag myself over disguised as a prince or a beggar. I don't know what photographs of me have been handed out to them—perhaps they gave them a small album with all my currently deciphered transformations. However, I am an artist, so I never repeat myself. The immortal Sun-Tzu taught me the art of hiding and transformation. You must sneak in as quietly as a shadow and attack as suddenly as a tiger. Watching the residua of Gorgeous Rože, I don't attack anyone, nor even sneak anywhere. I simply become invisible for several hours, even though I see everything around me perfectly well. I become one with the trees and grass, if necessary—with drops of rain or tufts of dust. Look around—look around very carefully—you won't see me anyway. But I see you all the time!

Don't get excited—at the moment I'm not the least concerned with you, I'm completely immersed in research on my mother, the Angel of Death. She looks like a store mannequin hung with colorful clothes that were fashionable five or ten years ago. She still wears Prada or Escada suits, but maybe they're Versace or Joop—I've never been enchanted with fashion houses and I don't distinguish their productions. My mother's nearly bald head painfully resembles a lifeless mannequin's head. She has hung maybe three or five amber necklaces on her thin neck and perched giant eyeglasses with green-tinted glass on her nose. She rules the terrace of the old folks' retirement home, makes the nursing attendants dance, and sometimes, for no reason whatsoever, remembers she once had lesbian habits.

Once, holding my breath, I watched her attacking a poor nurse—an insanely beautiful brunette. It occurred to me that she had learned from Sun-Tzu, too: she stalked her prey quite masterfully. The true mastery of stealth is to never hurry, to advance towards the prey a millimeter at a time, maybe even a micron. A true victor never worries about the time of victory, only the very fact of winning is important. You must emerge from obscurity like the Angel of Death, and fall upon your victim like lightning. That was exactly how my mother stalked, furtively and fatally.

The brunette nurse really was insanely beautiful—I could see that even through my spyglass. She sat in a wicker armchair tired and relaxed, her legs spread a bit and her head thrown back—most likely resting with her eyes closed. My mother snuck up to her a centimeter at a time. If there was one or another sexual hormone remaining in her death-like body, it had to be already hot and moist from the pleasure she imagined. She fell upon the completely unprepared brunette like a stinging, bespectacled cobra. She stuck a hand between her thighs at lightning speed; the girl was so shocked that she had neither the strength to stir, nor even to start screaming. Meanwhile, Gorgeous Rožė's residua unmercifully fell over on her without releasing the brunette's crotch out of her bony hand's grip. My Angel of Death mother tried so fiercely to suck that girl in with her lips that her green-tinted cobra glasses fell off her nose.

I don't even try to guess what kind of smell comes from the Angel of Death's mouth—I just smell it. I don't even try to imagine the horrible convulsion that cramped the brunette's thighs—I literally feel it myself. My mother always loved shocking and surprising. For that, I mortally hate her—for that, I love her desperately. I'll always remember how she literally pulled me out of Karoliniškės by the hair and threw me onto the rostrums at the freedom rallies. She crashed right into the bedroom; Laima and I were still lounging in bed. The world was, in any event, frozen and stopped, and there was nowhere to hurry to. I thought Gorgeous Rožė had broken in the door or climbed in the balcony, even though Laima's apartment was on the seventh floor.

"You're lying around at a time like this, when history is being made?" My mother screamed, shrieked, and screeched all at once. "Don't you realize it's just exactly your day that's dawned? The sun of your possibilities is shining. You could rise so high you'll be blinded. Your hour has come... Gee, what boobs—absolutely awful."

I believe I also tried to defend Laima from my mother's mockery, but our powers were extremely unequal. Gorgeous Rožė wasn't even fifty yet, she hadn't even hit menopause, so she pushed me over as easy as pie. She pushed my Laima over just as easily; that metaphysical frog obeyed astonishingly easily, and gave in as soon as she heard my mother's brilliant plan.

I alone opposed that plan with all my heart—you see, I was still a long way from transforming into Sun-Tzu. I still didn't even know the basic rules of battling with the world. I hadn't even entirely understood the deep truths of Aleksas's preachings.

I was still no more than a grown juvenile, an innocent infant of the spirit: I was shaken by Gorgeous Rožė's double, triple or even quintuple cynicism. I couldn't even imagine that after barely a few years quintupled cynicism would seem banal to me—I myself would, quite calmly, manage to be at least seven times as cynical.

"Wake up, you fool," my mother lectured me in my still half-naked state. "Can't you see what's going on in town? The security service is allowing demonstrations next to the Angarietis monument now. You can say aloud that Lithuanians were taken to Siberia. Big changes are coming, my son. And you will play a leading role in them."

Back then I thought no one could play any role at all, in either Karoliniškės or in this entire God-forsaken city. At the time it seemed to me that Laima's froggish body was God's greatest eternal gift. In gaining her, I no longer had to do anything; I could now calmly await Death the Liberator. That late morning Gorgeous Rožė turned all the convictions of my gray period into nothing. She told me: Get up and go! She ordered me to march forward, proudly carrying my father's severed head under my arm. Perhaps even more sacrilegious—to carry it stuck on a spike, like a national totem.

"Think of it—it's unique starting capital!" Aleksas insistently explained to me, "So, let's sketch your publicity biography in general terms. You are the son of a martyr. Your father organized a modern spiritual opposition movement and died in an unequal fight. He was the prophet and forerunner of all today's movements. He must become that tribe's totem. And you yourself will become that totem's bearer. You're destined to take part in the great game, my son."

As I had not seen Aleksas in person in a rather long time, I again unwittingly felt charmed by him. My second father had grown even stouter; he wasn't at all wormlike anymore—he looked like the good wizard in a fairy tale: graying but thick hair down to his shoulders; his face a bit puffy, but overflowing with a special goodness. He gave off a strange smell, resembling nutmeg; I knew it really wasn't perfume.

"Just think of the little creatures who inhabit this country. They are, after all, worthless little creatures; it's a nation of sheep that needs a strong and intelligent shepherd. You could be the minister of souls, the supreme secret organizer of this country. You could rule the entire world network of Lithuanians—from Siberia to Chicago. You'd be like a spider perched in the center of that network and tugging everyone by the threads of the web. You could finally get even with those little people, my son. After all, the ashes of your father and your Jewess are knocking at your heart, banging on it, no less."

You could accuse my second father, that merciless bisexual caterpillar, of practically anything—but not that he didn't know people. He knew them all too well: he nonchalantly arranged them like exhibits in his collection. That's exactly the way Aleksas understood people: he assigned everyone their own spot on the shelves of his collection, with their own worth or concrete price. I was no more to him than a graceful chess figure in his collection. Aleksas didn't even suspect that his game piece could have its own free will—and an extremely powerful one at that. Sun-Tzu's teachings were truly not among the many philosophical theories Aleksas knew. Among the numerous handsome young men he used so disgustingly there really was no other like me. He only naïvely thought he knew me.

I believe I did, secretly, really carefully think over what use that bisexual caterpillar could be to me. I believe I did really deeply sense the direction the voice of my ancestors was leading me. But the very last crucial shove was nevertheless given to me by my own Laima. Until her pivotal word I kept trying to talk myself out of it, to shamefully dodge my fate.

"No one knows me or recognizes me," I pleaded pitifully. "They'll get to know you. They'll get to know you better than their nearest relatives. After all, that's what a free press is for. We'll introduce you, my son, introduce you so all the devils will laugh. You'll learn so many amazing things about yourself, you'll be blown away. You'll fall in love with yourself."

"I don't know how to strut in front of a crowd. Demonstrations and soirees make me sick to my stomach."

"You'll get used to it. You'll get used to it and even feel good about it. After all, that's why they came up with image consultants and clever psychologists. My friends and I won't spare putting good money into you, but we'll create a truly good product."

"I'm not handsome," I flailed, practically in hysterics.

"You'll get miraculously better-looking. After all, that's why people came up with so-called inner beauty. We'll fix it so to these little people you'll become a great inner beauty. We'll turn you inside out, and we'll make your inner side silk and gold. Girls will love you, old biddies will pray for you, and pop groups will write songs about you." Aleksas knew how to tempt, even if he was only a caterpillar, and not a serpent. "It's the last and only chance of your life. You'll have not just fifteen minutes, but fifteen months, fifteen years of glory. You'll never be forgotten."

"You mean to say that it'll be my head carried around like a totem? You think I'll enjoy being on a totem pole? You think I'll experience a Lithuanian nirvana that way?"

"My child, we're truly not going to stick your head on a post in the Šventaragis valley. We'll make a political golden boy out of you. You'll play the piano, paint pictures, and amaze the crowds with your analytical intelligence. If necessary we'll prepare questioners for you, whose questions you'll answer with stunning accuracy and grace. Without, of course, avoiding your characteristic paradoxical spontaneity."

I knew remarkably well where I was heading and what

awaited me. I didn't have the slightest illusion or virtuous intentions. I was secretly already enjoying the mallable crowd I could despise and command. A crowd of people didn't seem like a band of sheep to me; they reminded me more of a pack of hyenas. Whining with obsequious pleasure in sight of a more powerful beast. Immediately tuck in their tails and disappear if those more powerful ones roar even a bit more angrily. But attack and tear into whatever carrion with the greatest boldness. If only someone doesn't move, can't defend themselves, and stinks to high heaven—a crowd of hyenas with foam on their lips rush upon them, and probably even experience a special hyena orgasm. I wasn't afraid of those hyenas; they merely disgusted me. Back then I was still capable of being disgusted by a thing or two.

As far as I remember, I felt nearly nothing and thought absolutely nothing. I was convinced I was in a strange dream; dreams like that had beset me earlier, too. I felt like I was acting in a movie whose script and events it seemed you could change a bit, but you can no longer turn the plot in a completely different direction. So you just look around and wonder at what's going on now without your willing it. It seems all you need to do is move, yell louder—and the course of the film will turn in an entirely different direction. But you never do move, you never yell; you helplessly give in to the movie's dreamy flow.

At the time, inside that waking dream, Laima determined my decision. She swayed into that dreamy film from some corner of the movie frame, wrapped in some strange scarf/not a scarf, embroidered with red hieroglyphs and yellow dragons. It seemed she listened to what Aleksas was saying to me; it seemed she brewed some tea for us. I was shocked by her jewelry: an antique enameled brooch and earrings with diamonds. Unexpectedly, my hideous frog Laima completely adapted herself to Gorgeous Rožė, who, like the real director of the film, didn't show up in the frame at all.

That shocking change in Laima is what I remember best.

She suddenly seemed to become unrecognizable, even though we had already lived together for nine years: oppressively and mysteriously unrecognizable. Up until then I had slept with a somewhat sad, poetic frog who lived for the day, sweated in a miserable office, and suited shabby Karoliniškės remarkably well. But suddenly, appearing in the corner of the panoramic frame and constantly drawing nearer the center, a noble lady who had grasped the absurdity of life's flow appeared. A lady with great taste, sending me signals of luxury with the select gems in her rings and earrings. I immediately understood that you wouldn't take a lady like that home to shabby Korals anymore. A yacht would have suited her much better.

She became strangely like my mother. As my mother is now similar to the very young Laima: sickly and insane, with giant eyes overflowing with unearthly pain. I'm still watching her through the spyglass, and I badly want to see her suddenly start undressing like she did in my childhood. I want to see her little dried-up arms and legs, the withered shreds of hanging flesh. I want to convince myself with hideous reality that worldly beauty passes by painfully and is meaningless. I want to see the Angel of Death, who will probably come to cut me down with its scythe, too.

At least for today it isn't my fate to be cut down. By now I've gotten pretty tired of being invisible; probably I'll shortly turn into a prince or a beggar again. For the hell of it, I pinch a pine cone off a branch and pitch it into the back of the security agent's balding head. He nervously looks about, but doesn't see me: after all, I'm absolutely invisible. As unreadable as the hieroglyph of a language he doesn't know.

21. Father's Head

I resolutely pulled my first father's head out of the dark nooks of the soul, where it had sat through two absurd decades of my life. It had to serve me as an authorization into the world of the future state. I dragged my father's bleeding head under my arm through all the silly political demonstrations. I was highly irritated by the strange people hanging around who hysterically convinced the crowds that they fought for freedom and justice. A third of them were agents planted by the security service, a third insanely and cynically sought power, and the remaining third were simply irredeemable fools. The all-knowing Aleksas used to warn me about specific security agents; I carefully avoided the fools myself—I was interested only in those resolutely seeking power. Not a one of them carried their severed father's head around with them—in this respect I was unique and incomparable. In this respect I could shellack them all.

"And now someone well-known to us all will speak," the demonstration leader would announce in the voice of a well-trained showman. "Our wrathful prophet, our merciless conscience will speak. Our angel of revenge."

Other orators didn't introduce me so thunderously, but I was the golden nail of every political show. They used to hammer me last into the coffin of Communism, to the huge delight of the public. Aleksas and Gorgeous Rožė really knew how to organize a publicity campaign: I became one of the crowd's symbols, which was why I was always surrounded by either stunningly hypocritical cynics or complete lunatics. But even in their midst I was the only one who dragged my first father's decapitated head everywhere with me.

I carried it, stuck on a sanctified pole, through every hysterically ceremonial street procession. Several lunatics would drag crosses on their shoulders in a circle around the Cathedral, while I would haul my first father's bloody head around like some prisoner's ball and chain. I had been alone throughout the gray period of my life—right up until I met Laima. But in the course of that year and a half, I had become a hypocritical, many-faced actor, patiently playing my act in the agitated swarm of people.

I had already turned toward some understanding of the world, but I was still stumbling around in the dark. I didn't really understand why I was mingling with all those honor-hungry psychos, and why in my enthusiasm I lied to the shallow faces of the crowd.

"What the hell am I doing here?" I'd ask Laima, the only person whom I could still truthfully ask.

"You're making history," she would answer, weirdly serious, "and history will make you."

All that eloquent fervency was no more than the hallucination of the mythological white mare, the dream of the severed head. I'm practically convinced I really did sense the dreams of my father's severed head. After all—dammit!—he really did form an intellectual underground and had stunningly naïve dreams about the historical role of the Lithuanian nation. However, his severed head didn't comment on my behavior in that period. It was as dead as dead could be; it never tried to come to life and never spoke, teaching me ponderously and reproachfully. Father's head retained a thoughtful but calmly indifferent expression on its face; the frozen features didn't inspire thoughts about graves, death, or the other world. Father's head gave off the scent of a painterly calm; it seemed to me it felt it wasn't just a tribe's totemic symbol, but a macabre work of art as well.

I knew quite well that from the other side, he attentively examined all of Lithuania's uproar and calmly deconstructed those parts he didn't like. I was scared to even think of the size of the shelf my first father erected for himself in paradise, and what means he used to arrange people and events from one shelf to another according to a deconstruction plan known only to himself. At night I dreamt of those shelves so suggestively that afterwards they'd loom in front of my eyes all day—I didn't even need to close my eyes. All of those little people noisily rushing about, all the marches and protests, took place on those endless shelves constructed by an unknown hand, which no one was destined to escape. All of those dilettante politicos looked to me like the agile lizard people or rat people from my father's secret room. The problem was, I was one of them myself.

22. The Quiet Search for Eros

No one wants to be a rat person of their own free will. Visions of the all-encompassing shelves constructed by Father or God were nothing more than a subconscious alibi, a deplorable self-justification to myself. It was time to throw father's bloody head over the fence and come to terms with what I was doing. Undoubtedly I was an exhibit in some sort of collection. I was also the secret sign of the Lord's general proclamation to the world. I was being mercilessly exploited by some sort of power for its own purposes, whereas I was, after all, the one who ought to be exploiting others. That was what the entire merciless game with my first father's head had been conceived for.

However, even in the course of an entire year of crushing hypocrisy and strutting on meeting platforms, I never did become reconciled to the role that had been thrust on me. I hauled Father's head around like Hamlet with Yorick's skull, but I hadn't believed in my monologues anymore for some time. I wasn't seduced by the sacred eros of power over a crowd. The crowd always seemed stupid and dangerous to me, while being greeted or spoken to by people I didn't know merely irritated me. I'd recover only with Laima, my eternal love, whom I'll never abandon. Maybe I'll even take her with me into my real coffin, since she didn't want to move into my interim underground one.

"I'm certainly not going to follow you wherever you may

go," Laima said to me a thousand times, "because you're a madman, and who knows where you'll go. I won't give you any children and make you a sweet family, because you won't support any family; maybe you won't even be able to feed yourself. Maybe Rožė and I will push you into power, but even that's questionable. You're incorrigible and monstrous, but I love you. I'll love you always, even if I end up ten thousand miles away. And you'll never find another woman who would suit you so well."

To me the only eros in the world was the magic of Laima's froggish body. I would plunge into her as soon as I got near her, even after the toughest days. That body was my gate to the Other World, my road to the Moon. Inside it, I would melt, die, and come to life again. Before that, for years upon years, all I could do was return to my interim coffin in Karoliniškės. I didn't even have a television in my coffin, so I used to spend endless evenings lying on a creaking couch and staring at the ceiling. You can't say I didn't do anything. Most often I created new, better plans for the Universe. Sometimes I'd forgetfully play with myself, splattering sperm on not just the walls, but probably the ceiling too. And sometimes I'd solve abstract mathematical problems. Hilbert's fourteenth problem, or something similar. A heap of unsolved mathematical problems had been left to me by both of my dead: my first father, and the one and only Sara. If I thought about mathematics, for some reason I'd remember my young mother undressing. If I shamefully masturbated, I never saw Sara's miraculous vagina before my eyes, only my father's severed head.

So Laima wasn't just a woman to me, but a threefold or fivefold salvation: it was only in her that I saw a deep meaning, as I hadn't seen any meaning in my life for a long time. The daily walk to the Mathematics Institute or splattering the ceiling with sperm couldn't have meaning. My ruined talents for art and music didn't have any meaning, either. Through all the years of my gray period I didn't draw the slightest sketch or touch any musical instrument. My only instrument was Laima. For a long time the only work of art that attracted me was my first father's severed head. I dragged it with me onto the political stage, too. By the way, on that stage I touched the keyboard of a piano for the first time in twenty years. In Kaunas, hardly believing it myself, I sat down on a creaky stool and played several phrases of Chopin as if it were an addition to a just-finished speech. Several hundred people, disarmed and dazed in surprise, sat in the hall holding their breath. Really holding their breath—not at all like at the time of my teenage concerts or competitions. The outburst of applause was so strong that it almost knocked me down. For a second I was on the verge of feeling the mysterious eros of a raging crowd, but that feeling instantly disappeared. I wasn't ready yet to experience an orgasm from the joy of ruling people. Sometimes the eccentric Artūras Gavelis helped me to make music; he would always start singing at meetings in a completely decent dramatic tenor. He stood at Sajūdis's very wellspring, but later began quickly distancing himself from the powers-to-be. He was an idealist, but not a fool—an extremely rare specimen. He wasn't stuck in there by the security services and wasn't seeking power; he simply found it enjoyable to feel the flow of history. He was likable; the two of us struck up a solid friendship—sometimes it's nice to know there are still idealists in the world. Even today, he's the only one I trust at all; I'd look to him for help first—and probably from him alone.

I had already moved into the red period of my life, but hadn't realized it yet. The red flashes that painted the scenes of my life looked like danger signals to me. The first to redden were the love games Laima and I played. It was maddeningly disturbing to sense this: the color of blood suddenly got mixed up in love and bodily pleasure.

That was indeed a portentous sign. I realized with horror that Laima's body no longer gave the usual sublime satisfaction, the joy guaranteed to encompass everything. Suddenly it occurred to me that her movements while making love had turned lazy, and all her body's muscles had gone disgustingly limp. She no longer pleased me with all the little corners of her body at once; I would unexpectedly come to in the very heat of the act of love and with murderous clarity think there was something missing in this sex. The incomparable eros of Laima's body unhappily faded, as if it had hidden itself away from me.

"You're not giving yourself up to me anymore," Laima complained too. "You're not giving yourself up with all your being, like you used to. Your movements are like a robot's; you're not making love intoxicated—you're probably thinking about something else entirely, not about me at all. Are you so tired and snowed under by those politics? Maybe we just need to make love less often, so you'd miss me more?"

I couldn't even explain to her that every thing I saw was imperceptibly painting itself in red. At the time I couldn't even manage to describe to myself what was going on with me. Only now, long after turning into the immortal Sun-Tzu, can I wisely explain that my body had simply been taken over by a quiet search for a new eros. The brain in my gut could no longer be satisfied by a woman's body alone. It had already been infected by the crushing virus of the thirst for power, just that I didn't know it yet myself. In order to understand what was going on with me, I first had to get close to Patris.

23. The Ill-fated Steeds of Socrates

Getting close to Patris seemed completely impossible back then because I found him disgusting. He was more of a caterpillar than that caterpillar of caterpillars, Aleksas, and more KGB than the ass-faced KGB agents who cut off my father's head. A disgustingly graceful brunet with thick hair and the face of some movie actor or another. Just so: no one specific, but just some movie actor—as soon as you saw Patris, you'd immediately think he reminded you of some actor: perhaps an American, perhaps an Italian, or maybe even a Latvian. But you could never manage to remember exactly who, or from what country. That's the peculiar way Jogaila's wretched charisma expressed itself. Patris's magic attractiveness was something like a word hanging on the tip of the tongue that you think you'll recall now at any moment, but in the end you never for the life of you remember it. It's as if he were many-faced and completely faceless at the same time. Only his eyes are stunningly interesting and deep; the true evil of existence lurks in them. Patris's gaze exists apart from his face: the eyes of a cynical philosopher in the face of a screen heartthrob.

I sincerely hated him, and he hated me even more. My hatred was naturally justified: I hated him because he was a heartthrob, a horrifying cynic, and a pathologic misanthrope.

And he hated me because at political meetings, my first father's bloody head would sometimes outshine his own thoughtful little face. The little women who wept at the fiery public speeches would kiss my hands afterwards, but only enthusiastically applaud him. Those were truly funny and hysterical times: you didn't need to work or create; all you needed to do was wag your tongue and stitch together political resolutions or fiery proclamations one after another. The fools rising on the national wave thought this would last forever. The KGB minions had long ago realized it wasn't the Communist Party that needed to be saved, it was its wealth. It was left to the smarter ones to divvy up the future state.

It was the omnipotent Aleksas who hitched Patris and me to the same wagon. He was the only one who could unite us, only his bisexual power forced us to love one another.

"I'll introduce you," Aleksas thoughtfully announced, after inviting both of us to his residence. "You're simply made for one another, you just didn't know it until now."

I really didn't think the disgusting heartthrob Jogaila was made for me; I didn't in general feel I was made for anyone on this Earth—except perhaps for my Laima. The fat, graying caterpillar Aleksas shone with all the brooches and necklaces pinned to his body; it was impossible to resist him, those flashes and flares had drearily hypnotized me all my life. Besides, Aleksas was my second father; I had to at least listen to what he had to say.

"Here sits Jogaila Štombergas, my son. He hates both individual people and all of humanity, so most of all he wants to be a uncontrollable tyrant. But he's truly unique: he's an intellectual tyrant. His bottomless soul would very much like to guillotine a thousand of his fellow citizens, but his cold intellect whispers to him that unfortunately, it's not possible. On its own, this nation is sufficiently slavish that it would be possible to guillotine them en masse, but neither Europe or America would allow it. The world's fashions are completely different now. Take a close look at this pervert, my son. His biggest public fault—on rare occasions he loses control of himself and tears or cuts apart some girl he's fucking. Although it's true he makes such an impression on the girls that so far, they all forgive him. Jogaila is one of a kind: there's such passionate hatred for people lurking in his eyes that the people he hates mistake it for love. It's the eyes of a person who's in love; the murderer Štombergas's essential charisma lies within those eyes. He hypnotizes the people of Lithuania like Kipling's boa constrictor hypnotizes monkeys; they don't even realize that his surname isn't in the least Lithuanian. He simply has no equal, that's why you'll join forces with him, my son. The two of you will plainly be an unbeatable tandem. And I'll hand over some priceless assets I managed to buy phenomenally cheap to you, too. I'll present you with the KGB agency files on the Sąjūdists, parliamentarians, and every stripe of minister. No one will dare to so much as meow in front of you. You'll be holding everyone by the balls."

Charmed, I watched Patris's intelligent face throughout Aleksas's long tirade. Despite it all, the man was maddeningly handsome and compelling. Whatever his words, whatever their meaning, they broke into pieces against his shapely looks and stunningly deep gaze. A practically uncontrollable wave of influence flowed from Patris. In horror I realized that I was beginning to fall hopelessly in love with him. Suddenly I started to vaguely sense where my unrealized eros lay.

"You, Jogaila, take a good look too: here sits my one and only son. This man is woven from a thousand talents and five thousand flaws. He's totally indifferent to both people and humanity as a whole; his hate is directed at the Cosmos itself. He thinks God created the Universe incorrectly and unsuccessfully; every night he gives birth to an abundance of plans for reorganizing the Universe. His biggest problem is that he only plans, but does nothing. He hasn't read Machiavelli's writings, so he doesn't know that you must try to cheat the entire world. He'd destroy all of humanity with pleasure—but only theoretically, completely pie in the sky. In practical terms, he's not preparing to do anything at all; he has no practicable notions whatsoever. He even restricts himself to fucking only one woman because he hasn't made the effort to find others. He lacks charisma in all aspects of his life, all the more so in public politics. But he will make a simply incomparable gray eminence. He's so abnormally intelligent and so full of talents and miscellaneous aptitudes that he'll be of more use to you than the most powerful computer, Jogaila. You two will be an epochal tandem; it isn't just that this country has never had anything like it, it will never give birth to such again. You'll rule ordinary people with your unequaled cynicism, and government people with old KGB files. The two of you can express this country's essence best. So kiss and be friends from now on."

I'm not entirely sure that Aleksas said everything exactly that way. I'm not sure that Patris and I really did kiss on the lips. But I remember all too well that afterwards an entirely new epoch of my life began. I completely forgot the likable innocent Artūras Gavelis. He slowly fell out of politics altogether. I joined forces with the incomparable Jogaila Štombergas and became even more attached to him than I was to my Laima. In fact it was Patris who slowly awakened a boundless eros for power in me. He radiated that eros so intensely himself that at first I mistook it for a sexual summons. I even started furtively looking over Jogaila the heartthrob's little butt. But I quickly understood that all his erotic energy wasn't directed at me at all, or even at women. Power alone eroticized and inflamed him. Only power could arouse a real orgasm in him. That's exactly why he occasionally lost control and tore up some girl; he kept naïvely hoping to get the same perfect bliss from her as he would experience when completely conquering some person, or an entire crowd.

"Sex doesn't bestow either real fulfillment, or a real

orgasm." he openly admitted to me. "Even when you rape a woman you won't conquer her completely. It's just a pathetic imitation of conquest. A worthless imitation."

Patris didn't drink, didn't smoke, and categorically refused cocaine, even in moments of the greatest exhaustion or disappointment. He was almost perfectly monogamous to power, just that he constantly allowed himself to be seduced by women. I had already nicknamed him Patris earlier, at an election gathering in Kaunas, when a fat woman with a hoarse voice yelled into the microphone:

"Jogaila—our number one patriot!"

"If a man's a patriot, he's nearly unavoidably an idiot," Apples Petriukas likes to repeat edifyingly. "But if he just pretends to be a patriot, then guaranteed he's a cynical villain. It's banal. It's the ABCs of life. Your Patris is being carried by the ill-fated steeds of Socrates."

The Ill-fated Steeds of Socrates is the title of one of Petriukas's books—one of the earlier ones, where there was still a bit of text. It's simply an essay about the emptiness of existence and power. Socrates was the first to understand that people are irresistibly led to tyranny and dictatorship by the same feeling that leads others to philosophy or poetry. That feeling is love: the eros that smashes everything in its path. It draws one person to the soul, or to heaven, others to the earth and the body. It's the two painfully different Socratic steeds of eros: one drags you down, the other pulls you to heaven. The more powerful one decides your fate: you fly to the heights of the spirit, or land face-first in the mud of earthly desires. Everything depends on what type your soul is. Petriukas named some nine types of Socratic souls: the highest he assigned to philosophers and poets, the lowest to politicians and tyrants.

Patris is almost perfect: his soul is carried through life by a single solitary earthly steed. Most likely he bumped off the Socratic steed that carries you upwards back in his childhood. He absolutely ignored the existence of the higher spheres of spirituality and gave himself up exclusively to his second brain. Jogaila Štombergas intuited every last thing in his gut, and for that very reason he rose to the very top.

24. The Second Brain

The discovery of a person's second brain was the result of my long and painful empirical investigations. I carried out my experiments carefully and tediously—at every opportunity that presented itself, whenever I managed to get a free minute. I experimented with people of various nationalities and sex, with transsexuals and hermaphrodites. Their reactions to the experiments were always different—and that's just what's most interesting. They moved differently and would always rest in some other manner; they would smell differently and were stuffed full of completely different organs, different mucilages and bodily fluids. However, I would discover the same thing in all of them: indisputable signs of a second brain.

The second brain is a subtle knot of nerves in the common tangle of the digestive tract. There are perhaps some hundred billion of those knotted nerve cells. I haven't counted them exactly, but there has to be roughly that many. In any case, there really are more nerve cells there than in the brain of the spinal cord—I've carefully researched spinal marrow, too. The gut's brain controls many of a person's spontaneous choices—not just food, but the choice of a wife or a lover. The choice of a favorite color or scent. Even the choice of a lifestyle. I say this without the slightest doubt, because I chose Laima only by the urging of my gut's brain. The actual brain in my head had no influence on this choice. Professor Wolfgang Prinz of the Max

Planck Institute in Munich completely agrees with this conception of mine. Not to mention Levas Kovarskis, undoubtedly the discoverer of a person's anatomical essence, the most frightful monster of Vilnius's secret laboratories. I won't hide it; I was always secretly charmed by Levas Kovarskis—the way Plato was charmed by Socrates. Kovarskis didn't just discover the secret parasite of Vilniutians' brains—he also was the first to theoretically predict the certainty of a second brain. I myself discovered it quite ordinarily, almost crassly.

Kovarskis's history is dark and mysterious; I myself don't know everything about it, much less understand it. He was a divine surgeon who became an anatomical pathologist of his own free will. He founded a giant laboratory in the Vilnius clinics where no one knew what mischief he was up to. Macabre legends spread about his experiments with corpses. According to some, he cut off those poor souls' heads and ate them with garlic, while others maintained that he was up to no good with the corpses' sexual organs. Still others furtively said that he discovered some kind of secret Vilnius parasite that ate people's brains. But I was mostly interested in something else: he had dissected a person into tens of thousands of pieces. There was barely enough room in his all of his laboratories to set them all out. With that collection of his, Kovarskis indirectly reminded me of my father: he was trying to deconstruct too, just a single person instead of the entire cosmos. But after all, a person is an entire cosmos too. And he was remarkably close to me because, in dissecting a person in that manner, he really had to fully know about the second brain.

Most of the time, a person doesn't even realize that any given choice he makes in his life is determined by the gut's brain. The noble brain of the head can be satisfied with the image of a beautiful woman, a wise book, God, or some other illusion the world tosses at you. But in the end all the gods and all the beauty of women turn out to be a deception most foul. It's unbelievably easy to hoodwink the credulous brain of the head with them. But you won't deceive the depths of the gut's brain so easily! It doesn't take up the intricate games of the intellect; it immediately rips off all the veils of deception and instantly, unerringly, comprehends the world.

"I feel it in my guts," Apples Petriukas likes to say, and he's philosophically correct.

A person feels and decides everything first of all with his guts. By no means are the empires of the world and the fate of nations determined by complex constructions, but rather by the state of the entrails of demented leaders. Historians can't say anything about the actual development of the world's past because they haven't grasped the secret of people's second brains. Hamlet weighed the metaphysical problems of existence only with his first brain. But all of his behavior was determined by the second brain in his gut: he was deathly afraid of concrete action, he avoided properly loving Ophelia—he was simply afraid; afraid he wouldn't succeed, afraid to show himself to be a rather poor lover. As soon as he tried to make a decision, the brain of his gut would take his breath away, smother his vital powers, and the prince himself would rush headlong to the toilet with the runs. All he could do was talk a lot about action, just not act.

I keep thinking about Hamlet because for an entire two years I dragged father's severed head around with me, like he did with Yorick's skull. Apples Petriukas and I never did like Hamlet, even though he really wasn't such a bad kid. Unfortunately, he was a melancholy impotent with strange deviations towards bisexualism. The second brain completely suppressed his masculine rudiments. It had expanded too much and oppressed his soul. I've seen second brains like that from up close many times. The meaning of that type of hypertrophied brain of the guts was probably best put into words by Levas Kovarskis during his grand visit.

"If the brain of the head were to swell up and balloon that way," he explained in the tone of a mentor, "a person would lie there like a log, in a complete state of coma. He'd literally be a vegetable. But with a hypertrophied gut brain, he walks, lives, and makes fateful decisions with it. When a man suffers from hyperplasia of the prostate—at first he urinates every half-hour, and later can't urinate at all anymore. When he suffers from hyperplasia of the second brain—at first he talks like he's wound up, tossing silly thoughts in all directions. Almost all politicians are of that type. Later, the carrier of a hypertrophied second brain can no longer stammer out any thoughts at all, or take any action. He simply becomes a vegetable in the highest political post. We've seen hundreds of these in Russia and China. Unfortunately, no one lets us dissect them or make ourselves taxidermy specimens. The science of the world has turned in entirely the wrong direction. Everyone's fascinated by the secondary brain of the head, but they've utterly forgotten the primary brain of the gut."

Jogaila Štombergas's gut brain is perfect by nature. Patris is a born master of presentiments and hidden influences. A genius chess player and intriguer, what my collection of charming little monsters most lacks.

25. Ruined Memory

My memory is quite ruined, but that's completely irrelevant to the sequence of world events, as well as to the collection and burning of the world's cockles. All that's relevant is that my memory is constantly fading. The rest of its metaphysics are of no vital importance to me. Of course, memories are directly dependent on the fact that the flow of time is one-directional and nonrecurring. Put another way, on basic rules of thermodynamics and entropy. Memory mercilessly enlarges the world's disorder and condemns it to a slow and hopeless thermal death. But let those things interest scientists and aficionados of prophesies.

I haven't made any prophesies for quite some time now, because I remember very well what will shortly happen. In my brain, all the seasons and directions of time's movement have gotten confused, so frequently the past comes after the future. Confused that way on the inside, living is difficult and dangerous, but exceptionally interesting. My memory whispers to me that I should be eating steak, grilled *saignant*. But I cannot believe that suggestive whisper without reservations, since my mechanism of memories is multilayered and multidirectional. Some ordinary fearful person, when he remembers something, would immediately know it really happened in his past, that it's factually confirmed by and directly influences his present. Once you've burned yourself, you won't stick a finger in the same flame again, because you would thoroughly remember the previous pain.

All that logic of memory is valid only when the past really did exist earlier and directly influences your present. But that logic absolutely no longer applies if your past is still to happen: the future pain of a past burn just can't influence your present. And the pain that was of the future is unknowable and is therefore essentially meaningless.

Have you understood anything of this ponderous confusion? I don't understand anything anymore now. I know just one thing: my memory is getting weaker, so some past events take on ever stranger forms, repeat themselves differently every time—with different people and a different me. All those events of the past hide in my future, that's why it's so difficult for me to figure out or foresee anything. And even harder to simply live and simply act.

26. The Disguise

It's horrible, but perversely pleasant to watch your face in the mirror turn by degrees into who knows whose face. This is how I make an offering to the world on the other side of the mirror, the world the Yellow Emperor imprisoned for eternity and forced to repeat the features and movements of our world. I allow the inhabitants on the other side of the mirror to vary their facial features. They remain imprisoned anyway, but at least they don't have to incessantly repeat the same me. They get a tiny little chance to improvise a bit. They cannot leave their prison cell of the other side of the mirror, but they can make some mischief and mock me at the same time.

I'm a man without a single real face. All the more a man without a single real name. You could call me the Archangel Gabriel. But you could call me Abaddon, too, even if I don't destroy the world with my gaze. Only Apples Petriukas destroys cockles from a distance with the help of his Voodoo. I'm not Apples Petriukas, but the gods allow me a great deal regardless. I can have a host of names and a multitude of faces. If you meet me, you wouldn't recognize me for the world; it might even seem to you I'm some distant relative you haven't seen in a long time. I'm likable and attractive—so attractive that I'm deathly sick and tired of it by now. Not so long ago, when I was going out into the street I'd make myself up nicely and even dress up, in my own way. But for many weeks now

I no longer pretend to be a prince, just a beggar. I started to like it when people follow me with cursory somewhat annoyed glances, when they turn their noses away from my well-considered stench. Each time I strive to stink in a special way; I collect changes of stench the way perfume maniacs select each day's special fragrance.

In this way I strive to be especially human. Apples Petriukas has written a book called *Man's Scent*. I haven't looked at it for a while, so I can't quote it word for word, even though the entire book is no more than maybe three pages long. It's simply a short parable about how man decisively differed from the Lord's other creations in evolutionary development. Why he fell out of the harmonious world of animals driven by inborn instincts, and started living apart from other living creatures. According to Petriukas's concept, an unbearable stench separated humans from the world of natural fauna. Any normal animal finds man's smell so unbearable that all living creatures run away in panic. The moment they smell a man's fetor, wolves, bears or tigers run away headlong, because from that stink they would be seized by terrible cramps and an irrepressible horror. Even the hungriest predators can't bring themselves to eat human flesh. Only completely mad pariahs driven out of the company of animals can manage, by some unknown means, to overcome their natural revulsion to man.

It was only because of his incomparable stink that man resisted the dangers of the ancient jungle and survived as a separate species. It's man's unique trait, and perhaps even more important than consciousness. That's why an exceptional person must reek exceptionally in order to survive without being eaten in the human jungle. In selecting a different specific stink for each day, I am especially human and can rise to an entirely new level of natural selection. With my looks and my smell I insistently prove on a daily basis that it isn't a person's exterior that's most important, but only his inner being and his spirit. Belonging to the circle of great righteous men of the world, I walk around stinking and tattered on purpose—unfortunately, no one even tries to look into my shining soul. All of them, like complete little idiots, turn their noses away from me. People in all ages have paid more attention to form rather than content.

Today I'm going to go watch my Angel of Death mother while gussied up in a beggar's costume of a fundamentalist professional dumpster diver. I've pulled on a jumpsuit with the camouflage pattern and hues of an unknown army, and on top I threw a robe fortified with a lining. The robe is a dirty blue, and the camouflage uniform was once green and dark brown. It would probably hide a soldier secretly lurking in some forest. But paradoxically it hid me too—a righteous soldier in the middle of a sad city.

The most important part of the ceremony still remains: to find a suitable smell for today. When complete hopelessness overtakes me, I behave traitorously and shamefully—I borrow Albinas Afrika's smell. I simply put on some vest of his. Some time has to pass before I recover from its stench and stop gagging. But that's just an extreme solution: Afrika's smell doesn't belong to my collection of smells, and besides, with his vest on I immediately get an irrepressible urge to bang on some bongos or congos. These substitutions of real smells are suitable perhaps only if I just want to go for a walk around Vilnius.

If you are preparing for a serious cockle hunt, a scent must be selected both carefully and with inspiration. Sun-Tzu didn't write anything directly about the selection of the smells of war, but after all, you have to read between the lines, or more accurately—between the columns of hieroglyphs. Your scent decides whether the hunt will be successful, or whether someone in the human jungle will themselves hunt you down. My collection of scents is hidden in the most scentless place in the world, in my room of homunculi, the delicate cocoons. Only Petriukas and I can enter. Inside is our private bath, our splendid bar and quite a decent collection of grass. A dim, even light shines there night and day, reflected thousands of times in a multitude of mirrors. My homunculi are reflected a hundred times in them; they seem to be everywhere, but Petriukas and I are the only real people here. In that two-person private club we sometimes discuss the problems of the world, and there I select the day's special stink for myself. My collection's cocoons stand there nicely lined up; so far there's exactly eleven of them. I really don't go in for quantity; I'm only interested in a true maestro's quality.

There's zillions of cockles in the world; if I were to try to burn all of them out of the world, I'd only make a joke of myself and ruin my great mission. I must select them extremely carefully; I'm limited by the size of my interim coffin, my tenacity, and even by the length of my life. I calmly decided I would assemble exactly twelve of them—at this moment I'm lacking just one, but it's the most important one. But I will surely set it there—I simply don't have the right to die without completing my collection. Although I'm not obliged to die immediately after I've burned the twelfth choice cockle out of the world, either. I could still exchange one of the less important cockles for a new one, a truly incomparable one. For the time being, there's exactly eleven of them, but I know full well who will occupy the twelfth plinth. The room has been readied for him a long time ago, and there couldn't be a better exhibit.

"Hello, my dears," I say to the homunculi, shutting the heavy armored door. "What's new in purgatory today? What fire is burning you from inside?"

They don't answer; only their eyes gleam angrily. They're too arrogant and furious to amicably socialize with me. Sometimes I chat with them for a while, comfort them or tease them, but this time I don't have the urge for it. I planned in advance what stench I'll assemble today: I mix pig pancreas, a bit of ambergris, and polecat secretions. It's truly a knock-out cocktail: if I were to board some trolleybus, the passengers would either faint immediately or instantly rush out. But I'm in a good mood today, so I won't torture people, I'm only going to be walking under an open sky.

Today is a beautiful and tormenting spring day. The passersby avoid me and occasionally swear. I stink unbearably; I'd say, sophisticatedly. The more those little people avoid me, the more they don't see me. They're vehemently spiritually blind, so they never see the essence anywhere. Knowing this perfectly well, I can hide myself, even in the middle of the largest crowd, without any difficulty at all.

Without hiding myself, I pass through the courtyards of Žvėrynas and Karoliniškės, and when I tire I calmly sit down on a little bench. Completely feeling my part, I sometimes even rummage in the garbage dumpsters, raising a real concert of flies that I alone in the world am capable of conducting. In this city I do whatever I feel like under the nose of all the authorities and the ass-faced security agents—they'll never catch the immortal Sun-Tzu because they're miserable dolts. The history of the world, as well as my own life experience, inarguably proves that people, in general, are not inconsiderable dolts.

27. People are Dolts

Patris and I have discussed this inarguable postulate many times. Jogaila also liked to call this the Law of Accumulating Idiocy. It's a rather strange, exceptional, and nearly astounding characteristic of humanity. Randomly taking a single person out of a crowd and examining him carefully, you'd probably turn up only a modest dose of complete idiocy inside him. Sometimes the quantity of that natural or acquired stupidity is so meager you wouldn't detect it with any apparatus, if not for Jogaila Štombergas's unique intuition. Of course, by chance you could always open up the very brain in which a critical mass of idiocy has accumulated. But on the whole, even an ordinary little Lithuanian is by no means the incarnation of stupidity.

The brain of the gut in Lithuanians is disproportionately well-developed, so taken individually, Lithuanians most often act driven by so-called common sense. Even in twos they most often turn out quite wise: Kovarskis and I tried this out more than once in our laboratory. Even cut into pieces and reassembled anew Lithuanians—like those sexy worms—would of their own accord miraculously grow together again, thanks to some unknown energy. They didn't just grow back together, but instantly turned into an individual, a normal, completely understandable person, or at least a harmonious creature. Kovarskis and I really liked these experiments. We used to carefully bind those folks, cut up into small pieces of the most varied shapes, and then with wonder and true scientific curiosity endeavor to track them slowly growing together again. We'd definitely sew together the brain of the gut for them: a person's growth and conformance started there. And then we'd slowly admire the way they turn into a whole, a real *homo sapiens*. Individual people are always *homo sapiens*. But just not gangs! Just not crowds, and not packs. Patris and I were frequently obliged to meet with real gang representatives: we'd smoke a pipe with Boria, and with little Igor, too. But I don't have gangs or provincial mafias in mind—those aren't the worst kind of gangs. An incomparably worse gang would be some delegation of provincial teachers. Those biddies probably didn't have a lot of intelligence individually, but when six or so got together they could strangle or rip anyone to shreds. Jogaila and I would be in the greatest danger when we ran into gangs like that. But we were courageous; we were still fairly young and actually extremely courageous. We even weren't afraid of rioting crowds of peasants. The great leaders of the time would lock themselves inside the Seimas with their tails tucked between their legs and hermetically seal the shutters—they supposedly feared snipers—while we'd go out in their very midst to chat with those peasants. We acted the way the great Sun-Tzu taught. You see, we knew a secret worth a lot of gold: that entire crowd was absolutely stupid, just like their rowdy little leaders. All together they were complete dolts. You could buy them for a box of bonbons or a spool of thread. They were a crowd; their thick-headedness was astounding, but at the same time it allowed Patris and I not just to survive, but to constantly rise upwards. Upwards, only upwards—to the very heights of absurdity.

So, the Law of the Accumulation of Idiocy, discovered by Jogaila Štombergas, indisputably declares an ordinary truth of the world. The more people gather into a pile, the larger their combined idiocy will be. Two advisors attached to some minister can be an entirely sensible pair. But take any board, any commission, any committee—now it's a collection of pure dolts. All of those people on their own aren't at all bad, but thrown into a pile they instantly get infected with incurable imbecility. Patris and I kept trying to determine the magic critical number beyond which a qualitative leap in idiocy occurs. But that miraculous number doesn't exist—it's different in every concrete case, although it is a clear and finite whole number. Six provincial teachers is already a doltdom of dolts. For the complete doltification of a government ministers' meeting, you have collect a couple more, but eleven is usually sufficient. Above eleven, a meeting like that turns into a colorful farce of imbecility. But it used to get most horrible for us when we met up with a really large crowd.

A crowd's thick-headedness is most astounding when looking from above, from a rostrum or a platform. Jogaila and I frequently worked as a duo—or in tandem, as Aleksas liked to say. When working as a duo, the crowd's eyes and face would astound us. It wasn't even the sort of emptiness of the eyes I remember from my childhood concerts. It was a cosmic thick-headedness. It was on account of that metaphysical thick-head-edness that Kovarskis and I, along with Kevorkian, created our theories. In my childhood days, all the listeners and even I, the player, were connected by music, and music, one way or another, is humankind's highest accomplishment, stolen from the gods. Unless perhaps Sun-Tzu's art is higher still. Maybe someone else would say that Sun-Tzu was a politician and a warrior, but he turned politics into an art. It's as if with the wave of a hand you were to turn a pile of shit into a mountain of live roses—with trees, springs, and charming rock gardens.

That's exactly what Lithuanian politics was, a pile of manure. In that pile of manure Patris and I were the darlings of all the dung beetles and the white shit worms. For a long time I traipsed around with my father's head like Hamlet, but Jogaila was simply a natural playactor. He literally didn't have his own personality; he could turn into whatever he wanted—or more accurately, whatever others would want. He was a genius. Now he isn't anymore because he has gotten too much power, which he fears for every minute. A true genius must improvise artistically, not just count boring chess-like intrigues. Sun-Tzu taught: power is nothing; victory is everything. Back then we reached truly harsh victories, because people are dolts. You can buy them with the silliest legends; you can finish them off entirely with an ordinary Chopin prelude. They dreadfully want to believe in fairytale warriors, they want to believe in a happy ending, and most of all they want to believe in princesses and princes on white horses. They become incurable, irreversible dolts as soon as they gather into a big pile.

Once Laima and I made love right on the stairs, completely ignoring our neighbors.

"Where are you going? What do you want to be?" It was the first time she'd asked me outright. "To finally go nuts and run after your own shadow?"

"I'm going to be president," I shot back without hesitating.

"But why not economic minister or premier—at least you'd cash in a lot of money."

"But I want to be president. I want to be the greatest and play everyone such music... paint everyone such pictures... Tear off their skin and examine their guts..."

"It seems to me that you're just jealous of Jogaila because he outdoes you in everything; he's an appalling cynic and he'll achieve a hundred times more."

"Patris is a genius, but he's laughable. He doesn't realize the meaning of a frog leaping into an empty pond. He doesn't know what a frog's shadow on the moon is. All he sees is one single objective, and that's naïve. We all have only one objective—the grave. And until then you have to either play, or fight."

Suddenly, for the first time in my life, I sensed that she was trying to get something out of me through the erotic act. Laima ordinarily never tried to become my confessor, or a leader's accessory. I'd go to political receptions alone—at least as long as protocol didn't require a wife. On that night of lovemaking on the staircase, I found out a couple of particularly important things. Men really do rule the world, and women rule men. Laima had absolutely no need to go to premieres: she already ruled me indirectly, and in part even Patris, too. She didn't used to sneak around with Gorgeous Rožė to no purpose. The world of women's intentions slowly became comprehensible to me. People are dolts, but not all of them—some of them understand a thing or two. And I'm one of those who understand.

Laima forgot, or maybe she didn't even know, that as a teenager I was a genius. A painting genius, a musical genius, and a mathematical genius. A single one of those geniuses wouldn't have, on its own, succeeded in grasping many important things in the world. But all three together were a great strength. They were very different, and miraculously completed one another.

That night it was as if I had awoken from the deepest sleep; apparently, I had already discerned a little bit. I no longer despised people because they're complete dolts. If they are—then that's because they were fated to be that way. And I'm not a judge who would punish or elevate them for it. If Patris and I are engaged in total prostitution and hypocrisy, then that's our fate. If my one and only tries to elicit my career plans during the act of love—what can you do, that's the fate of all women. At least they're not complete dolts, which is why they always want to clarify concrete things. By that time, I no longer believed in Laima as my private goddess. By that time, I was already cynical enough that I could lie quite calmly, even to her. I just firmly knew that now I could fool anyone—perhaps even the Lord himself.

28. Petriukas's Legacy to the World

In order to check my metaphysical abilities, Apples Petriukas likes to catch me completely unprepared. I came upon him, as drunk as smoke, in the sanctuary for the eternal cosmic cocoons. Actually, "as drunk as smoke" is just a banal Lithuanian expression. People familiar with a lot of secret hieroglyphs know many more ways of characterizing drunkenness. Petriukas and I have thought up at least twenty-eight.

At that moment, Petriukas hovered between the state of "the red buffalo with painful teeth" and the level of "a turtle so drunk it can't stick its head out of its shell."

"A free market rules everywhere," he said excessively politely, "even in living nature and genetic competition. Richard Dawkins demonstrated this."

His tongue didn't tangle or stumble at all, and that meant he was almost perfectly drunk. At this moment he was no longer "the red buffalo with painful teeth," maybe more like "the giant snake lost between all three worlds." "At this moment" is a dreadfully unfortunate hodgepodge of words: time doesn't at all pour like peas or grain, it flows like a river and blows like the wind. It sorely increases the entropy of the world—and for that reason is particularly painful to me.

I don't care that Petriukas got drunk; I'm just afraid he

could ruin my collection. If I'm there, I'd stop him faster than he could stir a finger, but he could intrude into the sanctuary when I'm not. More than once I've allowed him to reflect on things in there and torment himself—to thoroughly chew on his liver. Reflection and meditation are sacred things, but Lithuanian self-torture is a thoroughly ridiculous occupation. But I can't, after all, order Apples Petriukas about: he isn't my assistant—he's an independent solitary warrior. Sun-Tzu always respected people like that.

He tortures himself because he has to hide from even his wife and children, because he ruined his luxurious life and is forced to hide with me in a stinking underground, and as if that wasn't enough, he's also being chased around by a horde of stocky boys with Kalashnikovs and maybe even grenade launchers. In this case, fate's paradox is this: they're chasing one of the most profound of today's Lithuanian philosophers. A person who realizes that a truly good book title exhausts the entire book. Sobered up, Petriukas slays those boys with Kalashnikovs with his Voodoo methods. It's just that it takes forever and tires him to death.

Ten years ago the poor guy threw in his lot with a certain deceptive little Lithuanian bank that collected people's dollars, promising enormous dividends. Philosophical wisdom rarely coincides with practical sense—the bank solemnly invited Petriukas to be a consultant and the oversight committee's chairman. In any event, he was, after all, considered the greatest theorist of the free market between the Urals and London. Some of his books are devoted to freedom—of course, in the sense of Isiah Berlin's negative freedom; others analyzed the free market with all of its manifestations—not merely economic ones. He wasn't at all surprised to be invited to consult for a supposedly truly free market bank; he consulted with inspiration, and even neglected his university lectures.

And now just a minor detail, so you would perhaps understand just a little who Apples Petriukas is. When the bankers, naturally, scattered after they'd grabbed people's money—he didn't weep, didn't shoot himself and didn't run to surrender to the police. Via his Voodoo methods, Apples Petriukas found out where the petty thieves' cash was held and got almost all of it out of there. He still has a large part of it. As half a Shintoist, part Buddhist, and part Muslim, I cannot believe in Voodoo. But even without my belief it exists. Explain to me how he found and took all that money. Explain how Petriukas obtained more than half my cocoon collection for me. And don't talk about happenstance: happenstance is an immensely well-planned logical action that's also blessed by the gods.

"I've gotten extremely concerned about my legacy to this world I'm slowly disappearing from. At the moment I've taken on modifications of the Decalogue," Petriukas says with an unpleasant politeness. "The primary conception would maintain there is no Decalogue in this world, only its prosthesis. Sort of a half-decalogue. If you murder only half-way, you haven't committed a sin. If you commit adultery only half-way, you also stay clean. If you don't desire your neighbor's house and don't want his wife, but you desire his servants and his ass—you'll be absolutely perfect. That's what my new edit of the Book of Exodus will be. I'll be the author."

Petriukas has drifted towards words again, and that's really bad. He was perfect when his books were nothing but a title. Now he's constantly deteriorating, and becoming more and more trivial. But perhaps there's no saving him: he got the urge to settle accounts with the world as if it were some office. And that requires heaps of all sorts of red tape.

"I've also begun a study of the basics of a general theory of deconstruction. It'll be a book in honor of your father."

"Pet, I don't need another of father's severed heads."

"You little idiot, it'll be my head—not your father's. I'll sprinkle it with herbs and stuff it with the most brilliant thoughts."

"Start with the stupidest," I advised him.

"Of course. Do you know why the gods created the world? Out of boredom. They simply got deathly bored in that darkness of darknesses and eternity of eternities. Like true old drunks and gamblers they decided to pull a fast one and create some billion universes. Do you want a drink?"

"You know I don't drink in the daytime."

"Because you're afraid that when you're drunk you'll create something else besides this panopticon of yours."

I was a bit insulted: it isn't a panopticon at all; it's a orderly and nearly perfectly prepared collection, my little cosmic cocoons. I look after them and clean them every day, and I particularly look after the burners. In the end, cockles need to be burnt anyway.

"So what's this about those gods and deconstruction?" I muttered carefully.

"When they sobered up, they realized what they'd done. They started to not like any of it. Besides, don't forget it was a creative collective."

"And what if there is a single solitary God after all?"

"My dear fool, that single solitary was that enormous creative collective. He started disliking his work, so he started fixing everything. To deconstruct every last bit of it. The purpose and destiny of every real God or person is to deconstruct. Change, alter, and change again. Some seek perfection; others change things for the sake of change itself. What do you think, which type was your father?"

Petriukas had reached the stage of a "worm dug into the earth"; it was possible now, it seemed, to socialize with him completely calmly. I'd hopelessly overshot: he unexpectedly tried to cut off a little piece of cocoon for a snack. I took the knife away from him faster than he realized what was happening.

"My father was a perfectionist. One of those who never do anything, because nothing would ever seem sufficiently perfect to him."

"But he landed an externally perfect mother."

"And screwed her once in three months. It always seemed to him that he wasn't sufficiently sexually powerful and proficient. He constantly deconstructed himself, too. He was a dangerous idiot. He created an underground national organization, for which they cut off his head and threw some dozen people in prison."

"You accumulated good political capital out of that severed head."

"And that's why I'm sitting here now."

"You're sitting here because you deconstructed yourself, kiddo. Because you are a real person, or a real God—if you like that better. So, we're really not going to snack on that mummy? It looks appetizing."

It's a bit rough sometimes with Apples Petriukas, but it's impossible without him. Without him I would have gone out of my mind a long time ago. Without him I wouldn't have found even half my cockles. It was only the two of us together who could build this interim coffin, this endless underground world that's not being deconstructed. It's our common legacy to this world—Petriukas needlessly worried he would be left forgotten by the gods. We're too memorable to possibly be forgotten. We've already recorded ourselves in the book of the world for all time.

29. Afrika's Two Problems

Albinas Afrika has two basic problems. First, he bangs nonstop on those bongos congos baradongos. It works very well
for intimidating enemies, but it isn't very appropriate for purifying the brain. His music is absolutely necessary when I'm
preparing for an ordinary deed of war. However, he beats on
those drums even when Petriukas and I are talking about the
fundamentals of the universal theory of deconstruction. The
fundamentals of the theory of deconstruction could turn out
somewhat noisy that way. No one knows how Albinas ended
up in this underground, but he always comes here to spend the
night.

And that is Albinas Afrika's second problem, which turns
into the common problem of our underground existence.
Everyone sees him in the city, but no one knows where he
spends the night, or where he lives. Half the city's security
agents are looking for me, and half the city's gangsters are looking for Petriukas. I don't know anything about gangsters. However, a true purebred ass-faced security agent would immediately start looking—so where exactly does this drum-beating
louse spend the night? Just for the hell of it, for the general
sense of order. In the end it wouldn't be difficult to find out
where Afrika lives, and they'd smoke all of us out of here.

However, we're all still alive and well. And if that's true,
then it's worth considering this in a political light. Maybe

someone doesn't want me found at all, and that little show at the Astoria was no more than a deception and pretense. Maybe someone needs me to find my primary cockle and burn it up. Or maybe someone wants me to burn this entire city down. If somone is a politician, they could want anything, even the end of the world, the total deconstruction of every last thing. I was a politician myself; I had, and continue to have, little deconstructive, or even destructive, weaknesses.

30. The Endless Thirst for Knowledge

It has always shocked me out of my mind that I only see people from the outside, and not from inside. In my childhood I saw my naked mother only from the outside. Her body was brimming with the most secretive of nooks, but those were just superficial nooks, so their secrets were superficial. As much as I tried to penetrate Sara's very insides with my gaze, I still saw only the surface. Standing on a platform in front of an enormous crowd, I saw only those people's doltish exterior.

Ever since childhood I've longed to gnaw myself into and infiltrate a person's interior—the way my father penetrated the world's interior. No, I didn't pull the wings off of flies or poke cats' eyes out. I wanted to penetrate into people's real interior, and I didn't even know what angle to approach them from. They all seemed to me as if they were hollow inside, or else full of a solid mass of boredom. I didn't sense man's structure; perhaps that's why I could never become myself. I didn't sense people's vibrations; to me, everyone seemed to be made of stone. Sometimes I wanted to tear my own belly open, so I could convince myself there really was something pulsating inside me, that life and the mysterious soul dwelt there.

I walked among stone men up until the moment I met Laima. For the first time in my life, I really understood pulsating life when, one maddeningly humid night, we butchered the cosmic frog of Karoliniškės. For despite everything, we couldn't stand it; we stalked it and caught it on the first try, with a quick snatch. It was an ordinary little green frog—but only on the surface. When Laima and I remorselessly dissected it, an array of sounds burst out into the world from within; their strength probably outdid the roar of a jet aircraft—we were both temporarily deafened. When I came to my senses a bit, I realized I was holding the frog's little body, still kicking, in my hands. It was probably on account of that thunderous roar that I so desperately clearly felt its life departing for frog paradise, the last vibrations of its froggy soul.

After that evening, I suddenly miraculously started feeling Laima's interior. When we were making love, I'd penetrate into all of her: to her very nostrils, to her very ear lobes, to the very roots of her hair. Suddenly I sensed that she wasn't a single entity at all, but rather brimming with the strangest, most varied things, things that still needed names thought up for them. I felt all of my Laima's vibrations, her most secret quivering— always different, every day, every hour, every second. I loved her—that was why I felt each and every one of her quivers.

I suppose I love people very much, which is why I want to feel all their quivers. I want to understand their entire interior, to dissect them in all possible senses, to burrow into their kidneys and liver. My passion for amateur surgery is merely a tiny exterior expression of that all-embracing attraction. Perhaps I would never have taken a lancet in hand, but I was seduced by the cheerful drunk anatomical pathologist who dragged me off to his kingdom. I'll remember those half-drunk youthful attempts all my life: when I gained a high position in government, I intentionally made sure I would have the opportunity to examine people's interiors. To burrow into their kidneys and livers.

Being in power gives a person certain additional opportunities. At the very least, you can satisfy trivial whims, as well as slightly stranger predilections. Whenever I wanted I could get one of two operating theaters suitable for carrying out my research, and later for organizing the beginnings of my collection. Patris could get girls of whatever hue whenever he wanted. It was always a bit harder with mulattoes, but even they passed, or more accurately crawled, over Patris's great leather sofa. Jogaila consistently satisfied his physical predilections as well as his need to destroy people—particularly women—while I satisfied my cosmic curiosity and endless desire to know a person's depths. That was how I came across the second brain in a person's gut; that was how I found a number of things that cannot even be mentioned aloud. I know for sure I'm not the only researcher in this area. I communicated with Wolfgang Prince of Munich through diplomatic channels; I conferred with him about the problematics of the second brain. But I was even more successful: in New York I managed to lure out the legendary self-sequestered Levas Kovarskis, author of the famous book *There is No Soul*. This former Vilniutian, soaring through international spheres for some time now, is remembered in the clinics to this day for how he dismantled a human being into its tiniest component parts and arranged them on shelves. He separated every nerve, every smallest little muscle fiber, every tiny little bone. It's said it was a truly impressive collection.

In operating theaters and in morgues, without scruples, I acquainted myself with the physical interior of humans. It was even somewhat exhausting—now I look at everyone as a potential object of dissection. Some girl thinks I'm charmed by her breasts, when I'm really devouring them with my eyes because I'm dissecting her in my thoughts. It really is a bit exhausting, although in any event it hasn't turned into a mania. However, sometimes I even dissect my friend Apples Petriukas in my thoughts. I cut him up like some little corpse because he practically is one.

He lives entirely like a ghost because that's the way he likes it. He doesn't really show himself to living people; he

only haunts them. Besides, it's because he doesn't want to be
fried by some Kalashnikov or grenade launcher just yet. He
actually only sincerely socializes with other ghosts or deceased
people. He's the skinny medium of Vilnius, a self-taught Voodoo divine and the Columbus of all Vilnius's garbage dumps.
He doesn't drink water at all—only beer, wine, and tea.
He devours endless sweets because he's a diabetic, or perhaps
more accurately, a shameless slave to insulin. He's surrounded
by needles; he picks out a needle like a swell picks out a tie for
a pleasant evening: carefully and sensibly, and artfully simply at
the same time. That's the way Petriukas lives, plugged in to that
synthetic—or perhaps natural—narcotic, constantly drinking
beer and devouring sweets. The capillaries of his feet, retinas
and brain grow dreadfully narrower every day. The time is not
far off when they'll amputate Apples Petriukas' feet, but he'll
probably go blind, or nearly blind, first. Then he will finally
no longer be separated from his ghosts and Voodoo. However,
he'll have to move out from my interim coffin for all time. The
cocoons and I wouldn't put up with a disabled guy who needs
separate attention; we'll spit on his sickly, unhealthy little body.
We truly won't sacrifice a bit of our reserves for that scum.

I've dissected withered bodies like that. A diabetic's organs
are as dried out as a sponge and reek of acetone. Or maybe
they smell of something else—I don't remember very well
anymore. I'd love to cut those rotten feet off the friend of my
youth, Apples Petriukas, or even better, his legs right up to the
hip joint. Then I'd rename him Apples Ivan and set him rum-
bling down the street from Aušros Vartai on a cart. He would
become one of the most important riders of the Apocalypse,
bringing news of a dismal doom to the world. Then the world
would be forced to hear me out—there'd be no other choice.

But for the time being, Petriukas still has four limbs and
lazily rolls his still-seeing eyes. He is a philosopher by nature
and by nurture—a truly rare combination in this godforsaken
country. He's nearly the same as me—just that he's never been

in power. And that is his great deficiency. Power teaches a great deal, and can even enlighten. The magic of power enthralls, and opens a different view of the world.

31. To do Evil is Sweet

Jogaila Štrombergas and I based our entire political geometry on this unarguable postulate of the Universe. I don't have
Pythagoras's geometry in mind, but Hilbert's in its most basic
sense. The geometry of the Universe is ruled by an inherent
pain: the more complexity and hidden harmony you find in
the world, the less meaning you find in it. This pain torments
the world of human society even more intensely. Its alleged
meaning must simply be invented—and so we defined the key
postulate of our lives: to do evil is sweet. As sweet as honey. As
sweet as an orgasm. As sweet as an orgasm spread with honey.

"You cannot become attached to anything in the world,"
Jogaila explained to me gracefully. "You can't have either bud-
dies or real friends. You cannot have just one woman—that
destroys the very foundations of a just world. You must mete
out evil to everyone equally, and with all your might. To have
one immortal love is a prime obstacle to the entire conception
of the world. You surprise me, kiddo. You aren't consistent."

Patris was accustomed to give his profound lectures only in
his armchair, inevitably with it pushed up to the desk he ruled
from. Jogaila Štombergas's desk is worth more than merely a
separate portrait of its own; perhaps its own film, or even a
symphony. It was born and grew along with Jogaila himself,
and went through a complex and tangled evolution. An array
of items in shapes and colors difficult to describe stood, lay, and

projected from it. None of them had any apparent functional purpose, but within them hid a secret significance for government and power. That entire jumble of things was actually Patris's crown and scepter. A Bible, a statue of some unknown saint, and some kind of postmodern sculpture made of leather, buttons, and splinters of glass befit the place. Tomes of regulations and an archaic Stalinist-style inkwell next to a brandnew IBM ThinkPad. A picture of mama Alicija Štombergienė and some erotic souvenirs from Thailand or Burma. Behind Patris hung a sword—a real, live ancient Japanese sword that had to have cost an unimaginable pile of money. Jogaila's crude remarks about Laima usually made me furious.

"Mind yourself," I muttered grumpily. "Who's trying to lord it over us here when he has a scummy German last name? Who's trying to teach a Catholic country how to live when he's divorced and childless?"

"That's just where the beauty lies, where the aristocratic refinement of evil hides. Those degenerates must be humiliated on their own territory while the government breaks all their rules, kiddo. Well, if I had the name of some Lithuanian Grand Duke or count, well, I'd have a brood-hen with a flock of kids... It wouldn't be interesting anymore; it'd be like I was making an example of my own life. And look, now I'm divorced and childless and I'm teaching the nation to breed and multiply, thunderingly inviting them to conquer the genocide of childlessness. It's great, isn't it? Now that smells of refined, aesthetic evil. Evil for evil's sake. I don't just order these lice to breed—I avoid their fate myself. All of my girls are pumped out or scraped out the moment they dare get pregnant. It's a matter of principle."

"I'm not bringing any new dolts into this lovely world of ours, either," I muttered even more angrily. "But for some reason it's you sitting here in front of your altar desk and delivering sermons to me. At our next appearance, I'll wipe the floor with you in both the eternal dance and the ritual movements.

I'll hire both Andželika Cholina and Bukaitis to give me lessons. You'll be left in the shadow of a trained genius, big guy." I was just bandying words: at appearances with the voters, neither one of us was left in the other's shadow. Going out to the people wasn't a duty to us, and certainly not torture— those appearances recharged us with scintillating evil energy. Crowds upon crowds of dolts would gather to listen to us and look at us as if we were some kind of famous pop star duet or a pair of insane missionaries from some unheard-of religion. Patris would pour on his shameless propaganda in an erotically suggestive voice, constantly changing his mysterious magic poses. It really did work like magic: the crowd of unrivaled dolts would sigh and moan at his words, at the rolling of his eyes, at the significant raising of his eyebrows. He didn't like to gesticulate excessively with his hands: other parts of his body and face were enough for him. Many women would shove themselves as close as possible to the stage, and when he made his way through a crowd, they'd try to touch his thigh. I don't know what degree of orgasm they would reach, but their eyes would be glazed and unseeing. I kept waiting for one of them to fall into an actual trance and start talking to the gods out loud.

Patris was actually surprised. "You're funny. I dose everything absolutely accurately. Do you think I'm some sort of dilettante? Perhaps you think I lose control for even a second? That I don't see those moronic little eyes rolling in fat? Those heaving boobs? That I don't know in advance which girls' panties are completely soaked? I'm a professional, kiddo. Wake up. To an unbiased observer you, too, look like a shaman with a drum, or some character from Noh theater. But it's never come into my head, even for a second, that you've lost your mind: I can see your icy cold eyes very well. But come on, you aren't the only professional. You aren't the only one accustomed to an audience from an early age."

Jogaila's mention of Noh theater was quite close to the

mark. In our performance ritual, like in Noh theater, there was likewise a series of the same masks over and over, and likewise the repetition of a collection of the same plots and stories. Only Patris's words were always different, and I would always dance them differently. I would give my entire soul to the men gathered in the hall. I hadn't carried my father's severed head around for a long time, but they all still remembered it, so it would instantly come to mind. And with that non-existent head I could by now recite monologues worthy of all of Hamlet; that audience of thoroughbred dolts would instantly believe absolutely everything. My employment in duet with Patris was a conjuration of the brain. Jogaila would bewitch bodies; vaginas first, then the brain of the gut. Whoever was still unshackled and unstupefied would be left for me. I would gesture with my arms and even my legs, like mad. I would conduct the crowds like Seiji Ozawa conducts his orchestra. I aimed to transmit a hypnotizing system of signs to them that would win them over to our side for all time. Only then would I start speaking.

My doltifying system of speaking was extremely simple, but flawless at the same time. I used to start speaking very expressively, in short and clear sentences anyone could understand. Then the sentences would imperceptibly start getting longer; the words would begin to snuggle and weave themselves together more and more. I used to subtly speed up my speech's rhythm, speed it up and speed it up until the words started to climb over one another, stutter, and slowly lose their meaning. Then all that was necessary was to catch a completely hypnotic moment; from there on, my sentences would become endless, without any commas or periods. By then no one had been able to grasp their meaning for some time, because there actually was no meaning left in them. I wouldn't understand myself what I was saying anymore, but that is where the great magic lay: it was exactly from this kind of speech that they hypnotized themselves, like chickens turned upside down. From that moment, the entire hall was ours—not just for that time, but for all time. We could have led that crowd wherever we wanted: lay them under Russian tanks, send them to attack the Kremlin, or simply set them to butchering one another for Patris's and my pleasure.

Sometimes, with a bit more effort, that's what we'd do—we'd sic some wife on her husband. Patris was particularly proud of one of his creations: he got this woman from Panevėžys so wound up, she smacked her husband, who had bad-mouthed Patris, in the forehead with an iron. The husband ended up comtose and was left a vegetable, the woman ended up with a long prison sentence, and Jogaila bragged about this creation of his to the point of monotony.

"That scum think they're the only ones who manage to throw a crowd of children under tanks," he puffed up like some kind of erotic bubble. "We're capable of a thing or two ourselves. I'll sic some of those Kaunas dingbats on their own wives yet. A crowd is my third hand."

That awareness of the complete surrender of the crowd froze the blood and heated the hormones. It doesn't need saying that in hypnotizing the hall I would feel an ever-growing erection. The red eros now ruled me; with my eyes I would seek a body into which I could pour myself. After all, I couldn't physically love seven hundred or four thousand people at a time.

I noticed how covetously my assistant Elena followed me with her eyes from back in the wings. I understood without any uncertainty that she lusted for me painfully in those moments. I wasn't even surprised that the beauty Patris had selected could desire me: while playing in those Noh spectacles I was phenomenally sexual. At last I really did experience the great eros of ruling a crowd. The red phase of my life reached its apogee. With three gestures of my hand I could force the crowd to recite some magic word, or my name. On any television program I could crush my opponents, or even entirely friendly moderators, so badly that the viewers would completely forget there was someone else besides me on the screen. I ruled that entire crowd of blockheads with a true rule of the soul. I felt insanely good. Sometimes I even wanted to kiss that disgusting Jogaila Štombergas. Kiss him with a long, sticky kiss, sucking on the lips. There was such a quantity of erotic energy built up in me that I simply had to pour it into someone. Elena the assistant genuinely saved me. She fucked me so, on my own desk chair, that I could be heard howling throughout the halls of state. Suddenly I understood I was no longer the person I had been not that long before. Laima was no longer my only joy, nor the only possible woman. Dissecting and examining corpses in operating rooms arranged for that purpose was no longer the limit of my desires. I sensed that my world was not only becoming red, but strangely limitless as well. And I was in it all by myself.

A real man sowing evil has no right to attach himself to anything. He cannot have a single love, a single friend, nor real intimates. He can't even have a dog. I was sorriest about the dog. I have always had an extraordinary esteem for the neurotic dogs of Karoliniškės. I have always wanted to have one like that, but now I never will.

32. The Dogs of Korals

I'm convinced that not so long ago, happy wild dogs lived in the hills of Karoliniškės. They had their own independent republic there, which wasn't oppressed by any scummy people. They gadded about wherever they pleased and emptied their bowels wherever they saw fit. They didn't even know what a leash or a muzzle was. They could make love with whomever they wanted, entirely unconcerned about their breed's purity or their lover's parentage.

However, people got it in their heads to colonize the free dogs' hunting grounds. They treated Korals' dogs even more revoltingly than the American colonists treated the Native Americans. They didn't get the dogs drunk or drive them into reservations; they enslaved the poor free souls with handouts, with a miserable little pile of filling morsels. They took even the slightest expression of freedom away from the former libertarians and destroyed the very concept of doggy freedom.

With the eye of my imagination, I vividly see the proud and noble dogs of Korals growing irrevocably stunted and mangy. I see their unconfined pathways of indescribable complexity turn into barely a few little runways allotted specifically to that purpose. I see free and virtuous dog sex turning into coupling controlled by breeding-ground supervisors. From metamorphoses like that any creature would break down and turn into a dangerous schemer. That's exactly what happened to the dogs of Karoliniškės: they are all mortally dangerous neurotics taking revenge on people for their enslavement. Those poor doggies might not even remember who they are taking revenge on or why, but the genetic mark of savage revenge impressed on their brains can no longer be expunged.

Whoever has never seen a live Karoliniškės dog could never invent them or be able to imagine them. Incidentally, they wouldn't succeed in imagining a person from Karoliniškės, either. These two creatures need first to be seen from up close, and carefully examined. Even better is to dissect them and inspect their second brain. Then such gusts of fantasy flow out that you can't defend yourself from them anymore, to the very end of your life.

33. Degrees of Sliminess and Vilnius Poker

I couldn't keep a dog, but I could keep as many trained ministers as I saw fit. Patris and I divided ministers according to their degree of sliminess—like unusually specific jellyfishes. A minister of the proper sliminess could climb into the ass of whoever necessary without sticking and without squeaking. Those not slimy enough could get seriously jammed. As strange as it may seem, these kept turning up over and over. They couldn't attain even the second category of sliminess; they weren't sufficiently slippery, so they jammed in the first noteworthy ass. Or if they didn't jam, they started squeaking and chittering so badly the influential ass couldn't bear it. There aren't that many influential big business asses in Lithuania, but legions of suitably slimy or constantly jamming ministers went through the halls of state. The slimy ones rewarded themselves, while we'd destroy the jamming incompetents with gold hammers: that's what we called the giant retirement compensation packages.

Patris was the one who came up with distributing them: he never held back with the treasury's money, didn't much like counting, and didn't strive to directly enrich himself. I researched and tallied the degrees of sliminess and the phases of the gelatinous ministers' dementia. Jogaila and I always shared our work, our discoveries, and our entertainments. Later on, a third outsider attached himself to the two of us; the live doormat Minister Mureika. He belonged to the very highest, fifth category of sliminess—it wasn't just that he could make his way into any ass, but he could squeeze through a keyhole, or even the eye of a needle. Keeping him suitably close was unavoidable: at a bit more distance, Mureika could do irreparable and malicious harm. Slimy crawlers into strangers' asses have a very peculiar and painful psychology and understanding of honor. If they don't get to crawl into some favored ass for a spell, they don't just feel insulted, they get a peculiar sickness, and even decline considerably. At first they get depressed; later, they're overcome by an irresistible desire for revenge. Driven aside, a born jellyfish slime bag is even more dangerous than a rejected woman.

For one thing, we had to bear having Mureika nearby—one way or another, he was the Minister of the Economy; the entire property of this country of dolts slid through his slimy hands. For another, we got used to him, and even got attached to him in a peculiar way—like you get attached to an ugly and sickly pet. In a certain sense, Minister Mureika was a substitute for the dog I'll never have. Although it wasn't just that he had never lived in Karoliniškės—Mureika obsessively maligned it. Just like all the other new block housing neighborhoods. He felt he was a part of the rich upper class and brazenly despised ordinary little people. If he had known I'd lived in Karoliniškės myself only a few years before, he probably would have swallowed his tongue in fright—he had given vent to so many crushing analyses on the worthlessness of Karoliniškės' inhabitants.

Patris, listening to this drivel of Mureika's and quietly sniggering into his fist, would later suggest I cut off Mureika's head. To him the new neighborhoods simply didn't exist. Jogaila Štombergas had spent his entire life in a luxurious apartment right by the main boulevard; he was born there, grew up there, and was preparing to die there. I won't let him do that; he'll die somewhere else entirely. I usually keep my word—just as I did then, firmly promising Patris I really wasn't going to cut off Mureika's head; I would deal with him another way.

Ruling the country was fun at times, and at times irredeemably boring. Sometimes I would be overcome by an numbing metaphysical boredom: it made you want to howl, or write poetry. The Queen's three were left to me: illness, old age, and death. How do you like that line? Don't get excited, it's not mine, it's stolen. Like this one: this house hasn't been lived in by me yet, although I've walked through it, slept in it, and grown old in it. That's about my earlier interim coffin, where Laima still lives: a townhouse worth a million and a half, stuffed with oppressive idiocies of luxury. At one moment everyone in the halls of state went nuts over building themselves modern apartments and townhouses. Mureika would exempt the building contractors from taxes, and they built us houses for practically nothing. Then everyone was amused and even excited by an unspoken contest—who would come up with the prettiest little house in the very best spot in Vilnius. But I got bored of it very quickly. There was too little evil done in building townhouses. The despicable little men of the state were doing nothing more than erecting themselves pretty little houses. That was senseless—it would have been much more interesting and meaningful if they had destroyed and demolished other people's houses. Only doing real evil is sweet.

I began to understand Patris—why he would, in his fury, start tearing one of his nameless girls with his fingernails. He didn't call them by their names, just with numbers or invented nonsense words. He could call one Kanūcha, another Bomedelaina. Sometimes he'd screw them on his leather sofa right under the Japanese sword, even with me and Mureika in the office. He was so egocentric he never suggested we join in or taste of his morsels. If sometimes he started tearing one of them, her screams would be a bit disruptive, but then you could feel the touch of real evil on your eardrums. Jogaila tore up those cocksuckers out of pure evil, without any pretense or deceit. He hurt them because they'd been good to him. We were obliged to sow fundamental evil everywhere and at all times. Although sometimes I realized I'd gone all day without doing anything really bad.

It was the metaphysical boredom that was to blame. Perhaps no one else is as hideously bored as rulers are. There's a reason why French kings or Russian czars used to keep huge crews of professional entertainers. At least we were amused by Patris's multi-colored girls, whom he would afterwards parcel out to all the television channels. There was something of evil-doing in that, too: poor ordinary people couldn't figure out why those parrots with tiny chicken brains, who couldn't string three words together, were daily shoved onto their television screens. Ask me if you don't understand something: because some used to suck Jogaila Štombergas like a vacuum cleaner and others didn't mind being fucked in sight of me and Minister Mureika. Ask me if you don't understand something: all of those ministers climbed into influential asses not because they were born loving to soak in shit. They would pull millions out of those asses by their teeth. My God—how boring all of it was!

You can't imagine even a hundredth part of that cosmic boredom. Laima began popping up around me again, wearing dresses made by some designer; we acted in the grand operetta called "Vilnius High Society." Only a person with an artistic soul will understand what degree of decline it is, after Noh theater, to end up in a scene from a worthless operetta. My red eros had cooled off completely by then; I'd recover only when playing poker. We called it Vilnius Poker.

Killing our boredom, we'd wager gas pipelines, the docks at Klaipėda's harbor, the diamonds of Yakutsk or South Africa, sixteen-year-old girls, our wives, the widest variety of fates and careers of dolts and dopes, parcels around the Trakai lakes, and

I don't even know what else anymore. That poker sometimes still managed to heat my blood. You couldn't play Vilnius Poker just any old way—simply planning or arranging it beforehand. That poker had to be born on its own, like some living creature. The future players had to gather of their own accord, without agreeing beforehand, lazily discuss this or that, sip malt whiskey, maybe plan a weekend trip to Amsterdam. However, it would slowly dawn on everyone that Vilnius Poker would be played that day. Throughout the entire period there were only five players in Patris's office; besides the two of us and Mureika, only Uža and Uschopčikas played Vilnius Poker. In this country there were only two overgrown adolescents who were never short the wealth to wager at Vilnius Poker. Mureika would stake something from the bottomless sack of the taxpayers; Patris would despicably oppress us all with his situation— the worth of his bets would be ridiculously pathetic compared to that of the others. Some little black girl dragged straight from the television screen that Jogaila threw on the table couldn't possibly outweigh a four-acre plot by Lake Galvė. However, much was forgiven that scabby Štombergas. I myself started accumulating wealth just for Vilnius Poker. Elena took divinely meticulous care of it all; she looks after it yet today. Back then she was the only one who quieted my boundless schemes. If not for her, I would probably have played for the entire world, or my own life. Poker really did heat my blood. Only Elena used to somehow keep me grounded.

"You have only those four kilograms of the heroin confiscated from the Interior Ministry left, sir," she would say in a rather bored voice. "In your place, I wouldn't bet the house."

For some reason, her comments and observations made that villain Uža laugh nonstop; he'd start bubbling like a water heater in a sauna. Now we're not just poker partners, but profoundly related, but back them he was simply a wealthy gas magnate who always wore frameless eyeglasses. The fashion for those eyeglasses came, went, and came back again, but Uža never parted with them. He probably had a hundred of them. His eyeglasses were the one thing he never wagered. Incidentally, he was the one who put his wife in the pot first. I hope Vilnius Poker is no longer played these days. Uschopčikas directly or indirectly controlled three banks, but didn't know how to count at all. He played poker artfully, poetically actually—even more senselessly than I did.

"I'll raise," he'd say in his harsh voice, "After all, you need to rise. Rise to the skies, to the stars, to fly with Socrates's steeds, as that philosopher of yours says. If he were sitting here, he'd surely raise. I'm putting up four thousand Merrill Lynch shares."

I don't really know if the other inhabitants of the halls of state knew about Vilnius Poker, although I could wager they didn't know a damn thing. Vilnius Poker is a metaphysical game for the chosen, and in Lithuania there aren't many chosen. This country is simply too small to fit even a few more people who can truly soar. This country is unnaturally small; that's why there aren't enough people with truly honorable minds, truly free people, or true evildoers. Everything's in short supply there—not to mention Vilnius Poker players. Only those playing roles in the "Vilnius High Society" operetta are here in spades.

At some moment in my life I sacrificed myself to the idiocy of that operetta's *mise en scène*, too. I would come to myself in the toilet at the town hall or some fancy restaurant, looking attentively in the mirror. I had absolutely no idea any more what that round-faced man in a smoking jacket was doing in this world. He had come from the Yellow Emperor's kingdom of the imprisoned, so I wasn't in a position to understand him. He no longer played in the Noh theater, since he no longer needed to meet any voters. He no longer screamed when making love to his only good fortune Laima, as they made love, with some difficulty, maybe once a month. I hated that guy in the mirror with a mortal hatred. I was ready now to fight with the entire world. I had now half-way turned into Sun-Tzu.

34. Minister Mureika

He resembled a giant plastic bag filled with sticky starch paste. That bag was bizarrely twisted and had a multitude of nooks, weirdly similar to human body parts. He was even expertly painted the color of a human body. At dusk you could even be fooled into taking that bag, widening at the bottom, for a human being. A tall, sturdy man with clumsy paws and giant, weighty buttocks. The person who first nicknamed government officials the Great Buttocks had, without a doubt, previously seen Mureika in a dream.

No one could understand by what means Mureika had climbed the career ladder so insupportably high. Uschopčikas thought Uža had supported him, while Uža threw the blame on Uschopčikas and all his banks. None of the seriously rich could even imagine what nitwit would bet on a hopeless horse like Mureika. Someone even mentioned the late Boria, but he truly hadn't had a finger in it. I can testify myself: once they actually tried to evict him, with no concrete result. Mureika was a perfect metaphysical object: he had neither origin, nor history. No one knew who his parents were and no one understood where he got his power from, constantly holding out against the change in seasons and in governments.

He gave off the sticky smell of the starch paste that filled him. He could splash himself with any eau de cologne he wanted, but he couldn't hide that smell—at least not from me.

To me he seemed like a large and disgusting secret of nature. I always wanted to figure him out, to rummage around in his guts and research his structure, but I was afraid there could actually be only fatty, thick starch paste oozing out of him. It seemed hideously disgusting to me to get my hands dirty with him.

A person's blood can cause horror and or satisfaction, but it's not disgusting. The slimy mass accumulated in Mureika's guts could only cause repulsion. His second brain was steeped in that starch paste; it gummed up all of that brain's pores; from contact with the air it started thickening and turning into a hideous jelly. That jelly, that shining fat-covered jellyfish of the gut, reflected the world destroying it, and primarily—my sweaty face leaning above it.

35. The Loathing of the Face

I loath my face, because that person in the mirror is most certainly not me. My eyes never manage to decently impregnate any mirror, which is why those shining villains either show nothing at all when I glance at them, or else show an entirely different person. The sorcery of the Yellow Emperor doesn't work on me; for some reason, like in a bad dream, the inhabitants of the kingdom beyond the mirror aren't obliged to repeat all of my movements. They don't even bother to accurately replicate the shape of my face.

That nearly idiotic, fat little face cannot be my face. Those sad, tired little eyes really don't belong to me. I wouldn't get mad at mirrors if they didn't show me at all, and instead showed just a grayish, formless mess. But that's not enough for that kingdom from the other side: it has to also show me some entirely other shallow and despicable person. And it was precisely that fat senseless face that was once all over the newspapers and television. It was just exactly that soft little inflatable toy of a face that people took note of. That is my great humiliation and torment.

I stand opposite the mirror in the room of delicate cocoons and I cannot get over my disgust at myself. It's entirely untrue that a person's noble aims and desires purify the lines of his face and make his gaze bottomless. Alas, no aims nor efforts can change a person's face—only perfect makeup or death can.

Even when I turned into Sun-Tzu, I didn't come to resemble a Chinaman, not by a long shot. As much as I contemplated a deep restructuring of the Universe, I didn't start resembling my first father. As much as I immersed myself in the the intoxication of power, I didn't start resembling my second father, either. My body did not cover itself in gems or enameled brooches. I didn't grow thick gray hair down to my shoulders.

Sometimes, out of the depths of the mirror, a vision of Sara's spirit floats towards me; it's possible this mirror is an expression of Sara's vagina. I was probably born of Sara's womb, or maybe my mother didn't give birth to me at all. On the whole, I probably don't exist. That's not a person looking at me out of the depths of the mirror at all, just a human prosthesis. An archaic yellow prosthesis, thirsting to poison and destroy its owner. Believe me—I have a stellar understanding of the intrinsic nature of all prostheses. Divining the depths of prostheses like that can only be done by a representative of their family.

36. The Prostheses' Intentions of World Hegemony

I will always remember the pale yellow wooden prosthetic leg my uncle, my first father's brother, took off in Grandmother's garden. Bees buzzed and gooseberries, apple trees, and cherry trees flourished around us. The pear trees grew a bit further off, on the other side of the old thatched house. The entire clan was eating fresh honey with fresh cucumbers; everyone was absorbed in the sweetish flavors and smells, so no one paid attention to Uncle's yellow prosthesis. In the meantime, it secretly came to life and began its grim macabre activities.

The prosthesis came to life slowly, but hideously and inexorably. First it carefully moved a bit and just barely drew a breath: the tall dry grass swayed fearfully from that breath. Then the yellow prosthesis lazily stretched and stirred all of its straps and belts. And at last, by now violently, it extended itself and straightened out its entire yellowish body in order to finally collect itself for its villainous attack. It didn't rush to bite us all; it didn't run away into the gloomy thickets of the woods; it just sprawled there, rhythmically pulsating and continually changing its color. It would turn somewhat green, then bright yellow, and sometimes even a bit reddish. That was how it sent signals to the other prostheses of the world; they were all planning a hideous conspiracy against their owners.

Even though I was only eleven or twelve at the time, in that instant I saw right through the entire essence of the prostheses' revolt. I had to explain this to everyone; I was already opening my mouth to announce this terrifying news, but I suddenly understood no one would listen to me. Feasting in the garden that afternoon, my first father's relatives were enjoying life too much, were too far immersed in a hedonistic *dolce far niente* to hear the voice of pure reason. Yes, at that moment I was pure reason, even if I was only eleven or twelve. I had grasped the essence of the conspiracy of the world's prostheses, but at the same time I understood that no one would actually listen to my screams. I felt dreadfully hurt and atrociously helpless. I knew the real truth, but I couldn't convince anyone of it. Many years later, in the gray period of my life, a painful helplessness like that became my daily frame of mind.

But that afternoon I just swallowed my saliva in despair, not daring to open my mouth. My first father's family was enjoying life. That's the way I remember them—like in some Lithuanianized Bruegel painting. A white tablecloth with long fringe was spread on an outdoor table. My first father sat with a plate set next to him of a yet uncatalogued exhibit for his deconstruction room resembling the severed foot of a frog. My legless uncle, as always, didn't even take a plate of food, just a sizable glass of vodka. Grandmother flitted about the table; even back then she liked to fly. And the yellowish prosthesis just glared at all of them from under its disgusting prosthesis eyebrows. By no means was it a artificial piece of Uncle's body; it was an independent predatory beast lying in perpetual ambush. It was a yellowish hyena feeding on corpses. That hyena was relishing the taste of my uncle's corpse in advance; it had already infected Uncles' body with poison and knew the day of his imminent death.

That prosthesis had rubbed the stump of my uncle's leg raw and injected its poisonous saliva into the little cut. My thunder-voiced, rowdy uncle thought it nothing, but in reality it was a mortal bite. My uncle was hit by a lightning-fast sepsis; he didn't even manage to grasp that he was already dying, he simply got delirious, and then didn't even know he was already dead. Uncle lived all by himself, so no one missed him until the neighbors couldn't stand it anymore because of the unbearable stench of the corpse. All that week or longer, the yellow prosthesis hyena ate his corpse. They say it chewed off the entire stump of his leg, up to the hip, up to the very crotch, and even started feeding on his right gonad. My first father kept that bitten, blackened testicle in his collection. Sometimes he would look at it for a long time, trying to understand the signs only he could see on that macabre exhibit. I don't know how my father understood that story of the prosthesis, but there was a great deal I grasped all too clearly.

In order for me to grow into that comprehension, I needed more than to just mature and live through all the colored periods of my life; I needed to turn into a prosthesis cannibal like that myself. I needed to worm my way into high-level politics. To understand what is what in this dreary world, from the inside.

I share this grim secret with everyone: all the politicians, all the men and women of officialdom, are not people, not by a long shot—they're just yellow human prostheses. They developed out of ordinary wooden leg prostheses by a special method of selection. Inside them is the exact same amount of spirit, and the exact same soul of a corpse-feeding yellow hyena. I know what I'm talking about because for several years I had turned into a hyena like that myself.

We, the yellow hyenas, feed on the corpses of people and nations. There's absolutely no need to be surprised that we yearn so for the demise of individual people, entire cities, or even nations. It's simply that the Lord doesn't allow us to feed on live organisms like others do, nor does he allow us to feed on grass or leaves, like still others do. God created us to feed on corpses; it's not our fault. That's just the innate mechanism of our functioning. If we are no more than hyenas in Africa's barrens, then we feed on the fetid leavings of lions or jaguars. If we are politicians, the men and women of any government, we feed on the dead souls of people, or entire nations. And since we're aware and thinking hyenas, we manufacture our feed ourselves; we dependably and wisely destroy the spirit of entire nations. To live otherwise is quite impossible—it simply guarantees our natural survival.

It's really not pleasant to always feel like just a prosthesis or a yellow hyena. That was exactly why I so suddenly, and to the surprise of many, escaped the halls of state. They remained there to continue prosthesizing themselves, understanding nothing about their nature or essence. Only Patris grasps some of it, but he never lets on that he knows. He lingers in those halls like a thick fog, like the fundamental source of the world's evil, like the living reminder of my duty.

37. The First Bugle Call on the Road to Damascus

At the pinnacle of my prosthetic existence, I resolutely decided to run for president. Not just because I'd half-jokingly promised Laima this during a love session on the stairs. Actually, I was the one most suited to that post in this country. It seemed to me that the election campaign would revive my red eros. I would have been forced to ride around through towns and villages, perhaps I'd even manage to act in the sombre and mysterious Noh theater drama again. Besides, I liked the decoration of the presidential halls and the inner courtyard. I liked the idea of roughly fucking Lame Elena on the president's desk. But probably most of all I wanted to run away from the surroundings of the halls of state. I could no longer stand the coteries of revived mannequins persecuting me on a daily basis, and most of all I began to hate Patris himself. That was just when I determined and formulated the law of Lithuanian spontaneous selection.

This law is quite simple, but very sad. It asserts that in this country of dolts the spontaneous selection of people always elects and supports the very worst. The most degenerate and the least moral. The most dangerous and the least reliable. Lithuanian spontaneous selection drives the world in the direction of deterioration and ruin; it's the true triumph of the civilization of prosthetic hyenas. I know what I'm saying because I was a prosthetic hyena for several years myself.

We, the prosthetic political hyenas, developed from normal Lithuanians via the path of Lithuanian natural selection. However, our entire evolutionary development, steadily and purposefully, was such that we would be the very worst of the worst, the very stupidest of the stupidest, the most intolerant of the intolerant. We had to be truly choice specimens, so therefore we endeavored to become such as quickly as possible. The panopticon of the halls of state always pleased me in a weird way, apparently that was why I got the urge, in the end, to esthetically and conceptually surpass it. Perhaps it would be interesting to occasionally come by and bring the children, like going to some zoo or dolphin show. However, hanging around there every day, and sometimes going on until night—now that's an unbearable torture. It was oppressive even to a prosthetic spirit; there's no need to imagine that political hyenas are simply yellow pieces of wood, old-fashioned leg prostheses come to life. That would be too ordinary and dull; that's why it isn't that way in the world. The world likes to be needlessly complicated and idiotically intricate. The world's self-contained aim is to completely confuse and crush people.

So far I still clearly remember my spirits and my mood back then. I knew well enough that I was a prosthetic hyena, a creation of Lithuanian natural selection. But that didn't diminish my narcissism nor my megalomania, not by a long shot. With all my being, I felt myself a ruler—perhaps a bit weaker than now, but nearly omnipotent. I experienced a metaphysically real boredom of sovereignty that wasn't in the least imaginary or a pretense. Sometimes I would disperse it with the never-tiresome Vilnius Poker, and sometimes with visits to an ever faster aging Aleksas, my second father. To an increasing extent he rarely arose from his beloved Prince Oginskis armchair; he would put his bare right foot with his swollen, deathly painful gouty big toe on a little silk-embroidered pillow and be silent—he only inspected me with his eyes. His gray hair spreading on his shoulders was limp but still shone; with its halo Aleksas resembled a pagan high priest.

"You should filch an authentic pagan Lithuanian staff from some museum," I once suggested to him completely seriously. "Maybe you could even pronounce all kinds of curses, or at least summon rain."

"I don't need rain," Aleksas answered, entirely seriously. "And you wouldn't be stung by any curses anymore. You've long ago escaped from my care and my field of power. Maybe you don't even know what a monster you've made of yourself."

"At least I haven't fallen to fucking underage adopted boys," I detestably replied.

"Oh Jesus—that's such a trifle compared to your behavior and all of your activities. You're not fucking some little boys or girlies by force—you and Jogaila have completely defiled the entire ethnos. You allowed the nation to turn into a crowd of beggarly fools. Do you often, when you've grabbed someone on the street, bump him off and cut him into pieces out of curiosity? Do you often sterilize some beauty queen out of envy, so there wouldn't be any more of them? What amusements have you thought up so you wouldn't go out of your perverted official mind?"

The irritated old man's anger cheered me in a odd way, although I would only experience real pleasure when mocking people actually in government. Patris supported me in this too, but I was the one who always showed the initiative. I liked to make those stinking hyenas dance; the higher the post some little guy held, the more impressive the pleasure I felt.

I made some of them dance in the literal sense of the word. The choice show number, the apotheosis of cosmic boredom, was making Minister Mureika dance. We'd quickly summon him from the ministry and force him to dance the Russian kazachok. Mureika panted desperately and his glasses constantly fell off his nose, but he danced—and how he danced!

What else could he do? Patris and I still controlled all of the old KGB archives—all of the secret information about many current Seimas members and ministers. This gift from Aleksas was truly priceless. The two of us embodied the triumph of knowing a man. No one could stand up against us, not even Mureika. That was how we got our revenge on him for our inability to get rid of him. We also liked to make former Communist honchos dance. Several of them have already become cocoons; they stand in my collection and astound humanity. They have finally found their true place in Lithuania's history.

I didn't mention Mureika without good cause. He was the one who, for some reason, became the backdrop to my destiny, where the first trumpet sounded: his Russian kazachok became my road to Damascus. It was just as Mureika danced that I, after much conceptual thought, determined what this country and the organization of this city's society was crucially lacking. It fatally lacked a human garbage dump. It lacked a special reservation or park where all of its trash could gather and retreat from the world. It could be a truly beautiful park with handsomely shaped little benches that were pleasant to the touch. Next to its entrance—and at all pharmacies—there would be suicide pills for sale. A single pink pill would be enough for you to painlessly move on to a better world. Anyone who wanted could buy themselves this kind of pill without a prescription. However, some would get compulsory prescriptions they would be obliged to take. For these, the pink pill would be given out for free. Somebody with a pink pill, obtained of their own free will or with a compulsory prescription, would sit down on a handsome bench in a sadly beautiful park and blissfully journey to the other side. The bodies of those who had withdrawn would be gathered by a special service agency, and the world would breathe easier.

I could even write compulsory prescriptions myself. I'd distribute them first to the most prominent politicians—those yellow prosthesis hyenas. Writers and musicians of all kinds wouldn't avoid their retribution, either, bothering the peace of a man's existence with their verbal inventions or unnatural sounds. I'd dispatch all the pianists, painters, and mathematicians with particular pleasure. But that would only comprise a tiny part of the death park's visitors. The most important ones would be those who would purchase the pink pills themselves, of their own free will. The fewer people in the world, the better.

To assist in suicide is possibly the most humane of all human characteristics. It was exactly because of this deep understanding that I became acquainted with Jack Kevorkian's system. Even now Doctor Death could help me with a lot of things, but alas, those American ignoramuses have planted him in jail again.

Back then I wasn't familiar with his theories—I just looked at Mureika huffing and squatting and sincerely regretted that no one offered or foisted some pink pills off on him. To me Mureika seemed one of the worst examples of human perversion. Of course, not including myself. At the time I had just lost Laima to that clever rogue Uža in that unfortunate hand of Vilnius Poker. It just so happened that I no longer had anything else to stake; Elena, with all the uncountable riches, had already safely left Vilnius, and an uncontrollable passion overtook me to the marrow of my bones.

"You can always bet your wife," Uža calmly reminded me. "I'd accept a stake like that. You do remember, after all, I've bet mine several times myself."

I had to win, I simply had to: I had three aces and two kings in my hand. Many times I've staked my entire life on much weaker cards. I really did have to win that time, but Uža had four nines.

"I'll return her in a week, alive and well," he arrogantly promised me.

He hasn't returned her yet. And back then I still needed to tell Laima everything. A poker debt is sacred, otherwise poker wouldn't be poker anymore. But I just couldn't bring myself to inform my wife of that shameful horror. I felt like I was dying: my entire life with Laima flashed before my eyes. I probably did die, and afterwards came back to life not quite the same person I had been up until then.

I announced the happy news to her in a breaking voice, but she replied entirely cold-bloodedly. That was what hurt me the most. She didn't shriek, didn't reproach me, didn't smack me in the face—she actually didn't open her mouth, just shrugged her shoulders. Only later did it occur to me that earlier she and Uža used to flirt a bit, too. She gathered up a few things and went to him in Klaipėda like she was going on some kind of vacation. The rules of poker don't require they sleep together, but they don't eliminate that possibility, either. I had to reconcile myself to that hideous loss, so out of anger and mortification I made Mureika dance, and he foisted Sun-Tzu's immortal work on me.

"They say this Chinaman is even better than Machiavelli. It's no use to me, I don't read English, anyway. Maybe you'll find it useful?"

I started reading it idly, but an hour later I was already a slave to that book. To me, it resounded like a trumpet awakening me from the sleep of ages. I felt like I'd suddenly seen drunken angels on the road to Damascus. I felt like I'd understood the world, and even some more significant parts of the Universe. For the first time in my life, I grasped all the cynicism of the world and the absurdity of seeking victory.

I read that book one single time and have no intention of ever touching it again. I don't want to spoil the incomparable first impression. I couldn't accurately recite a single line of *The Art of War*, but I thoroughly fathomed all of that work's soul— maybe even better than Sun-Tzu himself. Books survive their creators, and in different epochs they begin to mean something else entirely than what they meant at an earlier time. To me, *The Art of War* perfectly laid out the rules of war against the entire world. That little rat Mureika foisted real poison on me, a narcotic I've never been able to wean myself from. And I didn't want to, either. In one bound, I had leapt into an entirely colorless and perfectly finished stage of my life. And the stage in which my heroic life will end.

I don't know if it was Sun-Tzu who was crucial in that transformation of mine. I'm gradually starting to suspect to an ever greater degree that just about anything could have become the fateful trumpet on my road to Damascus. An autumn leaf floating from the branch of a tree or the babbling of a little spring-fed waterfall. A naked girl of incredible beauty or an ant crawling over my bare foot. All the necessary changes had already happened in the brain of my gut; all that was missing was an outside stimulus to the brain of my head. The evolution of the world transpired in such a way that Sun-Tzu became that stimulus. And eventually I myself became the Sun-Tzu of Vilnius.

At first I still held on in that abominable little world of government people. I was missing certain information and opportunities only the state could provide. I needed materials for fundamental experiments that are unfinished to this day. Only the opportunities of the halls of state allowed me to constantly labor in two exclusive operating theaters, to repeatedly select and come to understand man's kidneys and liver. Only money from the halls of state allowed me to properly welcome my last but probably most important guest.

38. My Last Guest

It's always desperately sad to remember things that happened to you for the last time in your life. A man remembers his last love, the kind he will certainly never experience again, with a tragic sorrow. The last stunningly perfect act of sex, the kind he'll never manage to repeat again—no matter what quantities of Viagra he swallows. Of those times, I'm not saddest to remember Laima, who abandoned me, but rather my last great guest.

It's sad to remember him because I'll never be able to welcome anyone that way now. There's no way to welcome anyone any other way, either—after all, I'm not going to invite Kovarskis to my interim coffin, or to the jail cell of a lifer. I would only be showing disrespect to him and trying to elicit ridiculous sympathy for myself.

I invited Levas Kovarskis to come from Minnesota with money from the government's reserve funds. I spread a red carpet for him at the airplane's deboarding ramp. Kovarskis was stunned.

"Have I unintentionally become the president of some country without my knowledge?" he carefully inquired.

"No, but I'm shortly going to become this country's president," I answered politely, although I already knew perfectly well I wasn't speaking the truth.

Levas Kovarskis was also stunned by the assembled honor guard and the modest orchestra there to greet him. In the meantime, I silently tried to understand why the most prominent people in this world are so often completely unattractive. Levas had gotten quite stooped, and as thin as Bertrand Russell. On meeting a person like that in the street, you wouldn't pay the slightest attention to him, or else you'd consider him a harmless eccentric. You'd never suspect that the man standing in front of you was possibly the greatest expert on humans of all time, the man who had foretold the existence of the second brain a long time ago. Who had a long time since dissected man into the tiniest little pieces and grasped his cosmic nothingness. I invited him to visit because I wanted to show him Lithuanian brains of the gut from up close, to let him feel them with his hands. You won't find such distinct second brains anywhere in the world. Lithuanians think with their guts; this determined the entire nation's history, and even determined that I was precisely the one who began to rule that nation. However, books on the history of the nation aren't at all prophetic; they didn't foresee either me or Levas Kovarskis, or that the two of us would unfortunately meet in Vilnius operating theaters contaminated with shigella.

I didn't let on to Levas Kovarskis that I had already turned into Sun-Tzu and begun a war against the cockles of humanity. Sun-Tzu teaches us that secrecy and consummate pretense is the guarantee of any decisive victory. I pretended to be seeking to take part in the presidential elections, while in reality I had secretly freed the wonder-working contractor Nargėla, who always managed to get involved in swindles, from prison. I pretended to be intensely considering government financial matters, while in reality, in complete secrecy, I discussed the principles of the universal theory of prostheses with Apples Petriukas. I frequently, and with longing, stared in the mirror, seeing with horror and astonishment that I was spiritually coming more and more to resemble an ancient Chinaman. It was purely a spiritual resemblance: on the surface, the same round, meaningless little face continued to stare at me.

"Oh Jesus, it's been so long since I last cut up Vilniutians," Levas Kovarskis sighed, gently slicing into the first Lithuanian belly. "Since those sacred times when I discovered that despicable parasite of Vilniutian brains, I've cut up nothing but sleazy American bellies for money. Sweet Lithuanian meat smells completely different. Lithuanian bones are of a completely different delicacy and daintiness. I feel like I've returned to my youth."

I felt like I'd returned to my youth, too. I remembered the ill-fated frog of Karoliniškės, whose dissection started my journey towards my transformation into Sun-Tzu. I kept thinking that at any moment an unstoppable avalanche of sounds, louder than the roar of a jet aircraft, was going to burst out of the belly we were disemboweling.

"We really must write a monograph about the field of Lithuanian brains of the gut," Levas calmly proposed when we'd already lost count of how many we'd opened. "Here, look at how some of the knots and some of the fibrils repeat. I'm practically convinced these knots and fibrils indicate specific stereotypes of thought and behavior. The person who makes the first map of the gut's brain should get all the Nobel prizes at once. Just think, it would open up an entirely new area of human knowledge. Do you realize we've grasped man in an completely new way? Neither genetics, nor psychology, nor upbringing, nor surroundings explain much of people's actions. But a detailed analysis of the brain of the gut would explain everything. Here, look at these growths. We simply don't know how to read this script. It's a gigantic loss for us. I think the hieroglyphs of the gut's brain are the genuine signs of God."

The observation Levas made wasn't just fundamental—it was brilliant. Sun-Tzu made a note of it for all time and wrote it in his books. When you've met someone on the road of war, begin by examining his second brain: it alone accurately indicates what you can expect of that person. It says straight out who that person is and what direction they're headed on the path of the world. Actually, to understand the second brain you first need to dissect the man's gut. Levas Kovarskis dissected people expertly, simply perfectly; you could learn and keep on learning from him. Quite likely I had invited him with the unconscious desire of definitively justifying my ruin and my transformation into Sun-Tzu. I needed a conclusive push to throw me into the bubbling whirlpool of hell. I needed to see the senior chef of hell, Levas Kovarskis, from up close, and receive his blessing.

Levas wasn't at all in a hurry to give it to me. He greedily sliced Vilniutians' bellies and kept getting more and more excited each time. The employees in the operating theater had long since taken to looking at us askance, but they were afraid to so much as let out a peep. I was still at the summit of power and glory, even though I was preparing my great exit underground. Apples Petriukas had already gotten into serious trouble financially and had sunk deep undercover. The wonder-working contractor Nargėla was toiling below the earth, finishing equipping my future interim coffin. Elena hadn't been lamed yet, but she'd already been sent away; not just from the halls of state, but from Vilnius, too, with all of my big money. All I needed was a last stroke, a last incision of the great Kovarskis's deft scalpel, his last quietly uttered words.

At least I had perfectly foreseen the last testament he accorded me. I dreamt of that testament several times. Overcome by creative fury, Kovarskis suddenly slings the person we're dissecting aside and cuts into his own belly. It isn't some kind of hara-kiri; his slice is slow, accurate, and scrupulous. He is simply, like a real scientist, sacrificing himself in the name of knowledge. He has long since suspected that if he wants to best analyze the second brain, he must dissect a living body. While it's still just dying, the brain of the gut is already rapidly disappearing, but a dead person's has become entirely puny. You can find it; you can examine it; but it's weirdly ridiculous compared to a live person's second brain. In slicing open his own gut, Kovarskis wanted to show me a real, live, pulsing second brain. That was his last testament.

Besides that macabre testament, I got an astonishing gift as well. Levas Kovarskis brought me the accountant Eleonora's amputated breast. Over a bottle of wine, I had told him the story of my childhood observations, and Kovarskis suddenly got hung up on Eleonora's breast. It turned out it was a record-breaking breast tumor, which is why Eleonora's enormous boob was preserved and ended up in the clinic's unofficial museum. Eleonora Rogova, nineteen sixty-two—everything fit. Besides, I quite plainly recognized that breast—there aren't many like that in the world. So I already had the beginning of a collection—only that madman Kovarskis, who used to go completely nuts over a human body part, could have given me a gift like that.

That's why Kovarskis would try so hard to get into the operating room to cut up people who were still alive, intimidating both the professors and the staff physicians. He was insane—like every genius or anointed wise one. I badly wanted to become someone like that, too, so I could save humanity. I don't suffer from delusions of grandeur, but I've created this theory based on an old legend. According to this theory, God always wants to destroy humanity—he's so tired of it, it's starting to look so hideous and unbearable. But a few dozen or a few hundred of the anointed wise ones keep appearing in the world, whose very existence proves to God that it's worth letting humanity live. In a way, they justify humanity's existence, never mind all its vileness and weaknesses. They do all kinds of different jobs—not necessarily good ones. None of them know each other. Some of them suspect the existence of other anointed ones, while others don't have the slightest idea.

It seems to me that I have an essential understanding of it. Levas Kovarskis didn't have it: he was simply a genius of a researcher, able to discover the gut's brain, the parasites of the head's brain, or even a hundred devils on the point of a needle.

I did not take him to live and work in my interim coffin.

39. The First Definition of a Cockle

I had to find the first sacrifice all by myself, so that I could finally become an anointed one. Just don't get the idea I wanted it, much less desired it. I am no more than God's sign, and I do only what the Lord has prescribed for me. If it had been prescribed for me to get drunk day after day and at night hallucinate in delirium tremens, I would have done that. But I would have been a leader all the same, because I was born to be a leader. My insane Angel of Death mother put this into my head. She so devotedly believed me to be a genius in all possible respects that I started thinking that way of myself as well. They cut off my first father's head because he was no leader, just the deconstructor of the world. He deconstructed entire universes, but he'd barely gotten the urge to deconstruct the Soviet Union and his head was immediately cut off.

Then there's my second father: now there was a real, true leader—a bisexual emperor with innumerable connections and inscrutable intentions. Probably up until his or my deathbed, I'll never exactly understand why he pushed and shoved me into government. Afterwards he didn't demand anything from me in exchange. Aleksas didn't in the least resemble a politician or a manager of leaders. He resembled a retired painter, or a composer with a bushy white mane. Perhaps he was simply gathering yet another big collection. He had everything, and his heart got the urge to pin live, working politicians into his collection, too. That's why he had no intention of ruling over me and Patris: after all, you don't start re-throwing a Ming dynasty vase acquired with the greatest difficulty, or up and repaint a Vermeer. He simply found the two of us and added us to his collection, and then didn't bother with us anymore. You see, that's what Aleksas was like—no doubt he could have understood the significance of the second brain too, and the importance of my cocoon collection. He is truly an interesting and valuable sign of the Lord.

However, I had absolutely no need of a sign, just a sacrificial bull or sheep. He was so close by, so at hand, that I wanted to dissect him alive. You could kazachok him so, he'd explode from overextending himself. You could feed him such quantities of fatty salmon and ice cream that he'd finally have a stroke. But it was no accident Minister Mureika held out against all the Lithuanian governments, however many there were. He ate and drank like a dragon; he was uncontrollable and scandalous. That was exactly why it was fitting that he be the first to be sacrificed—because he was indisputably a cockle.

I've thought a lot about the definition of a cockle; Apples Petriukas helped me out there, too. After all, he could blather nonstop, wisely, for hours upon hours, on any topic. Once, when somewhat irritatedly asked about the blathering, he quite calmly explained:

"The words I say out loud I will never put in a book anymore. That's why I jabber so much, so that perfect emptiness will be left over for my books. That's the whole secret to it."

Meanwhile, the first definition of cockle turned out quite ordinary: it's simply a weed that must be pulled out and burned. Apples Petriukas rolled with laughter, trying to imagine how Minister Mureika should be pulled up out of the ground and burned. But I had completely different plans. I dissected him flawlessly, the way my master Kovarskis taught me.

It was the last corpse the two of us cut up in his beloved operating theater; it was just that this time, I cut him up on my own. I didn't kill anyone: Minister Mureika had in the end croaked on his own, from overeating, over-drinking, and fear of a higher power. There wasn't just a single layer of fat under his skin, but at least six; in place of lymph, fat oozed out from all of his tissues. But I was most interested in the brain of his gut. It was huge, like Mureika himself. He thought with his gut, made all of his decisions with his gut, probably even loved with nothing more than his gut. Mureika was truly a superb first exposition for my collection.

However, in that instant my public life ended. To disembowel a minister's corpse, and then to contrive a thing or two out of it, was not permissible, even for me. Probably not even for Patris. I sank deep underground, where I'm holed up even now. And I don't have the slightest chance of climbing out of it some day.

But I don't want to, anyway. I'm entirely happy constructing my collection of cocoons. It's fun to hold forth with Petriukas on lofty matters over some good whiskey. It's fun to listen to Albinas Afrika's music-making. Besides, I frequently go out into the light of day, even though probably half of Vilnius's policemen and security agents are after me. In that case, it's of primary importance to really make yourself up properly. After that, everything depends on the recognition time.

40. Recognition Time

Every human is understandable to the very bed of his nails, to the marrow of his bones, to the very last fibers of his brain of the gut. Every human is a bottomless chasm; however, the depth of that chasm can be measured with an infinite ruler. That ruler is indeed fundamentally infinite, but a person's recognition time isn't in the least infinite. You can recognize and figure out all of the people close to you in the course of your despicably short life. And the majority of people you merely come across can be understood in a laughable few years, or even months. Their recognition time is despicably short.

Every human's worth depends upon his recognition time. Upon how long that human can deceive those around him, particularly his intimates; upon how long he can remain unrecognized.

Women's recognition time is usually longer. There is no equality of the sexes—I announce this categorically. Women are more mysterious and much more froggish than men. And frogs themselves are even more froggish and inscrutable. You shouldn't think that recognition time is an exclusively human property. Every living creature, every tree, and every configuration of clouds has its own recognition time. Even the Universe has its own recognition time, just that it's infinite.

I am among the few thinkers who are thoroughly aware of having a concrete recognition time. Actually, an entire complex of recognition times. When I disguise my face, I am only seeking to lengthen the banal moment of physical recognition. However, you can disguise feelings as well as the spirit. You can even disguise your soul in an attempt to infinitely lengthen your inherent time of recognition. The deeper you hide from everyone, the longer you'll remain at the summit. The summit of love, sex, or the state. Or all the summits at the same time.

But, as you are enjoying those summits, don't forget for a second that those so-called summits are actually no more than chasms. It's this joke of God's. He likes to amuse himself that way on evenings of godly boredom. But regardless, lengthen your recognition time as much as possible. Act like me, act like Sun-Tzu; the longer you remain unrecognized, the better the possibility of winning your own game of life, or war. After all, war is nothing more than a bloody game—just like my life.

41. Divine Beauty

The world is the artistic creation of the Founder of the Universe. Many things in this world are pointless and senseless exactly for this reason. Apparently beauty, as Kant once wisely pointed out, cannot be purposeful or meaningful from a logical or utilitarian point of view.

The divine beauty of the world cannot be sweet or pretty. A toad or a hyena can seem disgusting and horrifying to humans because they are neither pretty nor sweet. However, these creatures are—like all others—divinely beautiful. God created them not for any particular reason or purpose, but just on account of his concept of beauty. To the Lord, only humans are ugly. If not for the anointed wise ones defending the world, humans would be long gone.

42. God's Signs

By no means is the entire world the sign of God. That mistake is made by mangy French deconstructionists or other vacuous blatherers. The world is, in great part, a fairly amorphous soulless mass, while signs are a spiritual structure. Some tigers are undoubtedly signs of God. But a drunk at the Karoliniškės fountain is not a sign of God. And not because he's a drunk—it's because he's a soulless amorphous mass. I'm acutely aware of this; I researched this metaphysical problem for a long time. What do you think—to what purpose are Serioga and Braniukas hanging around my interim coffin, and getting drink, too?

Even Sun-Tzu cannot read God's signs, but he must distinguish what are signs of God and what are not. Moses Malone from southeast Chicago with his Morgan Freeman face was such a clear sign of God that I dream of him still. I could enumerate a number of God's signs I've come across in my life that I wasn't able to figure out. My amber-necklaced swinging mother is a sign of God. As are both my fathers. The lizard people or rat people from my father's collection room are tiny little signs of the Lord. Jack Kevorkian's machine of death is an obvious sign of the Lord. Just like that red carpet I had laid down to meet Levas Kovarskis, like Kovarskis's own stomach, severed in my dream. I have the carpet in my interim coffin, but then Kovarskis is far away—in Boston, I believe. My frog

Laima is truly an incomparable sign of God, but Apples Petriukas exceeds them all.

"I create signs of God myself," he likes to say, modestly
lowering his eyes. "Of its own accord, my Voodoo is a manu-
facturer of the Lord's signs. Who would find you cockles, my
dear fellow, if not my Voodoo? How would you assemble your
collection, which is also a plucky little sign of God?"

Sun-Tzu tells us that in war it is extremely important to
distinguish the signs of God from various garden-variety signals. You can ignore secondary signals, but it's best to engage
particularly carefully with the signs of God. The entire success
of your war depends on it.

43. The Concert of the Flies and the Hideous Procession

The crux of my war fundamentally depends on Vilnius's most significant concert. Music inspires many people, but it inspires me like a superman. It wasn't in vain that at one time I used to collect one prize after another. My divine super-concert of inspiration is altogether unique. Let the naïve know-nothings wander through symphony halls and musical congresses; the most important musical happening in Vilnius—and therefore the Universe—is the brilliant concert of the flies over Karoliniškės' garbage containers. It is considerably deeper and metaphysically purer than Tarasov's famous fly-sound installation. It's a true live concert brimming with improvisation; its sounds determine the movement of the stars, the smells of Vilnius's streets, and Vilniutians' sexual mores.

Those flies buzzing above the new gray containers are numberless, but only a complete idiot would say they're identical, or more or less identical. If that was all they were, they certainly wouldn't determine either the movement of the stars or Vilniutians' sexual moods. Those flies are much more varied than humans: from the tiny Drosphila to the impressive horse shit fly. When Apples Petriukas went looking for the meaning of life in the garbage dumps, he counted one thousand seven hundred thirteen varieties of flies. I go up to Korals' reeking garbage containers and simply wave to that surreal orchestra with my hand—I don't even need a baton. The domain of the flies greets me with a majestic *fortissimo*, in which individual musical themes diverge only later: humming, whining, buzzing, as well as all the other fly sounds. But this is merely the beginning of the beginning—the buzzings will out-buzz one another; primary and secondary motifs will be born, as well as fly self-disclosures and leaps into infinity toward the Absolute of the flies. And on top of all of that, you need to add the smell! Only the *concerto grosso* of Vilnius's flies synthesizes a flawless musical sound and an artistic smell. The reek of that concert is simply unmatched—almost as amazing as that of my attire.

The sounds and smells of that fly concert rule the city of Vilnius. Vilnius essentially is also a gray garbage container, beset with an enormous variety of whining and reeking human flies. That is this city's incomparable beauty. Vilnius is a godly city, and God's beauty is never sweet or glossy. God created Vilnius the way it is, and designated me as its only Sun-Tzu.

That morning I, as usual, savored Karoliniškės' fly symphony, but I was slowly overtaken by an unpleasant premonition. Neither good nor bad premonitions ever deceive me, because I am Vilnius's Sun-Tzu. I wouldn't have won a single battle if intuition were to deceive me, and so far I've won them all. And that morning I instantly understood the danger was hiding in the hatch for the drunkards' fountain. That fountain is peculiar in that water never spurts out of it, but drunkards are always swarming around it. They take care of their drunkards' business and guzzle beer, mash, or surrogate booze. They live there. It was empty that morning by the drunkards' fountain; only a lone lame dog wandered about. Lone like a sad dream, like an alcoholic's painful morning hallucination. He was all by himself, but he treacherously pretended he was wagging his tail for others, ingratiating himself in a friendly manner with a world that despised him. That pretense of his instantly attracted my attention. At that time I had already discovered one basic rule of the world: pretense means camouflage, and all pretenders inevitably have evil intentions. It's entirely irrelevant who is pretending in front of you: a human, a lame dog, or a withered plant. After the fall of the free dog republic of Karoliniškės, the dogs of Korals turned into liars, just like this wretched neighborhood itself. All of Karoliniškės' dogs are quietly insane, and so unpredictably dangerous. They're murderous dogs with poisonous teeth and eyeballs that hypnotize their victims-to-be. That lame morning hallucination was from that wretched tribe of pretenders, too.

I instantly named that dog Hephaestus; even from a distance he looked like a real blacksmith of hell. Imagine a nearly meter-high monster with prickly, coarse bristles and a crookedly healed right hind leg. Imagine that monster constantly sniffing the ground, wetting the bushes, and then scurrying around again in nervous zigzags; the broken leg didn't allow him to run straight for even one tiny step. That dog of hell was obviously investigating enemy territory. He was a scout of the satanic powers, an advance combat soldier of the gray emptiness, or maybe even a saboteur.

That dog immediately reminded me of Minister Mureika; he was equally as huge, equally as scruffy—but even more lame. A spiritually lame cockle—I hope you understand what I want to say by that. Mureika used to scurry around enemy territory in the exact same way, sniffing everything and mercilessly urinating on everything. The whole world seemed like enemy territory to him, so in passing he would piss all over absolutely everything. Once Patris and I, after careful consideration, shoved him into a ring to box with an entire detachment of communists. We were delighted that the communists, without exception, were left covered in pee.

I didn't doubt in the least that the lame morning dog of Korals was Mureika's after-death reincarnation. I recognized him—it's not that easy to hide from me. I just couldn't understand what he was after in this dilapidated district. Minister

Mureika always loved luxury; when driving through grim high-rise districts he would demonstratively hold his nose and screw up his face. Apparently everything there was already pissed on without his assistance. But that morning he stubbornly scurried around the bushes of the drunkards' fountain and kept marking territory like a madman. He was preparing the ground for a dangerous landing party of hellish powers. Even now that soul-crushing sight keeps appearing before my eyes. I expected a great deal, but all the same I wasn't expecting that the emissaries of the gray emptiness would open a hatch straight into our exhausted world. Reality always exceeds the capabilities of even a painfully experienced person's imagination. The lame hallucinatory dog of the morning finished examining and marking his territory. He froze like some scruffy disheveled statue; even his constantly wagging tail was still. Turned to stone, he sent secret signs to his co-conspirators. Korals' murky air trembled and thickened, but people walked or stood about the drunkards' fountain without suspecting or feeling anything. They missed probably the most important event of their lives. They neither smelled nor heard that event. I alone understood every last bit of it.

Unfortunately, it's my fate to fully perceive things others cannot even see. It would be better if I didn't have those mysterious abilities. This occurred to me at the time, too, as the stream of hideousness emerging from underground was most certainly not a pleasant sight. The lame dog Mureika clandestinely opened the cover of the dismal hole, letting the conspirators out. They climbed into the light of day straight out of the opening to the drunkards' fountain—without trying to hurry or hide themselves. The appalling little monsters surged over the frozen landscape of Karoliniškės like ghastly little beetles: from afar they didn't seem at all that big to me. To this day I cannot understand how, at a distance of several dozen steps, I could make out all the details—unless perhaps I'd say that for a short period a third eye had opened on my forehead.

My third eye saw quite a spectral sight. The procession of little monsters was led into this world by a legless World War II invalid on a cart. He came straight into gaping Karoliniškės from Vilnius's Old Town of '53, and blinked sluggishly, searching with his eyes for his beloved runaway legs. He was the same height as the Hephaestus-Mureika dog. Except that the dog wasn't rolling on a rattling bed; instead he limped along in front of the line, constantly turning back and with a nervous movement of the head inviting them all to conquer the world. Behind Minister Mureika the sad prostheses horrors of the Universe hobbled, stumped, and tottered. I particularly liked the reduced-size copy of Patris with a gigantic head tormented by hydrocephaly. The resurrected skulls from old Mejerovič's painting lent a macabre mood: two larger ones of adults, and one of a child. It seemed to me that even from a distance I could count every remaining tooth: the adults had fourteen and eleven, the child seven. The worst of it was that they were absolutely, perfectly alive, and there was no way they had come into the world to sow good. It goes without saying that among the general company there was a dissected frog trumpeting the end of the world. And the disgusting rebellious snails boiled in wine—they were nearly a meter in height, too. I was driven to complete disgust by a yellow leg prosthesis in the shape of a hyena that was constantly biting at its companions. The entire procession was accompanied by ass-faced security agents surrounding them. Even I, Vilnius's Sun-Tzu, couldn't entirely understand whether they were guarding that band of freaks from running away, or just shielding them from possible attacks on their flanks.

However, I was perfectly well aware of something else: if all kinds of apocalyptic horrors were now starting to gather in Vilnius, the end of the world was not far off. As strange as it may seem, I got the urge to warn Laima first. Earlier, when I was an ordinary human, like everyone else I inevitably used to hurt those most, whom I had earlier humiliated, deceived, or betrayed. When I became Sun-Tzu, I fundamentally transformed myself: in my idiosyncratic way, I love and, as much as possible, protect my incomparable cosmic frog. I had exchanged her froggish love for the crushing Eros of the state. I had left her on her own in a hostile and stupid world. And in the end I lost her to Uža on account of that wretched Vilnius Poker. Earlier in my life, if I had done someone that much dirt, I would have screwed them over again and again, however I could, probably hiding my shame that way. Since I became Sun-Tzu, I don't know what shame is anymore—so I don't have anything to hide, so I no longer need to humiliate or hurt my Laima. I hurriedly flew to her house to see her.

That was the biggest mistake and idiocy in the entire history of my war. Sun-Tzu wouldn't have forgiven me for it—thank the gods he's long since in paradise. A warrior cannot go into a territory where there's guaranteed to be an ambush waiting for him—no matter how perfectly he may have disguised himself. On the other hand, the greatest victories are achieved precisely when you show up in the most unexpected place. It was most unexpected for me, pursued by all of Vilnius's security agents and half its policemen, to show up at my house. You see, Uža, who's from Klaipėda, is a thrifty man, so he didn't buy another house in Vilnius; he just moved into the one Laima and I built. Sun-Tzu teaches us: if you've acted spontaneously and without thinking, then it's best to continue relying on pure intuition. And intuition unavoidably led me to the wall overgrown with wild grape vines. They're inedible and make no sense, except for the masochism of melancholy memories: the exact same wild grape vines grew on the walls of my first home.

But at that moment I really didn't need memories, although there was masochism there: I felt a strangely pleasant tingle when I thought of what they'd do with me if they caught me. Either the same as I did with others, or something more idiotic and far less meaningful. I didn't hang there like some stupid bunch of grapes—I climbed a bare spot on the wall ninja-style, my back to the wall so I could see everything around me.

Laima's lack of surprise is perhaps her consummate characteristic. When I glided into the balcony terrace, she was sipping fresh Beaujolais. Without so much as blinking an eye, she nodded her head and looked me over from head to toe.

"I'd pour all my perfumes on you, but I know that would just make it worse," she said calmly. "Don't remind me, I know, you compose your polecat stench according to the most discriminating schemes. Maybe you showed up here because you accidentally splashed hallucinogens on yourself? Do you know how many agents of various kinds are lurking in the bushes? Some fifteen."

"They're all gaping fools."

"I know."

"And I can go straight through walls."

"I know."

"I still love you."

"I know. I know. I know."

"But I won't ask you to move in with me, into my interim coffin."

"Thank you."

"But there's a mortal danger threatening you. The end of the world is coming, because the riders of the Apocalypse have already arrived on the surface of the earth."

"Are these the ones whose guts you've dissected?"

"All kinds, mostly the spawn of hell. And they're not just after me, but you, too."

"Would you like some Beaujolais?" Laima suddenly inquired. "The nouveau in Vilnius is all gone already, these are the last bottles."

"You know I get diarrhea from Beaujolais."

"And now you've got diarrhea of the brain. Do you have any idea what you're blathering? You're a wanted Jack the Ripper; you're completely insane; you're defending me from the metaphysical spawn of hell; and at intervals you invite me to move in to your underground and cut up people with you in the name of some second brain and some kind of perfect wisdom. And I don't press the alarm signal, I sit with you and offer you some choice Beaujolais. Do you need money?"

"You know I don't."

"Do you need help from Uža, plastic surgery and a passport in some other name?"

"You know I don't."

"Then get lost, out of my sight and out of my heart."

"I came to warn you about a menacing mortal danger. The end of the world is coming."

"That's your end that's coming, my mad beloved. Get lost, I have to press the alarm signal, otherwise I'll be explaining things to security for the rest of my days."

"I warned you."

"Thank you, my dear."

Before disappearing into the air, I still had to ask her the most important thing:

"If you think I'm a madman and a monster... If you think I butcher people—why haven't you given me away? You've had a million opportunities."

"I could shit on all those scuzzballs you've done in. They're degenerates, they're garbage. Scram, I'm pressing the button now."

My divine frog Laima said what she had to say. She is an immensely wise woman.

44. The Miserable Craft of the Butcher

I did not become the president of Lithuania, but I did become Lithuania's purifier, the great agitator of the world of humans. The Americans nicknamed Jack Kevorkian Doctor Death—I wonder what those fools would nickname me. I'm not just a mystic or a philosopher, but I'm not just a warrior, either. I'm Vilnius's Sun-Tzu, so sometimes I reach a perfect balance between the most distant and most unrelated things. That balance can only be reached by one who thoroughly grasps the system of equilibriums between Nothing and the Void.

It's not at all easy to select the personae in my collection. Just the definition of a cockle is itself an extremely slippery philosophical and moral concept. Apples Petriukas wore my ears out by constantly discovering new descriptions of cockles and then delighting in refuting them himself. I know only one thing: I must first come to love my collection's exhibit. To come to love it with all possible cosmic hate. Besides these most characteristic human feelings, my sacred wheel of work depends as well on pride, fear, and ignorance. But in any event, love with hate is the most important.

My love with hate is best supported by the mysterious rhythm of drums. The incomparable concert of the flies is the source of my inspiration; that music is essential to me when

I'm looking for the best aesthetic decision for one of my dear cocoons. But when I want to get fired up, when I hunger to rouse myself before a feat of war—I must have drumming. All the furious congos, bongos, and a mass of other drums and drumlets whose names I never learned. I bought Albinas Afrika a collection of instruments possessed by no one else in all of Lithuania. I bought them to my own undoing: by no means does he beat those drums only when I need it. Afrika says he cannot exist otherwise, that the boundless collection of inter-weaving rhythms is the meaning of his existence. Only that lovely pronouncement appeased me: my collection is also the substance and meaning of my life. All collectors understand one another to some extent.

Albinas Afrika doesn't know about my collection—and he doesn't need to know, either. He probably thinks I've taken up some kind of alchemy, or I'm trying to find the philosopher's stone in my secret room. Only Apples Petriukas knows everything, or almost everything, about me, but he's merely a wretched theoretician—it's on my shoulders to carry out all the real work on my own. This is difficult, both spiritually and physically. Apples Petriukas never helps to drag some cockle into my interim coffin, and after all, some of them are really stout and weigh a lot. Petriukas only helps me scan cockles with his astral Voodoo—evidently he really likes this occupation.

Otherwise, I do the most important things on my own: I take all the troubles, difficulties, and horrors upon myself. See, human innards look ugly—no matter how colorfully anatomical atlases lie about it. It's simply a hodgepodge of meat, like that collection on the table in mismatched-breasted Eleonora's misty Old Town kitchen. I remember Eleonora often—if for nothing else than because her monstrous breast sits in a corner of my collection. However, it's a singular example; all of the other exhibits in the collection are prepared cocoons.

It's possible to prepare human viscera in all sorts of ways, but it's vital that the brain of the gut is exposed as best as possible. Ultimately, in a certain sense it's the reason for my collection. In any event, these are all no more than technical details that are actually of little interest to anyone. What may be of interest is the logic of the selection of the exhibits, the essence of my dear little cocoons, and God's unavoidable revenge, which still awaits me. The Lord doesn't like it when something is taken care of for him without asking. He doesn't like those who remind Him that perhaps humanity deserves to exist, either. With my insanely righteous deeds I constantly knock the Lord's beloved toy out of his hands: the button which, when pressed, could in an instant destroy all humanity and even every hint of the human genetic code. I know I will inevitably be punished horribly for it, but all the same I collect and prepare my collection of human cockles.

In my secret room I have exactly as many cockles as I need, but the most important one is still missing. Patris defends himself from me with every resource at hand, but I'll get him sooner or later anyway. I can lie in ambush for an indefinite time because my patience is unlimited. I can turn into a rock or the wind. My pride won't allow me to give up or mendaciously pretend there are more important goals in my life. It won't allow me to get tired—tired of hiding, of disguising myself, of changing my voice or stealing cell phones.

But I'm also suffocating, wallowing in fear. I fear I won't carry out my mission, I fear getting sick or dying too early, I fear being caught. I get up with fear; I lie with her, too—we've been joined in a perverted everlasting marriage for a long time now. Like real spouses, the two of us will die together, too: I'll die first, and then, after a brief, elegant pause, my fear will die as well. My fear does not smell—like my cocoons.

The most scentless place in the world is the room of my homunculi. The cocoons of my collection stand there nicely arranged; there are exactly eleven of them so far. I truly do not pursue quantity; I am concerned only with true craftsmanlike quality.

I immediately checked on how Minister Mureika—that wretched scruffy metaphysical dog—was holding up. His transformation into a lame dog and transformation back into a cocoon sculpture was making me increasingly nervous. Mureika was obviously hatching serious havoc; he'd ushered the soldiery of the Apocalypse into the city, even while standing there glued to his pedestal. Undoubtedly he's standing there yet—so far I haven't burned cockles in the literal sense, even though there's a special burner outfitted next to every one. So far I simply collect them; I'm researching not just their kidneys and livers, but the second brains of their gut. The contractor Nargėla's gut brain turned out to be entirely puny—that born thief and manipulator did everything in life consciously and exceptionally rationally; he obeyed only the brain of the head. When he was little by little stealing everything out of Trakai Castle, it was an internal matter between him and the ghosts of Lithuania's Grand Dukes. Nargėla wasn't afraid of any ghosts or devils. However, when he was yanked out of prison to outfit my interim coffin, he cleaned me out, too—probably out of gratitude. Now that was not just my business, and not just my accountant Lame Elena's business, but the business of the structure of the Universe. To that wretched cockle it came more naturally to steal than to breathe; I incorporated the money swiped from me into his exhibit. Nargėla placed no value on bank accounts or credit cards; he recognized only actual dollars, rolled into bundles and tied up in the Russian manner with a thin black rubber band. A good sculptor could perhaps create a more consummate work from material like that, but I'm entirely content with my aesthetic decision.

I create each of my delicate little cocoons in a different way—you see, their lives and deaths differed like the sky and the earth, like night and day, like music and art. Some were hated by possibly millions; to this day prayers and thanks are offered to me for their disappearance, without even realizing it's me they're actually thanking. But other great cockles seemed to many to be wonderful people, truly flora from the Garden of Paradise; every day hundreds of thousands curse me because of their death—again, not knowing it's actually me they're sending to God. I am the greatest unknown of this country; everyone seems to know me, but for the longest time now no one has any idea what I'm actually doing.

So it's about time I introduce myself: I am called Sun-Tzu, I am a military leader, and my field of battle is the entire world, artificially compressed into the holy city of Vilnius. In addition, I am a collector: I collect and spiritually burn the cockles of the world, all the miscreants and scoundrels—all that is left of them is wailing and the gnashing of teeth. My collection of surgical instruments is no worse than Albinas Afrika's collection of drums and drumlets. My only friend and supporter Apples Petriukas agrees with my way, even though he's not prepared to battle with anyone—he only attempts to understand God's signs. He says this is how he begins the twenty-first century, while I begin the twenty-first century in my own way.

Just don't ask me if I'm afraid of making an error—I most certainly am. Any mistake of mine would be completely irreparable. Which is why I do not err: in four years I have collected only eleven exhibits—only Sun-Tzu can be so thorough and careful. You have absolutely no reason to fear me if you aren't a cockle or a lame scruffy dog, if you haven't cleaned out rulers' castles or houses or raped this country in the most perverted ways. I do not attack minor lowlifes or minor bribe-takers. I will never dissect Serioga or Braniukas. My clients are only extremely substantial people, because only extremely substantial and influential people can be truly cosmically damaging cockles.

Just don't confuse me with Robin Hood—my name is Sun-Tzu. When I mercilessly strike with a sword, human eyes aren't fast enough to catch its gleam. When I hide myself in a completely empty open field, I am completely inseparable from its dust and grains of sand. When I examine people's second brains, I devote myself to the task with all my essence and all my soul. A scalpel in my hands hasn't yet made the slightest mistake; all my cuts and incisions are precise. I have not spoiled a single one of my eleven exhibits. Some aesthetics were inspired by Henry Moore, some by the Lithuanian Vitalis who escaped to Paris, but in essence they are neither copies nor plagiarisms—they're entirely independent works of art. I've always wanted to be original and independent.

Take, for example, the Gentle Magnate. In life, his expression was truly astonishingly meek, but now it's simply angelic. Officially he's considered missing without a trace, although Patris and all his security agents know perfectly well who disappeared that gentle destroyer of people. In scanning for Gentle Gedutis I didn't even need the help of Voodoo: he had already filled all the halls of state with his grim fluids. Gentle Gedutis was a cockle of cockles, a silent ravager of people. First he would take away people's possessions, then their self-respect, and then even their hope. His plan of action was astoundingly oppressive and at least a bit demonic, but at the same time shockingly stupid.

Gedutis took over at least a couple of state banks, banks he pumped money from in a constant stream. With that money, he purchased state factories on a massive scale, and later steadily and quietly stole everything out of them. He had no intention whatsoever of revitalizing them or setting them on their feet; he didn't worry for a second about the people who worked in those factories. Gedutis meekly sold those factories' equipment at half price and its products at a third, and the money, after several banking manipulations, got stuffed into his pocket. The workers at his factories worked for almost or entirely no wages. In the meantime, others wouldn't do anything at all: he used to simply drive people into emptied or sold-out workshops and lock them in there for the entire workday. Gentle Gedutis needed to feign activity in the eyes of inspectors and comptrollers.

I have seen more than once that people are complete blockheads. I've already explained the flawlessly working law of the spontaneous accumulation of idiocy in this country. In the story of Gentle Gedutis, this law demonstrated itself to a nearly perfect degree: all of those nitwit workers either worked for nothing or hung around in empty locked-up workshops, smoking one after another cigarette purchased with borrowed money. I'm not at all sorry for all those helpless fools: they were born to be victims and victims are all they could be. But basically I didn't like Gentle Gedutis. He maliciously distorted the order of the Universe and the structure of the world. He was a vile cockle, polluting and poisoning the common sphere of human creatures. I prepared Gedutis with particular craftsmanship; he reminded me of a jellyfish or some other live slime. It's precisely those types of slimes that fool people; their stickiness is what glues together the accumulating idiocy of people. This kind of cockle must be destroyed on a mass scale; a methodical technology should be invented to chemically reprocess these cockles so not even a scrap remains. Meanwhile, I had to carry out a piece job with my own hands. Jellyfish Gedutis was so colorless that even his internal organs didn't differ from one another; it was nearly impossible to tell them apart. I only just barely untangled his second brain—at least that differed from the rest of the gray quagmire. It was swollen and flaccid, but truly gigantic; an entire factory of jellyfish thoughts lurked within Gentle Gedutis's gut. I outfitted his cocoon like a jellyfish or some other dehydrated slime, just that I didn't spoil his round little face: now he looks like a pink little angel. Sometimes I want to cut off that cocoon's head, but I always restrain myself from urges like that. Only a complete madman could harm the collection of his life with his own hands.

I arranged the conductor Katkevičius differently in all respects. It took many months before I convinced myself that he really was a malignant cockle. All my life I've intuitively hated any conductor: no one, absolutely no one, had the right to conduct others. All conductors are pale yellow prosthetic hyenas—as are politicians. It's just that politicians ravage people or entire nations, while conductors ravage music. Which one is more criminal is still unclear. Humans are nothing more than specific biological creatures with a consciousness, most frequently not at all used according to its purpose. But music is an expression of exactly that part of a human worth preserving. To spoil music is much worse than finishing off millions of people in concentration camps. Even if you finished off a hundred million, there's still another hundred hundred million left. But in irretrievably spoiling a single phrase of Beethoven, all of humanity's centuries of historical efforts to grasp the Absolute are lost. I really did sincerely try to talk Katkevičius out of spoiling music; I resorted to nearly impossible efforts, but that monster was not persuadable. That mangy cockle was infinitely enchanted with himself. It seemed to him that he was enlivening and modernizing music that had supposedly fallen out of the era's context. He played with rock musicians and even pop musicians. He himself sang a syncopated arrangement of Verdi. He destroyed music every day, every hour, every second. Katkevičius alone is to blame that the people of this country no longer distinguish music from a pile of manure. He'd never manage to conduct Karoliniškės' concert of flies, not even with three batons. He criticized Albinas Afrika's drumming during the one occasion he had invited him to perform together. Apparently, Afrika didn't obey his direction—that kid generally doesn't obey any dictate, which is exactly why I keep him close to me. But crucially—Katkevičius was constantly explaining the subtleties of conducting to me. To me, who had for years upon years conducted this entire shitty nation. To me, able to conduct the *concerto grosso* of Korals' container flies with no more than subtle finger movements! I butchered Katkevičius somewhat nervously and almost unappealingly—that's how horribly he tortured me by his very existence and his endless pomposity. Incidentally, I shaved off his beard—I don't even know why myself.

Sometimes I try to conduct dear Katkevičius's cocoon: I simply want him to feel the real rhythm of the Universe, the real vibrations of music. The hell he feels it; he just senselessly rolls his unseeing eyes. Some aren't fated to grasp the essence of music, even after death. People like that can be astonishingly good dentists or plumbers, but a great horror visits the world when they get the urge to become conductors. Their mamas ought to wipe out these desires of theirs when they're still infants, but alas, mothers are almost always mistaken in respect to their children.

When I remember my mother, I too often wonder whether she isn't a real, true cockle. And I always reach the same conclusion: she's not a cockle, she's just an Angel of Death. She doesn't poison anyone's life, she just comes to take that life away. Humanoid cockles are terrible precisely because they don't seem to do anything openly evil, but they spread secret poisons around, destroying everything that is spiritually alive. They quietly, silently, slowly, gradually ravage thousands or even millions. Gorgeous Rožė is an entirely different, pleasant sort of Angel of Death: she tenderly and erotically kisses her victim before swinging the scythe. She really has no place in my collection, although in general there are women there. That's my contribution to the general mania for emancipation.

I consider Television Monika to be the pearl of my collection: she is the only one of my little prepared cocoons that has neither a second nor a first brain. I was forced to cleave off a quarter of her skull so this could be clearly seen—if it's possible at all to see that there's nothing there and never was. But there really was no brain in her head. I, who have trepanned thousands of skulls, am telling you this. That's unique in itself. But Television Monika's real uniqueness, her oppressive cockleness is expressed in her truly miraculous ability: with neither a first nor a second brain, on the television screen she looks thoughtful and nearly intelligent. I sent an email to Levas Kovarskis, begging him to explain how this could be possible.

"There is no God," my mentor wrote back, "so no live creature is created in anyone's image. Your Monika imitated the external signs of so-called thought with some organ unknown to us both. Too bad you can't send me her body, and I can no longer travel to visit you. Don't be angry, but I still surpass you in the art of preparing and analyzing people."

Kovarskis is mostly interested in scholarly and biological things. I'm mostly fired up by my war with deathless cockles. The ratings of Television Monika's show were astounding. She convinced hundreds of thousands of people that what she was doing on the screen was real thinking. Her damage to the world was simply incalculable. She had to be destroyed as quickly as possible, but that was not at all easy to do. Her security was perhaps even more serious than Patris's. But when Sun-Tzu goes on the war path, not even an entire army can stop him. Be as quick as a rabbit, Sun-Tzu teaches us, but as slow as a snail. Attack from all sides at once, but do not strike at all, just wait quietly for the hour assigned by the gods. I snuffed Monika out in a perfectly ordinary way: in my real name, I let her know that I agreed to give an exclusive interview from the underground of undergrounds. She fell for it at once: one way or another, after all, she didn't have any brains.

My collection is beautiful of itself, but its idea is even more beautiful. The essential beauty of that idea is that it is blanketed in complete unknown. I do not know why I behave the way I do. The Lord God didn't appear to me in my dreams and didn't order me to collect cockles. Apples Petriukas agrees with me, but with rather serious conditions. Let's put it this way: he doesn't openly disagree, but his assistance is very limited. Just at the moment the two of us are sitting in the secret room and sipping Irish Clontarf.

"There's too many words in your book anyway," he tells me glumly.

"For what it's worth, there's only eleven. I'm impatiently waiting for the birthing of the twelfth, which will be the most fundamental one as well."

"The good thing is that you don't entirely know what you want to say. The bad thing is that you're trying to say it anyway."

"In any event, would you suggest the Himalayas and the seventh stage of the silent Arhat?"

"I'd suggest getting thoroughly drunk. We're starting to repeat ourselves a bit. We desperately need something new. Fundamentally new."

"New aesthetics? New ethics? New names? New faces?"

"When Lao-Tzu retreated to the mountains to die, he burned all of his writings. If you'd burn your collection, where would you go? You've become too much a part of it. If it were destroyed, you'd be gone, too."

I can't stand Apples Petriukas exactly because he's perfectly correct much too often. Correct when selecting a type of whiskey to match our mood, correct in the eyes of the nonexistent God, correct in his insane boldness. One way or another, Patris and his ass-faced crew of security agents are after me. All the gangsters of Vilnius and Panevėžys are after Petriukas. I change my appearance several times a day and know how to thoroughly change my voice. Apples Petriukas can get himself sloshed in public in a popular bar where he could be shot at any moment. He's freer than I am—I don't deny it; I envy him that freedom terribly.

I am a slave. A slave to my collection. A martyr to my own idea of purifying the world. The perverse spouse of my own fear. At once both the father and child of my great ignorance.

45. The Great Ritual of the Search

It's not just that I envy Apples Petriukas his real freedom as a person who doesn't fear even a painful death; I also feel a rather somber respect for him when he undertakes his astral Voodoo. He glumly explains that his Voodoo undertakings are a sign of discouragement and black desperation. If, for years upon years, you don't manage to read God's actual signs, you finally foolishly decide that on rare occasions you can simply solve them by chance. That the secrets of existence and nothingness, of life and death, can be digested with the help of a magic ritual, particularly if that ritual is associated with the primitive sacrifice of humans.

"I'm seized by a hopelessly naïve, but extremely powerful conviction," Apples Petriukas, weirdly seriously, explains to me. "It starts to seem to you that you clearly see mistakes in the Lord's texts. Undoubtedly your father thought exactly the same way. That's why he shuffled the locations of the world's things, memories, or sunsets around. My conception is different. I'm more inclined to shuffle people around, or more likely, to annul them."

"It's just more interesting to shuffle people around. You feel almost like humanity's conductor. A kind of little god, fallen out of a tree."

"Don't mock me, kiddo. There's no time left for us to mock one another. It's just that without being able to make out God's signs, you unwittingly start to assume you can see his mistakes. You've obsessively read and reread His inscrutable text so many times, that now you think you know all the possible correct combinations of divine signals. Combinations of people and events. Combinations of names and dreams. That's why, when you come across some clear deviation from the norm, you're nearly convinced you've found a correctable error. And its correction is possible only through astral Voodoo."

"So why don't I ever see any black roosters? Any dolls stuck with needles?"

"I can't stand those standard methods," Apples Petriukas sighs, "although others say they sometimes work quite well. Maybe that's true in Haiti or other islands, but just not in Lithuania. You know yourself that I'm taking a more complicated but more reliable way. I'm not sticking needles into wax dolls, but into my immortal soul. After all, I cry real tears sacrificing any live creature—not to mention people."

"Who knows if it's possible to call a cockle a person."

"But you call a weed a plant, don't you?"

"There's a lot I call anything," I shoot back, and that's the truth.

Petriukas and I torture ourselves before every cockle detection seance. These Voodoo sessions are a mixture of macabre ritual and boring work. Sometimes I make myself up as an old Chinese man especially for these seances, as if I really were Sun-Tzu. And sometimes I'm not afraid to honestly turn my round, absolutely unimpressive real face to the world. The results hardly depend on the alteration of disguises. I don't know what they depend on. No one knows that.

Petriukas and I seem to know beforehand who the most apparent candidates for cockles are, but that knowledge is too deceptive, and therefore dangerous. It depends on how long and from what perspective you know a person, which type has bored you somewhat, and finally even on who is physically attractive to you and who is repulsive. A number of secondary things get tangled in there, piles of obvious garbage of the consciousness. It's completely unallowable to make a serious decision that way. One way or another, we're talking about burning cockles, not liquidating all the characters whose physiognomy turns your stomach. The Vilnius or Panevėžys gangsters hunting Apples Petriukas occasionally like to undertake the latter work because that is their metaphysical purpose. Incidentally, you can't even call them cockles; they are specific plants in the overall range of people. Most likely not pretty, and even poisonous—but they don't pretend to be anything else.

The first characteristic of every true cockle is a fundamental pretense. A cockle first must pretend to be something entirely different from what it really is. It attempts to not just deceive the people around him, but professional cockle hunters as well. Of the eleven cocoons in my collection, I at first considered at least four of them to be people worth attention and even respect. This is precisely where the true art of cockles' deception and their great danger hides. Without Apples Petriukas's help I really would have been lost. I would have overlooked the most genuine of cockles. Even worse—I surely would have mistaken some pathetic bribe-taker or a teacher torturing his pupils for a real cockle. I really was drifting into trivial details, worthless revenge, and silly human emotions, but just in time Apples Petriukas raised me to the proper level. He's able to not just look at other things, but to look at himself from the side. He's able to chatter for hours upon hours without shutting up, but he wisely manages to be quiet just exactly when anyone else would want to blather mysterious nonsense nonstop.

"We won't find anything more obvious," he says to me for maybe the thousandth time, "Your Patris overwhelms all the others by a hundredfold. He's like a whale among minnows. He's like a mountain of lead among down pillows. We really must snuff him out, but he's got no intention of surrendering. He's a genius, kiddo. He's the only one in all the world who knows precisely what we're up to. He senses with the brain of his gut that we're hunting him with all our might. But he's grown armor I cannot surmount. I don't even believe it's possible to grow armor like that. That can only be granted by the gods at birth. I'll even say this silly thing to you: if you were to overcome Patris, Lithuania really would be free. Are you at all concerned about this country?"

"Who knows. Sometimes I almost am—particularly when I remember my first father. Sometimes I don't give a damn—particularly when I remember all those crowds of dolts who worshipped me."

Apples Petriukas heaves a big, big sigh, and that means he's immensely unhappy with himself. He badly wants to help me, particularly since he'd like to take pride in showing off the power of his Voodoo. But against Patris he's as powerless as a baby. He can knock off any designated nonentity from a distance of a hundred kilometers—as long he's convinced it's really a cockle. But with Patris, the very most he can do is make his teeth hurt. Patris is as invincible as the inborn idiocy of this country's people. As the nighttime howling of the yellowish prosthetic hyenas. Patris is our great shame, our hideous weakness, and even the mortification of the meaning of our lives.

"My Voodoo acts like a boring computer utility program," Petriukas likes to explain to me, "like some Norton Speed Disk or just some dinky Microsoft disk scanner application. I simply scan the hard drive of the world written by the Lord and come across incomplete files, lost sectors, or an erroneous layout of the file tables. I'm like a computer, or more like one of the programs serving to supervise the world's computer. The code written within me allows me to approach areas on the world's hard drive where no one else is allowed. It's not even that I've merited it; it's just the way I was made. My merit, if any, is that I managed to perfect it. I am scanning the world's hard drive increasingly more carefully and perfectly. But I'm unable to fix it. Fixing it is your task."

"So why it is we haven't been able to correct Patris?"

"Jogaila Štombergas is a genuine bad sector on the world's hard drive. Like every bad sector, he expands constantly, infecting everything around; he's laying waste to the entire surface of the disk, destroying and mutilating information. You've noticed, haven't you, how quickly he tries to rewrite Lithuania's recent history. You've noticed how he defiles and destroys the women around him. You know, of course, how many times he's falsified the minutes of Seimas sessions so that entries he needed would appear. He's a cockle of cockles, the future pearl of your collection."

Apples Petriukas, like a good doctor, explains everything methodically, whatever he's doing. Now he's adjusting the mirrors of our secret room for his Voodoo ritual. He must be reflected in them in a certain specific way in order for all of his diabolical energy to spread throughout the world, searching for flaws in God's signs. Or in other words: bad sectors and other defects in the world's hard drive. Sometimes I think Apples Petriukas helps the Yellow Emperor freeze the people on the other side of the mirrors. To them it's still something of an amusement and a diversion from everyday existence. They don't need to repeat anyone's movements, since when Apples Petriukas is immersed in his Voodoo he actually freezes completely. And even the Yellow Emperor cannot force the poor souls on the other side to repeat our thoughts, too. I believe it's precisely their psychic energy they return to Petriukas's Voodoo system.

"Banalities," Apples Petriukas mutters angrily, "It's that crazy Seimas representative again. That flower garden of doddering cockles will finish me off. But I always reach the easiest ones first. That's the way I'm programmed. The hidden defects appear much later, after another more careful scan."

I find it horrible to look at him when he's working. Some

people look beautiful, or at least sadder, when they're thinking. Apples Petriukas looks horrible when he's thinking: he winds himself up like a sea-shell, his face turns into that of a ruined drunken moron, and his cheeks start twitching excessively. And when he starts a serious Voodoo session, he looks altogether horrifying: to all of the aforementioned beauties, add hands quivering in a fine tremble and sweat pouring down his face. It's difficult to even imagine a more physically disgusting creature than Apples Petriukas when he's thinking or carrying out his Voodoo rituals. Laima, my Frog of the Universe, used to look a thousand times better in even the most difficult moments of her life. All my life I've been accompanied by perfect beauties or shocking frights. All of the people close to me go only for the extremes; not a single one wants to fall into the normal middle. The gem of that collection is me myself, the Sun-Tzu of Vilnius, who has announced war on all the cockles of the world. If the gods give me health and strength, I truly won't stop at just Lithuania. Madeleine Albright can start watching out—Apples Petriukas's Voodoo could do away with her even now. The only problem is how to transport her over the pond and adorn my collection with her. In Lithuania I can do anything; overseas I would find it much more complicated. After all, I'd need to get a stack of forged documents, and then to fly the coffin with the bloating Madeleine home to Vilnius. Not to mention that I must have all of her famous brooches—that's my fundamental aesthetic requirement. Without those brooches, Albright's cocoon would be entirely worthless; it has to be buttoned all over with those idiotic little brooches of hers. It's obviously the influence of Vitalis, whom I mentioned earlier, as well as my second father, but I simply can't imagine Albright's cocoon otherwise.

"And now there's all of your dreams," Apples Petriukas says with his eyes closed, "a complete gallery from America and other cockle lands. It seems there's even more of them than usual."

"Prodi's there too?"

"Certainly Prodi's there."

"And Soros?"

"Now, how could Soros not be there!"

"And that one, I don't remember his name, the French intellectual?"

"I can't say, kiddo, if you can't remember the name. But there's droves of Frenchies there in any case. Seems there's fewer Scandinavians—maybe they've started to improve somewhat?"

"What do you think—will we stumble across a serious, realistic candidate? It's been an impossibly long time since I've handled a real, accessible persona. Sometimes it starts to seem to me now that my life is worthless."

The sweat was now pouring in rivulets rather than drops from Apples Petriukas's face. The man was really trying, but even the gods can't do everything. Probably the seance and the inhuman efforts it required would once again be fruitless, as in all the previous weeks. Suddenly Apples Petriukas stirred convulsively, licked his lips, and tried to say something, but for the moment couldn't manage it.

"Now here's a really, truly bad sector," he finally spoke. "A very very very bad sector. Right next to the system zone—and right by the government again. We've got booty, kiddo—it's a fresh cockle, that's a rarity."

I look carefully at Apple Petriukas's changed face, reflecting in thousands of mirrors—it's unbearably disgusting; that's not a face, it's some other part of a human body. A face looking that way is unbearably disgusting, while someone's mirrored vagina looking exactly the same can be the most beautiful in the world. At this moment it really seems to me that Apples Petriukas's face has turned into the miraculous flower of Sara's crotch, and I have turned into my own hardened like a rock masculinity. Apples Petriukas and I, it seems, have hit upon real booty. I sense this not just because of his vagina-like expression. I sense it in his vagina-like scent, in his maliciously joyful voice when he finally, distinctly and no longer panting, says:

"I'm going to make you mortally unhappy, kiddo. I warned you many times, but you never wanted to believe it. Now everything's so clear there's just nowhere to hide anymore. The new bad sector on the Lord's hard drive is Artūras Gavelis."

I'm not one of those people who can be shocked by a single sentence or a single name. I instantly restrained myself, and didn't even attack Apples Petriukas with my fists. I didn't spit in his face or at the thousand mirrors reflecting it. I simply said quietly:

"You've picked on him because, after resisting the temptations for so long, he went into government anyway."

"I don't pick on people. I scan the Lord's hard drive. Artūras has been in government for more than a few months now, but so far he hasn't presented a problem. I don't know what he's up to specifically, but I have serious suspicions."

"And what are your suppositions?"

"Wait, I'm going to disconnect—I'm not going to manage any more today, anyway. Even if I badly wanted to, I couldn't finish off your Artūras. My energy level is limited. I'm getting old already."

This phase is probably the worst. Apples Petriukas slowly changes back from a cosmic mirrored vagina to simply a tired person. Deathly tired: he doesn't even manage to be reflected in the mirrors anymore, he's left all alone in the entire world— tiny, shriveled, and worn out by diabetes.

"I've unequivocally identified him. He is a cockle that must be destroyed and burned."

"Artūras got in your way because..."

"Have I even once been mistaken and misled you?"

"No."

"Have I ever surrendered to emotions and offered you someone I merely disliked?"

"No."

"Accept the reality of Voodoo, kiddo. Artūras Gavelis is a potential exhibit in your collection. As of today, the most valuable of the new ones."

"Listen, even when you're doing holy work, do you have to be betrayed by the most trustworthy person? By your only hope?"

"When doing holy work, your nearest and dearest, definitely and inescapably, betray you. It's a fundamental law of the universe. The next traitor ought to be me. It's a law; it's a rule of the Universe. The fate of all the holy ones."

I plainly couldn't destroy Gavelis; none of the gods would allow me to. The two of us created Sąjūdis together. I'm a hundred percent sure he wasn't slipped in by security: Aleksas's documents clearly show that Artūras Gavelis resisted all temptations and all blackmail. It's a hundred percent sure he wasn't looking to be in the government at first: for ten years he maintained a significant distance. The two of us used to give concerts in the provinces: Artūras, in an entirely decent dramatic tenor, sang old partisan songs; all I had to do was lazily select harmonious accompanying chords. I couldn't dissect and prepare Gavelis—Apples Petriukas knew this perfectly well. I didn't blame him, only myself: I never did clean out all the garbage inside me, so my soul never did become a pool of untroubled tranquility. I was and I remain a weak little human, undeserving of the name of Sun-Tzu.

"Can someone really mutate that quickly, that they'd turn into a cockle in a matter of months?"

"They can. Not just can; already have."

"How would you explain this yourself?"

"According to what conception? If according to a medical one—Artūras Gavelis has simply lost his mind. He's gone off his rocker. His eyes have looked like a madman's for three months now. For the last five months, his speeches have been like those of some demented person. And if Voodoo now indicates he's the worst defect in the world, the young man obviously has something in mind. He'll use the power he has and make some kind of trouble. He should be snuffed out as soon as possible. I don't have any strength left today, but I'll try to get myself together by tomorrow."

"I've already got eleven cocoons. The twelfth should be someone else entirely."

"Don't fool yourself. You've got at least a couple low-value specimens. In God's eyes, Artūras is a ten times more poisonous cockle than those two. Frankly, in the name of Artūras Gavelis you could even throw out the collection's initiator, Mureika. He may be the initiator, but on the whole, he's a totally pathetic cockle."

I was completely crushed—much more so than after Laima left me. Now the last person I still counted on to some degree had abandoned me. After all, I had envisioned the home of the divorced, solitary Artūras Gavelis as a possible refuge if I were at some point to be smoked out of my interim underground coffin. But if even Gavelis has become my sacred enemy, no road back, nor in any other direction, remains. Sun-Tzu clearly says: if no road remains, go forward in peace. It hasn't happened yet that going forward would lead nowhere. Actually, that's exactly where going forward always leads. But "nowhere" is my most accustomed place. It's not just that there's nothing sacred in the world, not just that there is no God—it's that from this point forth, there's no trust in anyone left, either.

"Pour me a quadruple of the Irish," I said gently to Apples Petriukas. "I'll try and dissolve in triple brewed and filtered malt. You've done me in. I'm barely two steps away from you. Maybe you could find the strength yet, start up your Voodoo and disengage me for all time—unlike the insanely temporary disengagement that Irish whiskey produces."

46. Paintings and Aleksas's Demise

I drank Irish whiskey until my paintings came back to life. In general, paintings are a distinct form of life. Some spit sticky saliva, like camels, as soon as you come near them. Others hysterically lick their lips, like some Maltese Bolo. Worst of all are the ones that bite, or even try to tear you to pieces. These need to be kept in cages. There were a couple of golden cages for paintings in my house—I don't have any idea now whether Uža kept them or not. He probably sold those cages without realizing they were more important than the paintings themselves.

My interim coffin is full of paintings, too. Some of them were gifts from Aleksas—just exactly the ones that start rampaging first. I thank the gods that at least the skulls from the Mejerovič's old apartment didn't come over to greet Mureika's doggy cocoon, their liberator from the hatch in the drunkards' fountain, or directly from hell. My grandmother probably attracted the most attention to herself. At my request, this talented young artist painted my flying grandmother for me. Most of the time that grandmother flies in the very corner of the painting and tries not to attract any special attention to herself. My gloomy uncle, dressed in white and sitting with a bottle of moonshine set in front from him, is much larger in the painting. The most important and most dangerous creature in the painting rolls about next to my one-legged uncle: the yellow prosthesis hyena, already sharpening its venomous teeth.

That's the way it is, as long as that painting doesn't start showing off an independent life. As soon as it comes to life, my grandmother instantly flies out to the very front and blocks out all the others. I don't think she would want to fly out of the painting into the real world, or to somehow harm the viewers so the painting would need to be enclosed in a cage. She doesn't try to slice through the flatness of the canvas, but she highlights herself so much she's all you can see. None of this sparks so much as a speck of life in her; she remains as much a painting as ever, but nevertheless she desperately tries to get to the very front, blocking out both Uncle and the yellow prosthesis hyena.

I'm not particularly charmed by Aleksas's gift, "The Journey," in which crowds upon crowds, an unending stream of pilgrims or ordinary madmen, crawl on their knees down a rocky path towards some goal known only to themselves. Every last one is naked and has turned as yellow as candle wax. It's not a pleasant sight even when those crazy pilgrims don't move. When the picture comes to life and those yellowish pilgrims actually start crawling, instantly scraping their knees bloody— you immediately know something nasty is coming into your life.

But most often I'm attacked by "The Birth of Virtue," yet another of Aleksas's little gifts. Some kind of an armless and legless person, even more pathetic than the war invalids on carts, was portrayed in that painting. But the poor soul had tried to fashion himself prostheses, too—or maybe some well-meaning relative stuck him with those prostheses. In place of one leg, an ordinary floor broom poked out; in place of the other, a grotesque stump from a rotten piece of ham. In place of one hand there was a thin little blue stick, and in place of the other a bloody blob which, when the painting came alive, would instantly started pulsating and spitting bloody foam. The armless and legless man also vomited blackish bloody froth, and worse yet, would start quarreling with and assaulting the viewers. That was one of those paintings I had to keep in a cage. It was just then trying to get out of the cage when a special doorbell rang. That meant I had a visitor. There was only one visitor I could have: Lame Elena. "The Birth of Virtue" had put me into a such a mood that I wouldn't at any price have agreed to either lame her other leg or make wormish or birdish love with her. However, Elena shocked me far more than I expected.

"Your father is near death," she announced hoarsely. "Actually, he should be dead by now, but he's not giving up until he's finished making all his worldly arrangements. I suspect you're among those arrangements. Find a way to visit him. I myself can't help you with anything. I just brought over a pile of things you ordered, that's all. My sympathies. Hang on, if you can."

There was nothing I needed to hang on to; to me, Aleksas hadn't existed for some time now. I would creep over to secretly watch my Angel of Death mother, but I hadn't seen Aleksas's noble gray head in ages. He was of little interest to me anymore—in any case, he was no more than my second father, a born caterpillar, and besides, no one had cut off his head. It seemed I had a lot to be thankful to Aleksas for, but all of his help and advice led to a single thing—that I am what I am now. I'm proud that I became Sun-Tzu in the holy city of Vilnius, but I wouldn't wish that fate on anyone. It's not the kind of fate moms prepare their children for. It's not the fate written about with delight in thick memoirs. It's the fate of a mortal warrior, and for the most part, warriors do not belong to themselves.

Whatever the case may be, I had to visit Aleksas on his deathbed and be the last to kiss him on the forehead, perhaps even shut his eyes. If someone imagines how it's done, you could advise me here and now. The first thought that came to mind was this: make myself up as Lame Elena, even if that required injuring my own leg. Only later did I think of Sun-Tzu's teachings.

If you need to get directly into an enemy stronghold, pretend you are one of your enemies yourself. Sun-Tzu doesn't indicate how to do that in contemporary Vilnius, but his writings aren't intended for complete blockheads, either. All I needed was to make one strong, nearly consummate assumption, and then believe that assumption myself. The latter point in the logical chain was the hardest of all. In the end, I forced the conviction on myself; I had no other choice, anyway. The worst of it was, it was entirely true—I really didn't have any other choice.

Perhaps I'm not the free man Apples Petriukas is, but if I decide to visit my dying father—even if it is my second father—then I carry out my plan. Unlike Apples Petriukas, I have not mastered Voodoo and I'm horribly afraid of a painful death, but there are things I've done without the slightest regard. Without the slightest regard, I lost the love of my life at cards. Without the slightest regard, I rejected my desire to become this country's president and chose instead the life of an underground hermit. Without the slightest regard, I went to Aleksas's deathbed. I'm not revealing openly how much time I had to spend disguising myself—you wouldn't believe me anyway. No Lithuanian would have that much patience. But for some time now I have been an ancient Chinese: I can lie in ambush for days upon days without moving; I can stand for hour after hour on one leg, with the other raised parallel to the ground. I can squat for hour after hour underwater, breathing through a hollow reed. And I can go to the performance of my second father's own deathwatch.

It was indeed an astounding performance. I'd perhaps never seen so many politicians and renowned businessmen in one place before: apparently Aleksas had decided to divvy up all of his wealth. He lay in a bed with a canopy, as dried up as a sponge, and his famous pagan high priest's hair was thinned and disheveled. Only his voice remained the same: imperiously commanding, but mild to the point of sweetness at the same time.

"To you, Aleksandras, I leave my entire collection of old weapons, as well as that pendant with diamonds you liked so much. The executors of my testament will hand over everything at the proper time. Consider it all yours already."

It was quite normal to me to greet everyone: everyone said hello to me first, I merely replied with a barely noticeable nod of the head. And if someone didn't greet me—ergo, I had already seen them today, although I didn't know when or where. It certainly wasn't just ministers and famous members of the Seimas waiting on Aleksas's decisions—these simply flocked in, hoping to get genuine valuables for nothing. But there were also men and women he had invited himself, the entire motley crew of his lovers. I had the opportunity to observe an inimitable performance of life's mockeries. Some of those balding potbellies were those same muscular hunks whose observed caresses under the shower drove me out of my mind thirty years ago. Some of those humanoids of indeterminate gender with drooping cheeks were really women that all of Vilnius had moaned over forty years ago. The damage of the flow of time on display in that hall was both despicable and hugely spiteful at the same time. The gods demonstrated what was waiting for you in ten or twenty years in a particularly spiteful way.

Everyone was inclined to allow me to proceed to the dying man's bed out of line, but I kept refusing with no more than a dignified wave. I looked around for Gorgeous Rožė, but she wasn't there. Everyone tried to let me take their place or politely move aside. I've always said that people are dolts: no one noticed that I had arrived without bodyguards or the usual several automobiles. That I didn't, as customary, rush through the hall like mad, pushing everyone aside, and late everywhere.

I nevertheless kissed Aleksas on the forehead. He was as parched and delicate as a dried mushroom. I pressed his creaking little shoulders and really didn't know what to say. I was more accustomed to listening to Aleksas.

"Now you're symbolic, like death itself," Aleksas hissed in my ear, "Jogaila's looks and your own insides. You're like a double genius of evil."

"And how do you know it's me, and not Jogaila?"

"He would be afraid to show up here for fear you would drag him off to your hell. And you anticipated that and counted on it."

Even on his deathbed the old man thought with precision. That was exactly what I counted on, that's just exactly what my general assumption was, even though convincing myself of it was particularly difficult.

"You came here purely out of meanness—or maybe you expected an inheritance?"

"One way or another, I am your only stepson."

"You're the only one of those who came here who won't get a thing. Besides, you couldn't take anything, anyway. It's like you're virtually gone already, aren't you, kiddo?"

"You're going to unmask me? Theatrically, on your deathbed?"

"No, I'll do something much more interesting. I'll eat you."

The old man still had a lot of strength, even though by now it was his last strength. But he caught hold of my neck so hard that I came near to suffocating. He wanted to drag me off with him to the grave. He spoke symbolically about eating me, or maybe he was just dreaming of it: although he furiously chewed on my ear, his mouth was completely toothless. He was a mummy, pleasantly and theatrically distributing the profusion of wealth accumulated in his lifetime. I had accumulated wealth, too, just that my wealth was different. I could dissect him and set him in with my delicate cocoons. But I didn't need him; I needed someone else entirely.

I'm simply astonished at how I manage to ruin everything in my life that I've so much as touched. I lethally scrutinized Sara, burned through her with my murderous gaze. I ripped off my first father's head and exchanged it for the questionable pleasures of a politician. And in the end I ruined my second father's pleasantly dramatized auto-funeral too.

The old man was still strangling me and still chewing on my ear—only at that moment did real mayhem finally break out. Some tried to pull me from his grasp, some ran chaotically about the hall, others shouted: "Guards! Where's the guards?"

All that universal mayhem was incomparably grotesque. Freed at last from that madman Aleksas and as I was being led by the arm through a side door, I convulsively but sincerely roared with laughter.

"How can you, Mr. Jogaila, really, how can you," someone kept repeating right by my ear.

But I, entirely seriously, thought: maybe I should put myself into my collection? Maybe Kovarskis could dissect me through the internet, right from Boston? I would make a choice specimen in the collection: part cockle, part cockle hunter, part ordinary madman.

In the meantime, I still needed to escape from that crush of real and alleged guards, the buzzing cameras, and the unbearable stink of the crowd. I was drawn to the interim coffin's peace and quiet. As well as to the reanimated paintings. Actually, the formerly reanimated paintings—one after another they froze, arranged into entirely new compositions. For the handless and legless one in "The Birth of Virtue," the benefactors attached a giant pinecone in place of the arm's bloody bubbling prosthesis. The foolish pilgrims in "The Journey" fared worse: they didn't just scrape their knees, they broke their necks, too. All of their heads, without exception, really did break off. Now they crawled on all fours, their heads hanging downwards. Only my optimist grandmother fared well: she was again quietly flying around in the corner of the painting. Apples Petriukas came across me meditating on the paintings' changes; I hadn't even taken off the Jogaila Štombergas makeup yet.

"You are a consistent madman, brother. Are you practicing how your collection will look in the mirrors when its principal persona is in it?" he pragmatically inquired.

The two of us didn't yet suspect, either how the collection's life would end, nor who would finally become its new principal persona. The two of us still cherished countless legions of naïve hopes.

47. My Gorgeous Beloved Angel of Death

In any event, I overdid it, and overshot all the marks. I left too many footprints all over Vilnius—from Korals right up to the house where Uža now lives with a lady by the name of Laima, devilishly similar to a cosmic frog. For too long and too sincerely I directed the *concerto grosso* of the flies and attracted unwelcome listeners. And for no reason whatsoever I clattered off to that accursed division of Aleksas's belongings: he couldn't disintegrate into dust in my hands, no matter how much I wanted him to. I left traces all over the place, and for that I must suffer. I suffered terribly: the gorgeous beloved Angel of Death finally found me.

I had no need to fear a straightforward attack by the security services on that account: my mother always was an alien from another universe, her senses and logic had nothing in common with this world. She found me by methods no security agents of this world could conceive of. However, that meant an invisible path of light was now stretching to my interim coffin. And paths like that aren't used solely by good aliens.

At that very moment I was walking around the sacred places of Old Town. I had aged myself somewhat and looked very elegant; I tried to resemble a curious Swiss tourist who was very interested in Vilnius's churches. The Angel of Death caught up with me right next to St. Casimir's Church, where I tried to chase off some unpleasant memories. At first I felt caught, but then I simply stared at my mother in curiosity. After all, I hadn't seen her up close for all of four years.

Gorgeous Rožė immediately lied to me that she had actually succeeded in making love to her beautiful nurse. Then she told the truth—that to her, girls had always seemed like a kind of oversized flower you could pick and smell, swooning, for a day or two. Like a kind of boat you could use to cross to the other side of the river, and then go far off into the forest, where men race and roar. She spoke practically nonstop; it became remarkably similar to an evening of reminiscences. And it was the last evening of reminiscences: after all, it was the Angel of Death visiting me.

I'll say right off that she was no longer wearing either the giant orange glasses or the decade-old yellow Prada or Escada jacket, nor her ever-present amber necklace. For the bright fall day she had selected an ordinary coat, but she fancied herself up with a little hat tied with a delicate scarf. I was also dressed simply, but quite elegantly: the two of us must have really looked like a pair of foreigners leisurely looking over Vilnius.

"I remember when you were a child, you used to secretly watch me undressing," Rožė explained. "I felt it all over my skin, and I liked it. It was like the flow of the fluids of moonlight, like the smell of the forbidden fruit... And now I feel it from a distance every time you're observing me in that retirement home... Listen, it's full of all kinds of agents there, they say you're no longer in government. Are you a famous partisan, or what?"

"A very unique partisan. Truly not Che Guevara."

"Oh, you were always unique. And with that lame Jewess of yours... and later with Laima... Maybe you should have taken up with men? Weren't you ever attracted to Jogaila's little butt?"

I had countless important pre-death questions for my beloved Angel of Death; I didn't even know where to start. Holy Vilnius invited meditation, not interrogation. But she spoke without being questioned anyway; Gorgeous Rožė was a particularly talkative Angel of Death. I wonder if all bony ones are that talkative, or if most do the work they love in grim silence. She particularly liked talking about her earlier victims—about both of my fathers.

"Your Dad was like some kind of bird, I had to warble in his birdish dialect to him. Otherwise he wouldn't understand. Sometimes we wouldn't say a single normal word all evening, we'd just warble."

"But why did you grab him up? It was you who grabbed him, wasn't it—I can't believe he would have courted anyone, and especially not such a beauty."

"It was because his name was Ričardas. In my youth I couldn't pass up any Ričardas calmly. And besides, he was a bird. Real people birds on this Earth are rare."

"What kind do you come across most?" I asked, having her craft as Death in mind—I'm not sure she understood the hint.

"Flying rats!" my mother instantly retorted. "Flying rats are by far the majority in this world. But come on, we're not talking about them, we're talking about your Dad."

We were walking in the very heart of Old Town, in the places of my childhood—I was even momentarily alarmed that my dead ones were going to start wandering about there any minute. My headless father, or Sara with the hole in her crotch that I burned through with my lustful gaze. Or that the secret apocalyptic soldiery summoned by the dog Mureika would close in on us and surround us. It's a complete lie that your dead ones look beautiful and young to you—they look wilted and rotten, particularly in Old Towns.

"All those mathematicians were part bird. But your father was the most special one. First of all, his name was Ričardas. Secondly, he collected those rotten things of his, including sighs, in glass jars. Thirdly, he fought for Lithuania. At least several unforgivable errors at once."

"So you knew about that laughable resistance of his?"

"From the first time we spent the night together. I sucked out all his secret information together with the first sighs of orgasm. I did say, didn't I, that he was a bird. It seemed to him that for a girl who performed fellatio on him, he could twitter it all out; that they had already been connected by a blood oath."

We walked across the Mejerovič's yard—and nothing happened. The terrifying Mejerovičius paintings didn't catch up with me; Sara's wailing ghost didn't fly by. Once more I convinced myself that the world is clear-cut and ordinary. My first father had his head cut off, and the day before yesterday my second father suffocated in view of several hundred people after trying to bite my ear off. If that wasn't enough, everyone there thought he was biting the ear of Jogaila Štombergas. Everything was as clear and as ordinary as a Japanese landscape.

"So why did you try to turn him from a bird into a house cat? Did you really think it would work?"

"I experimented. All my life was a great experiment. I was the first to be filmed in a commercial. I trounced the invincible Aleksas. I made love to women. I made my only son into nearly the most powerful man in the country. Those were all experiments. Or maybe games."

"Don't lie—women don't play. Only men play games. Women go after a tangible goal—most often through men's games."

Gorgeous Rožė was a bit sad that her elegant lie didn't pass muster—but not for long. She tried to lure me into our old courtyard, and I didn't resist very much. According to the perverted ritual of the Angel of Death, victims should be lured to the places of their childhood, or even birth, and finished off precisely there. But now I no longer feared our old house with its overgrown grape vines. It no longer seemed to me that my father's bloody head would roll down the little path from the house towards me. I had long since sold off that head wholesale and a hair at a time. Mother, climbing up through the triple monastery gates, talked about my second father.

"Aleksas most certainly was not a bird; he was a whale. You had to watch out all the time that he didn't crush you. Crush you with his money, his sculptures and paintings, even his muscular lovers. Undoubtedly you know he wanted to fuck your Laima, too? He drowned her in diamonds. She looked like dessert to him. That's the way that whale dined. A couple of young men for an appetizer. The main course—some collector priest from Kaunas. And for dessert he wanted your Laima. And just imagine—she didn't give in. Did she tell you that? Do you actually know anything about your Laima?"

"Probably not. Except that I love her still."

"When you lost her at cards?"

"I love her even more because of that. That betrayal completely drove me out of my mind. I even celebrated our silver wedding anniversary with her."

"You two passed each other in time, poor things. She loved you dearly precisely until that moment, and then... I don't know. The two of you suited each other, kiddo. You shouldn't have lost her. Living with her you wouldn't have turned into that... partisan..."

At that moment I was barely listening to her. We had finally stepped into our old courtyard. I was shocked by its cosmic neglect. In the Holy Old Town of Vilnius, where houses like that cost millions, our house gaped with broken window openings. Inside it was littered with the strangest garbage—even old mannequins. For a moment it even seemed to me that beyond those windows there were snipers watching us. Or all the soldiery of little monsters pulled out into the world by the dog Mureika.

But no one was watching for us there—and that was the saddest thing. There were no lingering old scents of our family, no echoing sounds of our old life. No memorial plaque hanging there, no sparkling mansion with our family name. No more than a neglected, completely dead old house sitting there. I suddenly felt grimly depressed that my real name had engraved itself so poorly on the world. I could have been a virtuoso pianist or a world-famous painter. But instead I became a warrior by the name of Sun-Tzu. That's a great honor, but it's a rare connoisseur who would value it. Suddenly I wanted universal honor and the adoration of the crowds.

"I didn't even become the president of this country," I complained to my mama like a little kid.

"And entirely unnecessarily. You speak foreign languages, play the piano beautifully. You could have taken back Laima from that oil man by a special directive. Laima would have been remarkably suitable as a first lady. And if she pulled all the diamonds that Aleksas poured on her out of her secret little boxes... By the way, have you ever noticed that she just slightly resembles a frog?"

"A frog princess. A cosmic frog."

"And the first lady of the country. Why didn't you make her that?"

"I chose a completely different way, Mom."

"You really are your father's child. You too, just had to get tangled up in a holy war, and you too, will just have to get your head torn off... You really don't love your head."

I was more and more oppressed by our courtyard's neglect. There was no life there. Even Sara's and my voices from the past couldn't be heard. Father's soul in its quilted office jacket wasn't hovering about. It was a dead courtyard, and Gorgeous Rožė and I were dead, too, only maybe we didn't know it yet ourselves. All that remained was for me to conclusively convince myself of it: I turned boldly towards the old talking stairs to Father's deconstruction room. It proved hopeless: the stairs not only no longer spoke, they plainly didn't accept me—the very first step was so rotten that my foot went right through it.

The Angel of Death was no longer waiting for me around the corner, but right here, perhaps even inside me.

"Why did you come looking for me?" I suddenly insisted of Mother. "What did you want to say? What else did you want to hurt me with?"

"I wanted to say goodbye, my little boy. I feel I'm going to die soon."

I knew full well that this Angel of Death was going to out-live both me and the Holy City of Vilnius too, but I kept quiet. I no longer wanted to say anything. You don't talk to Angels of Death; you just wait patiently until they do their work. Even Sun-Tzu himself didn't know any invincible tricks against Death. The bony one caught up with even him. However, there was one thing I had to ask Gorgeous Rožė anyway. It was one of the questions that had bothered me most in my life.

"Will you answer one question truthfully? You won't lie?"

"Ask."

"Why did you so mercilessly wreck and ruin Father's col-lection? Why did you destroy it? After all, that wasn't at all necessary."

"What do you mean, why?" Mother looked sincerely sur-prised. "I have a mortal hatred for any kind of collection."

Suddenly I realized that I had looked my mother straight in the eyes for the first time. There was no expression in those eyes—only perfectly graceful signs of death.

48. The Last Defenders of Duobėnai

Of course our stronghold was first nicknamed Duobėnai, the pits, by Apples Petriukas. Others have their Pilėnai, the castle hill defended against the Teutonic Knights, he liked to explain, while we have our immortal Duobėnai; we are the last defenders of Duobėnai. The time will come for us to burn ourselves up, too. Perhaps he didn't even suspect himself how prophetically correct he was. On the other hand, I used to occasionally think that Apples Petriukas didn't just understand the past; he understood the future, too. He really was prepared to defend Duobėnai to the end. When he would show off his collection of weapons, I would get the shivers. Judging from the amount, he had prepared himself to hold out against a small battalion of troops. Out of all his arsenal, I liked only the most modern gas masks. At least they couldn't smoke us out of my interim coffin like some kind of rats.

In any event, our military forces were truly impressive. For a bottle, Braniukas and Serioga would tie garlands of grenades to themselves and lie down under tanks. Apples Petriukas had a good regiment's worth of weapons, but didn't know how to use any weapon. Probably Albinas Afrika was the most effective: his psychological drum attack could scare off even the most terrifying enemy. Incidentally, it was precisely with

Albinas Afrika that everything started; he became the first sign of impending doom.

As was my habit, I was cleaning and polishing my collection. My delicate cocoons demand particularly painstaking care, and besides, each one must be cleaned and decorated differently, entirely individually. At least once, but better twice a week, I painstakingly tidy them up. First of all, the dust and all sorts of collected deposits need to be cleaned off all of them. That's a common hygienic requirement. And then comes the time for purely individual needs. Some need their little bones scrubbed and polished. The dollars incorporated into the overall composition for the builder Nargėla need to be checked every time, God forbid they should get damp and mold. Dampness is, in general, the mortal enemy of cocoons. I've burned a great deal of electrical energy keeping the collection room at nearly the microclimate of a desert.

Each time I invariably have to scoop out all the internal spaces of my beloved conductor: all kinds of uncleanliness and bugs collect inside them. Not to mention my beloved television star: she must constantly have her intimate places cleaned out, too. I have special little brushes for that purpose, similar to the ones used to clean pipes—just a good deal larger. One the one hand, it's a rather equivocal pursuit. On the other, I'm simply looking after my collection's exhibition. Left without tending they would rot, mold, and get worm-eaten. The physical tending of my delicate cocoons is a boring but unavoidable routine. Understandably, the metaphysical contents of the collection are much more meaningful; however, the soul is born only when the body is put right. Perhaps the cocoons' burners are somewhat more metaphysical. I strive to check them daily; they must work perfectly and without the slightest interruption. In the end, cockles must be burned; that is their divine fate, so the burners should be impeccably cared for. They must burn up the cockles instantly—by a special spiritual command, by a certain movement, or simply when it is very much wanted. I check the burners every day.

So, I was cleaning my delicate little cocoons as usual, but I began to realize more and more distinctly that something was missing from my interim coffin. Not some trifle, but some linchpin. That bad feeling plagued me for at least several hours, until I finally caught on: the quiet rumble of drums was missing. Albinas Afrika had gotten sick or fallen asleep, that's why I was having such a hard time cleaning the television star's intimate places. However, Sun-Tzu's inner voice immediately warned me: there are no chance noises, and neither are there chance silences. Every silence in the world has its surreptitious reason. Quite often the reason for an unexpected silence is betrayal. Silence is one of the essential hieroglyphs marking betrayal.

With my blood freezing, I slowly crept out into the common room, and then sidled over to Albinas's room. The worst thing that could have happened, happened: his entire drum collection was gone, the little room was wiped clean. You couldn't carry out that many drums and drumlets at once, nor in several trips: Albinas Afrika must have worked very hard, or at least had some assistants. I didn't even think of running rats or sinking ships, I simply considered what to do next. Suddenly it all became obvious to me. My interim coffin was already marked on someone's maps of war, and the nameless warrior chief was already planning the decisive assault.

Just a few days before I thought I had a backup route: Artūras Gavelis's bachelor apartment. Apples Petriukas's wicked Voodoo had toppled that naïve last hope too. I'm a stunning failure with people close to me: they either die, or betray me. I needed to escape quickly, but I could only escape into the void. I had absolutely nothing to do in the void, particularly without my collection. Probably all that was really left was to burn myself up—like the last defender of Duobėnai. However, first I had to make Apples Petriukas happy. He was meditating in his cell, at intervals glancing at some thick book.

"I know," he said sadly, without even allowing me to open my mouth, "I've known for a couple of days already. I used the secret connections of Voodoo and immediately understood the essence, although it's still not entirely clear to me. I ordered those who could to escape as quickly as possible."

"And not a word to me?"

"What for? What would it change? Maybe you've got somewhere to go? You simply got to live a few more days as usual and without fear."

"But you have places you could go. The world is big, and your bank accounts are huge."

"Don't be naïve. What country are you living in? If the fuzz scouted me out—they would have immediately sold me to the gangsters. I have nowhere to run. They'd come across me in any tiny Caribbean island. Besides, I don't want to run. I like Vilnius's garbage dumps and Vilnius's underground. All the rest of the world is crap."

Petriukas's eyes were large and sad, but by no means did he look frightened. More like intent and thoughtful—as if he were calculating or weighing something.

"I just don't get it. If they've already detected us, why are we sitting here like nothing's going on? Why are we still alive?"

"I haven't figured that out entirely, either," Apples Petriukas replied. "Maybe according to their idiotic logic they're trying to scoop up the entire supposed organization, all of our accomplices, so they're watching and waiting. But I'm not certain of that version."

"And how did they detect us? After this much peace and quiet?"

"You can thank your friend Artūras. I'm completely certain about that. He's Jogaila's right hand now, and once had you very well figured out. He knows your secret habits, your unconscious inclinations. He's scoped you out, if only while you were hanging around Korals. Or following your beloved mama. Or in one of your other sacred spots. All these last days it's been Artūras Gavelis I've been killing. Perhaps I succeeded to some extent."

"What does that mean—to some extent?"

"I've made him ill, I can feel that clearly. But will I have time to finish him off—only God knows. After all, you remember how much time it used to take to mess with some of the clients. Villains are as resistant as devils. I have problems with Artūras. I have revolting problems with Jogaila. It's going to be unbearably revolting to me to die leaving him in charge. Can you imagine the humiliation—the two of us dead, and he's thriving?"

It really was difficult to imagine a vision like that, but not because of Patris: I couldn't imagine myself dead. Sun-Tzu doesn't offer any special solution for retreating to a better world. He writes of war and victory, but not of complete defeat. I was a bit sorry for myself, and very sorry about my incomplete set of cocoons.

"In any event, I know perfectly well what my last book will be," Petriukas observed sadly.

"You're writing it now?"

"It will be written in a single instant. My last book will be the blast of a bazooka. A blast that will instantly finish everything. I think it's the very best form for a last book in this dear world. A title, and contents, and the end—all at the same time."

I remembered, remembered very well, all of our superb life and spirited war with the cockles. I actually palpably remembered my longing to conquer the unconquerable Jogaila Štombergas. I still didn't want to believe it was almost over now. I had to believe it after exactly eleven seconds, after eleven beats of the heart, after eleven lives. They attacked from all sides, through all the openings at once, as if they had thoroughly studied Sun-Tzu's teachings. They weren't prepared to kill us immediately; they even let us retreat into the gentle cocoons' room together with Apples Petriukas's bazooka. Most likely they had been ordered to take us alive.

It would have been better for Petriukas if he hadn't played with that bazooka of his. As soon as he tried to put it to his shoulder, one of the attacker's nerves failed, and Petriukas was picked off by a powerful automatic shotgun salvo. Some hundred shells at once plucked Apples Petriukas like a flower. Fate's mockery was complete: Petriukas wasn't finished off by gangsters, but by the gangsters' hunters. By some miracle, his head was still attached to his body—like my first father's head once held on by a strip of skin. I was always convinced that Apples Petriukas and my first father were astral twins. Petriukas simply had to end his life headless; that didn't surprise me at all. I was surprised by the attackers' slovenliness. One lummox suddenly ripped off his black mask and started vomiting right on the floor, and between heaves howling too:

"You see what he's done with them? Do you see? I can't... You see?"

After that inarticulate tirade, he started vomiting again, right on the floor in the sterile repository for the delicate cocoons. As a warrior chief, I was ashamed of the worthless people they select for the special units. That black-hooded puker was totally green, a lily-liver who hadn't experienced the real horrors of war. Sun-Tzu would never have put a weapon in the hands of someone like that. Unfortunately, they were the majority, and they were directed by an experienced hand and a most severely deviant brain. We had no chance of saving ourselves from Jogaila; all that was left was to methodically carry out my old metaphysical plan. When, with a single sacramental movement, I set fire to my delicate cocoons, the assaulters completely lost their heads; they no longer knew what to do. They simply had not been given any directions for a situation like that. I was impossibly sorry for my collection, but cockles must be burnt in live fire—it's the only proper end for them. The cockles burned beautifully, magically, much prettier than the giraffes in Dali's painting. The overall aesthetic impression was perhaps a bit spoiled by the black bands of smoke flapping around the edges of the flames. I wouldn't say the smoke reeked all that badly, but the assault kids broke down entirely.

They were beset by great weeping and the gnashing of teeth. They vomited, screamed, and writhed among themselves, completely forgetting me. Behind their backs, like victors, the apocalyptic characters of hell slowly gathered. I saw them all very clearly: the reduced-size edematous copy of Patris and the war invalids on carts, the gigantic rebel snails boiled in wine and the skulls from Mejerovič's paintings, the dissected cosmic frog of Karoliniškės and my uncle's yellow prostheses hyena, clacking its poisonous teeth. They all knew perfectly well why they had gathered there: to relish my defeat. And I knew perfectly well what I must do—what the incomparable Levas Kovarskis had taught me in my dreams. He left me that knowledge in a special testament. I had been holding the lancet in my hand for some time; baring my stomach took only an instant. My cut, as always, was calm, accurate, and nearly perfect. I finally saw my own second brain, still alive and pulsating. The brain of my gut was nicely developed, it moved and lived; just then it took in the last and fateful decisions of my life. The poor Aras anti-terrorist assault troops totally lost their focus and froze to the spot like fenceposts, while I studied and scrutinized the work of my gut's brain, feasted my eyes on them, and surprisingly felt practically no pain. Calmly and unexpectedly, the image of Moses Malone, the negro from Chicago, emerged from behind the apocalyptic characters; he applauded me for my incomparably human deed. I became the twelfth exhibit in my collection, although I had never prepared myself to be one. Perhaps that is exactly this world's meaning and truth. Perhaps I was exactly the one to embody the essence and beauty of all Vilnius. My last thought before I departed throbbed with a boundless regret that I never did figure out the secrets of my childhood. I never did determine what my first father fed those lizard people or rat people that multiplied in his deconstruction room. Those are exactly the sorts of questions that should most interest humanity.

49. The Righteous Ones

Thirty-six righteous souls live and have always lived on the earth, and their purpose is to justify the world in God's eyes. The righteous do not know each other, and in life they get by poorly. If someone finds out they are one of the thirty-six righteous souls, they instantly die a painful death, and their place is taken by another somewhere in an entirely different corner of the world. These righteous souls uphold people's existence in the world. If they didn't exist, God would have destroyed the human family a long time ago.

The righteous souls stubbornly defend and justify the world in God's perpetual court. With their very existence they patiently elucidate human imperfections and the inevitability of sins to God. Their very lives explain to the Almighty the rules of the world He himself created, and don't allow him to take up furious actions. The Almighty does not like the work He himself created. Like a true artist, He keeps threatening to bust it into bits—or more accurately, to decompose it into atoms and once again release them to scurry randomly about the boundless infinity of the Universe. So far, only the thirty-six righteous souls protect the world, without knowing it themselves. Possibly in secret half-dreams they come to suspect they have a special purpose, but only perhaps in the instant before death do they learn their real destiny. In the end, they do not receive any recompense for their righteousness: neither from God, nor from humans.

CPSIA information can be obtained
at www.ICGtesting.com
Printed in the USA
FFHW011844280119
50291381-55333FF

9 780996 630436